"What did Joey Ginzberg do," O'Toole asked, "knock over a bank?" He laughed. Good Jewish boys did not knock over banks.

Weiss shook his head. "Murder," he said.

"And this Joey is now—?"

"In the Tombs. He was caught at the scene."

The deceased was one Earl Grasser, single, age twenty-six. He lived in a two-room flat on the corner of 107th Street and Amsterdam, and according to his neighbors, was an unemployed salesman . . . shot twice in the chest.

"The judge won't be wasting the people's money on this one, Mr. Weiss. It's open and shut. . . . Now, if the lad had money," O'Toole said, "that'd be a different story."

"He doesn't need money," Weiss said.

"And how's that?" O'Toole asked. "He has the good fairy on his side?"

"No," Weiss said. "Better. He has me."

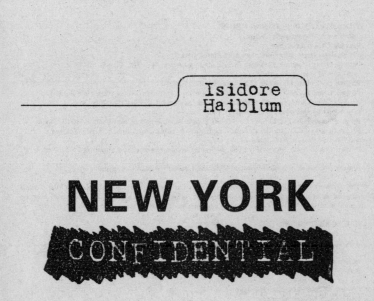

Isidore
Haiblum

NEW YORK
CONFIDENTIAL

BERKLEY PRIME CRIME, NEW YORK

THE BERKLEY PUBLISHING GROUP
Published by the Penguin Group
Penguin Group (USA) Inc.
375 Hudson Street, New York, New York 10014, USA
Penguin Group (Canada), 10 Alcorn Avenue, Toronto, Ontario M4V 3B2, Canada
(a division of Pearson Penguin Canada Inc.)
Penguin Books Ltd., 80 Strand, London WC2R 0RL, England
Penguin Group Ireland, 25 St. Stephen's Green, Dublin 2, Ireland (a division of Penguin Books Ltd.)
Penguin Group (Australia), 250 Camberwell Road, Camberwell, Victoria 3124, Australia
(a division of Pearson Australia Group Pty. Ltd.)
Penguin Books India Pvt. Ltd., 11 Community Centre, Panchsheel Park, New Delhi—110 017, India
Penguin Group (NZ), Cnr. Airborne and Rosedale Roads, Albany, Auckland 1310, New Zealand
(a division of Pearson New Zealand Ltd.)
Penguin Books (South Africa) (Pty.) Ltd., 24 Sturdee Avenue, Rosebank, Johannesburg 2196, South Africa

Penguin Books Ltd., Registered Offices: 80 Strand, London WC2R 0RL, England

This is a work of fiction. Names, characters, places, and incidents either are the product of the author's imagination or are used fictitiously, and any resemblance to actual persons, living or dead, business establishments, events, or locales is entirely coincidental.

NEW YORK CONFIDENTIAL

A Berkley Prime Crime Book / published by arrangement with the author

PRINTING HISTORY
Berkley Prime Crime mass-market edition / June 2005

Copyright © 2005 by Isidore Haiblum.
Cover design by Steven Ferlauto.
Illustration by Robert Hunt.
Interior text design by Stacy Irwin.

ISBN: 0-425-20360-3

BERKLEY® PRIME CRIME
Berkley Prime Crime Books are published by The Berkley Publishing Group,
a division of Penguin Group (USA) Inc.,
375 Hudson Street, New York, New York 10014.
BERKLEY PRIME CRIME is a registered trademark of Penguin Group (USA) Inc.
The Berkley Prime Crime design is a trademark belonging to Penguin Group (USA) Inc.

PRINTED IN THE UNITED STATES OF AMERICA

10 9 8 7 6 5 4 3 2 1

For my lovely wife, Ruthie,
my Wonder Woman and Supergirl
all rolled into one amazing package

ACKNOWLEDGMENTS

For this book, I have rounded up the usual suspects, whose help, support, and encouragement kept me going and helped whip this novel into shape. Any errors that have crept into the text are my doing (my lawyer told me to say that).

Stuart Silver's extensive knowledge of cars, guns, and antiques, coupled with his sense of design, helped give this book its special flavor.

Susan Husserl-Kapit's reading of the text strengthened and broadened its perspective.

T.E.D. Klein's honesty and fine eye brightened the copy and kept me laughing.

Judith Ann Yablonky's feedback helped shape the story.

My agent Nancy Yost's unwavering enthusiasm and energy made sure this book saw the light of day.

My editor Esther Strauss's encouragement and suggestions helped bring this novel to its happy conclusion.

And, my wife, Ruth Aleskovsky-Haiblum, ensured that my characters' emotional lines were consistent; that my gags produced, at least, a chuckle, and that everyone was appropriately coiffed and garbed.

I thank you all from the bottom of my heart!

CHAPTER 1

Morris Weiss—1948

Joe Louis was heavyweight champ. Jack Benny, on the radio, made the whole nation laugh. Heifetz had a date at Carnegie Hall. Bogart and Bacall were teamed in *Key Largo*. Truman was running against Dewey for President, but Henry Wallace, the Progressive Party candidate, was making the biggest *tumel* on the Lower East Side. More people read the Yiddish *Daily Forward* in this neighborhood than the *New York Times*. The *Forward* supported Truman. So did Morris Weiss.

"Please," Fineberg said.

Weiss shook his head. "No," he said.

"Morris, I beg you on bended knees."

"No is no," Weiss said.

"What am I to tell Sadie?"

"Tell her the truth," Weiss said. "There is nothing I can do for her boy."

Morris Weiss was a medium-sized man with broad shoulders, a thin mustache, and a full head of dark, curly hair. He had fought in the amateurs as a teenage middleweight and won all of his thirty-one bouts—twenty-six by knockouts. Approaching thirty, he still moved with the grace and speed of a first-class boxer. His heavy-lidded brown eyes looked out at the world with wry amusement. He wore a brown tweed jacket, an orange and green diagonally striped tie, and immaculately creased tan trousers. His brown shoes were polished to a high gloss.

"Who else is there if not you?" Fineberg asked.

Weiss said, "I hardly know the woman."

"You are a *landsman*."

"This," Weiss said, "is news to me?"

"It is true, Morris, you are."

"Fineberg, I am everybody's *landsman*. From all over the Lower East Side they come to me. Find my husband, he has run away from the job, from the children, from me. They are from *shtetlech* I've never even heard of. And they are always broke."

"You are a benefactor, Morris."

"And you, Fineberg, are a terrible pest."

From his office window Weiss could see the towering Forward Building in the distance. Nearby, wash dangled from backyard clotheslines strung between tenement fire escapes—shirts, pants, sheets, pillowcases. A billboard showing a penguin smoking a cigarette was visible from Delancey Street. "Smoke Kools," the billboard urged. Weiss did not smoke. He was not amused by the thought of a smoking penguin.

"Do it for me, Morris," Fineberg begged.

"No," Weiss said.

"Just speak to Joey. If you do not like what he says, when finished, walk away. What harm can there be in that?"

Irving Fineberg was a portly man in a gray three-piece suit. His brown eyes, behind thick glasses, always looked worried. He was only thirty-three, but already his hairline was receding.

"I know this Joey Ginzberg," Weiss said, "from the old days. He was never any good."

"That was then," Fineberg said, "before the war. He is a changed person. He now works for City College."

"He teaches crime?"

"Please, Morris."

"He's really changed?" Weiss asked.

Fineberg shrugged. "I give to everyone the benefit of the doubt. This is the way of the law."

"My business isn't the law."

"No, you spend your time chasing after runaway husbands. What kind of business is this?"

Weiss shrugged. "I make the husbands pay."

"If you find them."

"I find them," Weiss said. "Their wives, at least, are innocent."

"So maybe Joey is also innocent."

Weiss waved a hand.

"How can you be so sure?" Fineberg asked.

Weiss sighed. "All right. So I'm not so sure."

"There, you have said it yourself."

"Very smart," Weiss said, smiling. "I admit my error."

"That is good."

"Your Sadie, she has at least some money?"

"I will pay your fee," Fineberg said.

"You?"

"From my own pocket."

"Fineberg, you are feeling well?"

Fineberg pressed his thumb and forefinger together. "My wife and Sadie, they are this close. What choice do I have?"

"You know my fee?"

"I know, I know. You could get blood from a stone, Morris."

"True," Weiss said, "but it takes some practice."

"Well?" Fineberg said. "We are partners in this?"

Weiss rose to his feet. "You were always a sucker, Fineberg," he said. "And now you are making a sucker of me." Weiss stepped around his desk, went to the closet for his coat, reached for his hat on the rack near the door. "Come on, sucker," he said. "Let's go."

The cell door clanged shut behind them.

"Joey," Fineberg said, "I have here someone who maybe can help you. This is Morris Weiss, the detective."

"Hello, Joey," Weiss said.

Joey Ginzberg sat on his narrow cot and gazed dully at his two visitors. He was a short, muscular man in his late twenties. His nose was flattened like a boxer's, his shoulders were wide and sloped, his blondish hair crew cut. He neither spoke nor rose from his cot.

"You don't remember me, Joey?" Weiss said.

"Why should I?" Ginzberg said, in a hoarse, flat voice.

"You snatched a purse once, Joey. I caught you."

"Never," Ginzberg said.

"This was before the war. You grabbed an old woman's pocketbook on Orchard Street. You ran right into my arms."

Ginzberg got to his feet. "Maybe you should've minded your own business."

"That was my business," Weiss said, a half-smile on his face. "I'm a detective."

"I was just a kid."

"Sure. I let you go."

A radio, tuned to a soap opera, was playing somewhere in the cell block. Weiss could hear loud voices, a metal door opening or closing. The smell of Lysol burned his nostrils. Weiss hated this place.

Ginzberg said, "You here because of Ma?"

Weiss leaned up against the wall, hands in his pockets. He nodded toward Fineberg. "Him."

Ginzberg shook his head. "A pair of greenhorns," he said bitterly. "A pair of damn greenhorns."

"You don't like us?" Fineberg said. "So go hire yourself a Yankee lawyer. You got the money, Mr. Big Shot?"

"Go on," Ginzberg said, jerking a thumb toward the door, "beat it. I don't need your help."

"Listen, Joey," Fineberg said. "In this state, for murder, they give you the chair, the hot seat. You understand? We are all you have got. Take it or leave it."

Ginzberg suddenly sat down on the cot. "I was framed," he said.

"Sure," Weiss said.

"You don't believe me?"

"What is to believe?" Fineberg said. "So far you have given us *bubkes*."

"Look," Ginzberg said. "I'm a custodian at City College. I sweep. I mop. It's steady work. Why would I go looking for trouble?"

"You tell us," Weiss said.

A second radio began to play in the cell block. Kate Smith, the heavyweight soprano, was talking. *Better talking than singing*, Weiss thought. The pair of radios became a jumble of unpleasant sounds, mixing with the voices that had now begun to argue. Weiss had an urge to put his hands over his ears.

"It's crazy," Ginzberg said. "I get home last night, same as always."

"The time was what?" Weiss asked.

"Around six o'clock. I open the door and what do I find? This stiff lying in my living room."

Weiss said, "You knew him?"

"Nah, he was just some stiff. I never laid eyes on him before."

"So what did you do, Joey," Fineberg asked, "call the police?"

"Yeah, that's all I need. Listen, I've been keeping my nose clean. But I got a record from before the war. Two-bit stuff, but it makes me a sitting duck. I don't even think twice about calling the law. What I do is lug the stiff down the back stairs. I got my car parked in the alley. I shove him in the backseat, and I'm sitting there by the wheel, like some sap, trying to figure out where the hell to dump him, when suddenly the whole alley is crawling with coppers."

"So what happened?" Fineberg asked.

"What the hell you think happened?" Ginzberg said. "They pinched me. That's what happened."

The automat was beginning to fill up with the lunchtime crowd. Weiss and Fineberg avoided the steam table, which now had a long line. Instead, each put five cents into a slot; coffee poured out of a spigot inside a small metal lion's head and into their cups. A pair of quarters made two small glass windows pop open in the wall. Both men reached in their respective cubicle for American cheese sandwiches on white bread.

"Here is the restaurant of the future, Morris," Fineberg said. "No waiters. No menus—"

"No taste," Weiss said.

"Very funny," Fineberg said. "Eddy Cantor is sweating you will take his place."

"Tell him not to worry."

They shared a table by the long plate-glass window with two men in work shirts, overalls, and peaked caps. Outside, a horse and wagon moved slowly up the street. The wagon was piled high with junk. A newsboy was hawking the *New York Journal American*. Pedestrians in long coats with padded shoulders hurried by on their lunch hour break. Every man and most of the women wore hats.

Fineberg ate in hat and coat. Weiss took off his coat and neatly folded it on the back of his chair. As was the custom, he did not remove his hat.

Both men finished their sandwiches.

"*Nu?*" Fineberg finally said.

"This Joey is a peach," Weiss said. "You are his only lawyer, Fineberg?"

"I am."

Weiss sipped his coffee, looked at his friend. "You are a criminal lawyer now?"

"You know what I am, Morris. My office, it is a storefront on Rivington Street. I sit and wait for the customers to come in. Some I help with immigration problems, others with benefits, or maybe taxes. Also, I look over legal papers and give advice."

"From this you make a living?"

"My enemies should make such a living."

"So," Weiss said, "what is your secret? You are maybe a gangster on the side?"

"If I only knew how. No, Morris, I am the lawyer for the Delancey Street Democratic Club. There, many deals are made. And I am always making sure that everything is kosher."

"For this they pay you?"

"They pay me."

Weiss shook his head. "America *gonif*," he said. "It's you who are the benefactor, Fineberg, helping this *schlepper*, Joey."

"My Rosie, she would kill me if I did not."

Weiss said, "You'll really go to court with him?"

"Never will it come to that."

Weiss smiled. "So, Fineberg, you have something up your sleeve?"

Fineberg nodded.

"What is it?"

"You, Morris."

"Me? You're crazy."

"I am paying good money," Fineberg said. "More than you will ever see from your so-called innocent wives."

Weiss shrugged, put down his empty coffee cup. "I told you, Fineberg, from them I get usually nothing. But in the end I get. And that's plenty for me."

"Now you will get more."

"Who needs more?"

"You need. Everyone needs."

"You are a philosopher, too, eh, Fineberg?"

"I am what it takes," Fineberg said. "This case, it will never go to trial, Morris, because you will clear Joey first."

"I am a detective, not a magician," Weiss said.

"Then for the boy," Fineberg said, "you will become a magician."

CHAPTER 2

*I never worry about entrusting a case to Max.
What he might lack in experience he makes up for
by being very smart. Naturally, this trait runs in
the family.*

From the casebooks of Morris Weiss

Max Weiss—The Present

Boris Minsky was lodged in his favorite chair, namely
mine, when I walked into my office on Hudson Street in
Tribeca. Across the street, a men's clothing shop, a pair
of restaurants, a food store, and a card shop were visible
from our window.

We exchanged greetings.

Minsky was an ample man of seventy or so in a striped
brown three-piece suit and waxed mustache. He carried a

marble-topped walking stick, wore heavy tortoise-framed glasses, and parted his still-thick hair straight down the middle. He had begun working for my great-uncle Morris, when the office was still down on the Lower East Side.

Our current client was April Freid. And the reason Minsky had dropped in this morning.

Ms. Freid had found a flyer enumerating the wonders of the upstate Mannerdale Rehabilitation Center among her uncle's papers. She had never heard of Mannerdale. And, as far as she knew, her uncle was in no particular need of rehab. What she did know was that Uncle Felix had inexplicably dropped from sight without saying goodbye to anyone, including her. This was very uncharacteristic behavior.

April called her lawyer, who called his friend, a retired cop, who came up with Uncle Morris, of the Weiss and Weiss Detective Agency. As fate would have it, Uncle Morris, hale and hearty at seventy-seven, was off to Florida that very day, so the job fell to me.

Naturally, I'd put Minsky on it.

I seated myself in the client's chair and said, "Tell me what happened, Boris."

"Why, I simply drove up to Mannerdale and inquired as to their rates. I said my aged mother was in need of their services. They seemed eager to have my business. Especially when I told them she had excellent insurance coverage. On my way out I spoke with three people, a nurse, a woman who ran the recreation room, and what passed for security at the front door. I described Doctor Margoshes to each. Only the latter was of any help. A man fitting his description, I was told, was in room 3J. He had been there for less than a month. All that, Maxwell, and my itemized expense account, can be found in my report. It is being typed by the indispensable Marsha at this very moment, no doubt. And now," Boris said, "if I may be permitted a question?"

"Sure," I said. "At the usual rates."

"Most amusing, dear boy. What do you plan to do next?"

"Take a ride with my client. And I'm not your dear boy."

"Of course not, Maxwell."

CHAPTER 3

Morris Weiss—1948

Jimmy O'Toole rose and extended a fleshy hand across his desk to Morris Weiss. "Well, well," he said, putting on a thick brogue, "if t'ain't t'dreaded bloodhound o' East Broadway hisself. How're ya, Mr. Weiss?"

Weiss grinned at the performance, as he always did. "In the pink," he said. "And you, Detective Sergeant O'Toole?"

"Never better," O'Toole said, dropping the brogue. He seated himself and nodded Weiss to the straight-backed chair by the side of his desk.

Weiss removed his coat and, draping it carefully over the back of the chair, sat down. He continued to wear his fedora. "Your charming wife, beautiful daughters, and little Mikey?" he asked.

"Thriving, I'm pleased to say. It's a wonder they haven't eaten me out of house and home yet."

"Give them time," Weiss said. "How many are there now? I've lost count."

"As well you might. Four, I'm proud to say, going on five."

Weiss raised an eyebrow. "You are a hero of the bedroom."

"I can't deny it."

"My regards to the family."

O'Toole was a large beefy man with a florid face, small blue eyes, and dark hair. He had on a navy blue suit with a wide red tie. Weiss was genuinely fond of the detective. The pair went back a ways: O'Toole had once walked a beat on Broome Street.

"Now," O'Toole said, leaning forward, "to the real work at hand."

"Of course," Weiss said, a smile of anticipation on his face.

They commenced to chew over the Tony Zale–Rocky Graziano bout of last June when Zale regained the middleweight crown in the third round. Both held that Zale, the "Man of Steel," who had labored in the steel mills of Gary, Indiana, and who could stand up to the most fearsome beatings and still prevail, would easily defeat the Frenchman, Marcel Cerdan, in their upcoming match later that month. They talked about Willie Pep, the featherweight champion, who gained a decision over Paddy DeMarco last month at the Garden. Again they agreed: Pep would make mincemeat of Sandy Saddler in their October fight. The topic shifted to horse racing. Legendra, running in the Cherryola Handicap at Jamaica, was a cinch to at least place. Capote, slated for the Wakefield Stakes, was worth a two-dollar ticket. Glenwood Kid had looked good in his latest workouts. . . .

"And what, Mr. Weiss," O'Toole finally asked, "brings you to our fair station house today?"

"Business," Weiss said, "what else?"

Weiss took the folded envelope out of his wallet and slid it across the ink-stained green blotter covering the detective's battered oak desk. They were in the squad room. Detectives worked in a warren of small, pasteboard cubicles. O'Toole's was better than most. He was over by the west wall and had a window with a fine view of a small park across the street. O'Toole was vice president of the Sergeant's Benevolent Association/Superior Officers Council of PDNY. He had power and connections and could write his own ticket. It had been years since O'Toole had risked his neck on the streets. None of the other detectives took notice that money changed hands.

O'Toole did not glance at the envelope. It vanished into his desk drawer. He folded his hands over his ample belly and said, "Well, now."

"Joey Ginzberg," Weiss said.

"One of your lads, is he?"

"God forbid," Weiss said.

"In a bit of trouble?"

"More," Weiss said, "than a bit."

"What did he do," O'Toole asked, "knock over a bank?" He laughed. Good Jewish boys did not knock over banks. And the Jewish gangs had been broken by Tom Dewey in Manhattan and Bill O'Dwyer in Brooklyn. The pair of D.A.s had gone on to better things. Dewey was now governor of New York State, and O'Dwyer was mayor of New York City. For them, crime had certainly paid.

Weiss shook his head. "Murder," he said.

"Murder, is it now? Domestic troubles?"

"Not domestic."

"That's bad," O'Toole said. "It's not like fixing a ticket. What do you want done, Mr. Weiss?"

"I would like," Weiss said, "to know what happened."

"Working for the family, are you?"

"Their lawyer," Weiss said.

"Give me the when and where of it."

Weiss did.

"And this Joey is now—?"

"In the Tombs. He was caught at the scene."

"Our vigilant lads spot him?"

"Someone did."

O'Toole rose to his feet. "Stay put, Mr. Weiss," he said, and strolled off.

Weiss turned his chair to face the squad room. He stretched out his legs and clasped his hands in his lap. A half smile appeared on his face as he surveyed his surroundings.

The walls were pale green and in need of a fresh paint job. Yellowish light came from small, half-shaded bulbs dangling overhead. The desks were old and the chairs creaky. A few other civilians were here, mostly suspects, victims, or witnesses of some crime. Detectives interviewed them, shuffled through records, and used the phones, which rang repeatedly. People came and went. The place smelled of cigarettes and cigars, coffee, sweat, old police files. Not a Jewish face was in sight. New York's Finest did not hire Jews.

O'Toole presently returned, clutching a single sheet of paper. "Precious little I've got for you," he said, seating himself.

Weiss turned his chair to face the detective. "Anything will do," he said. "I am not choosy."

The deceased was one Earl Grasser, single, age twenty-eight. He lived in a two-room flat on the corner of 107th Street and Amsterdam Avenue and, according to his neighbors, was an unemployed salesman. Grasser was shot twice in the chest. The M.E. found two thirty-eight-caliber slugs. There was plenty of blood in Ginzberg's flat. No one heard the shot. An anonymous call had alerted the police. No connection had as yet been found between Grasser and Ginzberg. The case was still ongoing.

"No more?" Weiss said.

"It's only the third day," O'Toole said. "What do you think, Mr. Weiss?"

"A setup, maybe?"

"Ah, the anonymous tip. No more than some busybody looking out of a window. A great aid to law enforcement."

"Very convenient, too," Weiss said.

"We value such conveniences."

"Of course. What I need, Detective O'Toole, is Joey's mug shot, and a picture of this Grasser."

O'Toole smiled, and handed Weiss a pair of glossy prints. "I'm way ahead of you, Mr. Weiss."

"You I don't mind. It's the lowlifes I don't like." Weiss looked at the prints. "Grasser is no beauty."

"Nor your Joey."

"True. Only Joey is at least not dead."

"Not yet," O'Toole said. "The judge won't be wasting the people's money on this one, Mr. Weiss. It's open and shut."

"And if Joey is innocent?"

O'Toole waved a hand. "Your Joey has a hot sheet," he said. "They'll call him kike and send him over—even if the lad didn't do it."

"Kike?" Weiss said.

"You know how it is," O'Toole said.

"I know."

"Now, if the lad had money," O'Toole said, "that'd be a different story."

"He doesn't need money," Weiss said.

"And how's that?" O'Toole asked. "He has the good fairy on his side?"

"No," Weiss said. "Better. He has me."

CHAPTER 4

*It is always good to have a paying client. And even
better if the paying client is a beautiful woman.
Rich also doesn't hurt.*

From the casebooks of Morris Weiss

Max Weiss—The Present

April and I whipped up the West Side Highway and ex-
ited north on the Taconic. Soon the city was a distant,
smog-enshrouded enclave.

The trees out here were just beginning to turn. A nice,
inspiring sight.

"We would meet for lunch regularly every other
month," April told me. "We kept in touch. Last year,
when Uncle Felix went to Israel on sabbatical, he let me

know weeks in advance. So what if he didn't talk much about his personal life? We were friends."

"Friends is important," I said.

My client was a pert blonde in a neat teal suit. When she wasn't chasing around the countryside hunting for uncles, she was an off-Broadway publicist. Being her own boss meant she could chase all she wanted.

Dense woods and a stream were on our left, a few scattered barns and rolling fields on the right. A couple of ducks were swimming in the stream. It looked like an easy and not unpleasant payday. Those were the best kind.

"Well," I said, "your uncle hasn't the faintest idea that we're about to pay him a visit. You can play it any way you want when you see him."

She sighed. "He can be very difficult at times. What if he doesn't want to see me?"

"Relax, enjoy the ride," I said. "We'll handle that if and when it happens."

"Yes, can I help you?"

The prim lady behind the desk looked like someone's blue-haired grandmother.

I glanced at April. She was standing by my side, speechless. Maybe the thought of surprising her uncle had immobilized her.

"We're here to see Dr. Margoshes," I said, stepping into the breach. "This is his niece, April Freid."

The grandmotherly type smiled. "Of course," she said, turning to her PC monitor, and bringing up the patient file. She peered at it through her spectacles and turned back to us quizzically. "Would you repeat the name, please?"

"Felix Margoshes," April suddenly chimed in.

The woman searched again. "I'm sorry, there is no such person staying with us."

April looked at me.

"Who," I asked, "is in room 3J?"

Another glance at the screen. "Mr. Davidson."

"Right," I said. "That's who we want to see."

"I don't understand," the receptionist said. "You asked for a Dr. Margoshes. Is Mr. Davidson a relative, too?"

"I believe Mr. Davidson *is* Dr. Margoshes," I said. "Right guy, wrong name."

The receptionist stared at me as if I had suddenly begun babbling in Urdu.

"I'm afraid," she said, "you will have to speak to Dr. Kramer about that."

"Sure," I said.

We were directed to a waiting room. It was empty except for us, a potted palm, and a couple of modern abstract prints. It was not a room I wanted to spend much time in.

Presently, a lean, gray-haired, disheveled man in a white jacket hurried toward us. Slightly stooped, eyes bulging, mouth open, he resembled a mackerel out of water.

"I am Dr. Kramer," the guy said. "What is this about Mr. Davidson?"

I told him.

"That is nonsense."

"Look," I said, "all we want to do is look at the guy. He won't even know we're there. What harm can it do?"

"Absolutely not," Kramer said. "Our patients demand complete privacy. We always respect their wishes in this."

"Dr. Margoshes hasn't been seen in four weeks," I said. "How long has your Mr. Davidson been here?"

"I would have to consult my records," he said.

"Good idea," I told him.

Kramer turned on his heel. We trotted after him as he all but raced up the corridor.

In his office, he leaned over a computer terminal on his desk and punched a few keys.

"Three weeks," he said grimly, as though telling us we only had a few days to live.

"Still fits the time frame," I pointed out.

Kramer stared at us. "This means nothing. I must ask you two to go at once!"

"Okay," I said, "but we'll be back with a court order. You can count on it."

"Are you out of your mind?"

"And we won't be alone. The police will be with us. And so will the press. Mannerdale will be famous, along with you, Doctor. There's no way you can stonewall on this."

"This is an outrage!"

"The sooner you let us take our look, the sooner we'll be out of here."

Kramer hesitated, glowered at us, then furiously strode out of his office.

"Come!" he yelled.

A small elevator carried us up to the third floor. We trailed along as the good doctor hurried down the carpeted hallway.

He opened the door to 3J very quietly and gazed in. He remained standing there as if glued to the spot.

April and I peered over his shoulder.

An old Hitchcock movie would, no doubt, have a total stranger in that bed. A grade B thriller, and Dr. Margoshes would be stretched out on the same bed, dead as last week's donut. In my own mind I'd pictured April's uncle alive and kicking, but far from overjoyed at seeing his niece suddenly pop up.

All of these scenarios were wrong.

Even when we'd searched the bathroom and closet and looked under the bed, the room was still empty.

CHAPTER 5

Morris Weiss—1948

Morris Weiss got off the IRT subway at the 135th Street station and walked up the hill, past Lewisohn Stadium to Convent Avenue. A cold wind blew in from the north. He stood, hands in pockets, gazing up at the twin-towered Gothic structure that was Shepard Hall, the main building of City College. CCNY, he thought: Christian College Now Yiddish. Weiss smiled at the old gag. Harvard, Yale, and Columbia University had unwritten quota systems when it came to Jews. So Jewish students flocked to City. The place was a hothouse of ideas, many of them radical. At least the price was right. City College was tuition-free.

He crossed the street, entered Shepard Hall. The ceiling was high, the floors marble. A lone student climbed the wide staircase at the end of the hallway. A bell rang and the staircase suddenly filled up as students poured out

of classrooms on the upper floors and began to head
down. Some, he saw, were mere youngsters, others already adults—the vets here on the GI Bill. Weiss knew he
was eligible. He imagined himself spending four years in
this institution, sitting in a classroom, and shuddered. To
what end? He was a confirmed autodidact. And what
would he do with their degree? He already had a profession
and knew he was good at it.

Weiss stepped over to a window marked "Registrar"
and asked the woman inside where the custodian's office
was located. She didn't know. He tried two other windows before he was directed to the basement. *They keep
the place clean*, Weiss thought glumly, *yet nobody knows
where they are.*

A side staircase led him down two flights to the basement. It was quiet here. Naked lightbulbs were strung
across the high ceiling. An assortment of pipes, both narrow and wide, were laid overhead and on ground level. He
wandered by a boiler, a furnace, a coal bin, a large rusty
utilities sink with buckets and mops clustered around it.
The basement smelled of oil, steam, and damp wood.

Weiss came to a doorless room. A small, wiry man in
shirt sleeves sat behind a scruffy wooden desk, smoking a
cigarette and reading a tabloid. Weiss saw it was the *Daily
Mirror*, opened to the racing pages. Behind him on the
wall, an *Esquire* pinup-girl calendar was hung next to a
time clock.

"Trailblazer," Weiss said. "Third race this Saturday at
Belmont."

The small man looked up. "You're nuts," he said instantly. "It's Point Blank hands down."

Weiss shrugged. "Only if it rains. I'm looking for the
head custodian."

"You found him, mister."

"Weiss," Morris Weiss said, stepping into the room.

"Ned Luker. What can I do for you?"

"I'm here about Joe Ginzberg."

"What about him?"

"He's in jail," Weiss said.

"In jail? What for, he drunk again?"

"Not drunk," Weiss said.

"So what is it?"

"They say he killed a man."

"You're shittin' me."

Weiss shook his head.

"Hang on," Luker said, rising hastily. He hurried to a closet, returned with a folding chair. "Take a load off. We can talk for a few minutes."

"Thank you." Weiss folded his coat and hung it on the back of the folding chair. He wore his hat. He sat.

"Well," Luker said, "that sure explains why Ginzberg ain't on the job."

"It certainly does," Weiss said, a half smile on his face.

"You don't look like a cop," Luker said.

"I'm a private detective." Weiss produced the photocopy of his license and showed it to the custodian.

"Uh-huh. You workin' for Ginzberg?"

"His lawyer."

"Who's dead?"

"This man." Weiss reached into his pocket, took out the snapshot of Earl Grasser and held it up. "You know him, Mr. Luker?"

Luker stared at the photo. "Nope," he said. "Who is he?"

"Formerly a salesman," Weiss said, "now, unfortunately, a corpse."

Luker laughed. "No future in that."

"None at all," Weiss agreed. "Does the name Earl Grasser mean anything to you?"

"Uh-uh," Luker said. "That him?"

"That's him. How long has Ginzberg worked here?"

"Couple years, maybe."

"A hard worker?"

"He's all right."

"He drinks?"

"Sometimes."

"But," Weiss said, "he always shows up the next day."

"Not always."

"Ah," Weiss said. "But you don't fire him."

"Fire him? He's a Jew," Luker said. "Like yourself."

"So?"

"In my book, the Jews are a smart race."

Weiss smiled. "I would be the last to disagree, Mr. Luker."

"Yeah. So when I give Ginzberg a job, I know he's gonna do it right. Maybe not fast, but right."

"Ah-ha," Morris Weiss said, trying hard to imagine Joey the purse snatcher doing anything right.

"Not many Jews on my staff," Luker said. "So I make allowances."

"That is commendable, Mr. Luker," Weiss said. "How many Jews do you employ here?"

"We got two, Ginzberg and Irving Kabalsky. Kabalsky works hard *and* fast."

"They are close?"

"In a pig's eye. Kabalsky keeps to himself. He don't pal around with no one."

"Does Ginzberg have many friends here?"

"Friends? This ain't no social club. He gets along. Everyone gets along, even Kabalsky. I ain't got no time for troublemakers. I get me a troublemaker, I boot 'em out."

"And before here, Mr. Luker, where did Joey work?"

"Gotta ask personnel that one," Luker said, raising his thumb toward the ceiling. "Upstairs."

Weiss glanced over at the time clock. "The shift changes in five minutes?"

"Yep."

"I have some questions for your staff, Mr. Luker."

"Fire away. Only make it short. We got some tired men here wanting to go home. And the swing shift gotta job to do."

"Of course."

By the time the first worker appeared, Weiss and Luker were engaged in a hot debate regarding the merits of competing horses and jockeys at Belmont. Weiss reluctantly broke off and spoke briefly with the man, who knew nothing. During the next fifteen minutes he interviewed a variety of men of various nationalities, shapes, and sizes. Their command of English differed greatly, but they all had one thing in common: they had never seen Joey Ginzberg with anyone even vaguely resembling Earl Grasser. Irving Kabalsky was no exception to this rule.

"Kabalsky," Weiss said. "What do you do here?"

"I fix, I clean. I do what he tells me," Kabalsky said, pointing a finger at Luker, who smiled.

"And tonight," Weiss asked, "where are you?"

"Top floor. Here. Why?"

"Why not?" Weiss said. "Have a good evening."

When the last worker had left, Weiss retrieved his coat, put it on, and thanked Luker for his help.

"Sorry it didn't pan out," the custodian said.

"You never know," Weiss said. "Ginzberg work anywhere special?"

"Wherever he was needed. Around the campus, in the cafeteria sometimes."

They shook hands. Weiss left.

The personnel office was already closed. Weiss used the main staircase and climbed to the top floor. Night classes were in progress. He could hear murmuring from behind closed doors. Weiss walked down one corridor, then another. He found Kabalsky up on a ladder, working on a darkened ceiling lamp.

"Kabalsky," Weiss called, "it's me, Weiss, the detective. Come down, I want to talk to you."

"I'm working."

"Come down anyway."

Reluctantly, Kabalsky climbed down. "What is it? Be quick. They pay me to work, not talk."

"It is about Ginzberg," Weiss said.

"I already told you. I know nothing, nothing."

Kabalsky was a short, skinny man of thirty-five or so. His head was pear-shaped, with receding strands of black hair combed back over his skull. His nose was pear-shaped. He had large ears that stuck out like a pair of vestigial wings. His speech and movements were abrupt, filled with nervous energy.

"You have had no contact with Ginzberg at all?" Weiss asked.

"What contact? I work nights, he works days. How should we have contact?"

"Still," Weiss said, "you two are the only Jewish workers here—"

"It means nothing, nothing. I am from the other side, from Odessa. I was in the camps. Look." He pulled up his sleeve. Weiss saw the tattooed numbers. "I lose my family there. I lose everything. This Ginzberg, what does he know about anything, ha? He is from another world. Why should I be interested in him?"

"Mr. Kabalsky," Weiss said in Yiddish. "We are both *landsman,* I can speak plain words to you. Ginzberg is accused of a terrible crime. I am only trying to find out what happened. If he is guilty, I will have nothing more to do with him. But if he is an innocent person, how can we let him go to his death without even lifting a finger?"

"He is guilty, guilty. Just take look at him," Kabalsky answered in Yiddish. "He is not a refined person. What he is is a slugger, a hitter, a beater. Such Jews worked for the Nazis in the camps."

"You two have spoken?"

"We have not spoken, not even a single word."

"But you see things. . . ."

"What is to see? I mind my own business. I see nothing. My friend, listen, I do not want trouble. I have had enough trouble in my life for ten people, for twenty, for a hundred."

"I understand," Weiss said very earnestly. "Look at me, Kabalsky. I am a slugger?"

Kabalsky looked, shook his head.

"I am a hitter, a beater?"

"You are not."

"True. You and I, Kabalsky, we speak the same language. I was born in Lukov, Poland. My parents came here when I was seven. They were good kosher Jews. And I am like them. What you tell me goes no further. It is only between us. Never will you get into trouble because of anything you say to me. Never. I give you my promise."

Kabalsky stared at Weiss, then nodded very slowly. "Yes," he said, "I can see that you are an honest person."

"Thank you," Weiss said. "I would like to show you the photograph of the dead man again."

"Show me."

Weiss produced Grasser's photo.

Kabalsky took it in his hand, studied it.

"Well?" Weiss said.

"Yes, I see things. I am not blind. I keep my mouth shut, but I see things." Kabalsky took a deep breath. "I know him. In the diner by the 125th Street El, more than once as I go to work, I have seen him and Ginzberg through the large windows whispering together. They think no one sees them there."

"Whispering, eh? Like old friends?"

"Like criminals."

"You could tell?"

"My friend, when you have been in the camps you know this look. And you never forget."

"I understand," Weiss said. "They were always alone?"

"Not always. Sometimes there was with them a third person. Once I saw this man here at the college."

"And you could recognize him?"

"He limps. At the coffee shop, he was walking over to their table. The limp, it was very bad. Also he has a big mustache like a Cossack. I would not forget such a man."

"Where on campus did you see him?"

"The cafeteria, at night. I think he is a student. One of those on the GI Bill."

"He is older, eh?"

"He is no youngster. And he is like his friends."

"In what way, Kabalsky?"

"He is no good."

"Ah-ha," Morris Weiss said.

CHAPTER 6

*It often falls to the private detective to bring en-
lightenment to those who do not want it. My nephew
Max is especially adept at this.*

From the casebooks of Morris Weiss

Max Weiss—The Present

"I simply do not understand," Dr. Kramer said.

"Your patient's skipped," I said. "His clothes are
gone. The rest of his belongings are gone. *He's* gone.
What's to understand?"

"This is ridiculous," Kramer said. "Patients come here
for treatment, for rest. They do not skip."

"What have you done with my uncle?" April broke in.

"Paul Davidson is your uncle?"

"Felix Margoshes is my uncle."

"Then we have done nothing to your uncle, have we, Miss Freid?"

"How about Davidson?" I said. "You do something to him?"

"Do not be asinine."

We had returned to Kramer's office. He had used his phone to contact doctors, nurses, security personnel, the cleaning staff; he had ordered a search of the building and grounds.

I sat through all this, eyeing the bookcase, which held a bunch of medical works, and the window, which showed a nice expanse of manicured lawn.

Meanwhile, the phone kept ringing, bringing us more reports of no progress. When the final call ended, I said, "Admit it, Doctor, you've lost him. The question now is, do we keep this hushed up or sound the alarm?"

"You have no right to meddle in the affairs of this institution. Davidson is our problem, not yours."

"We're making it ours," I said. "Unless you want to go public. Then the police can take over."

"This is blackmail."

"Grow up, Doctor." I handed him my snapshot of Margoshes. "This your patient?"

The doctor sighed. Carefully, he removed a pair of gold-rimmed spectacles from his vest pocket, donned them, and took a long look at the photo, first holding it at arm's length, then bringing it clear up to his nose.

"Come on," I said. "The guy's been here three weeks."

Kramer's mouth twitched, the lines on his face rippled. He looked apoplectic, as though I had questioned his medical credentials. He said, "The man I treated was thinner. His hair was almost entirely white. His shoulders were stooped to a noticeable degree. This man is younger."

"He *was* younger," April said. "The picture was taken ten years ago."

"Is there any resemblance, Dr. Kramer?"

He shrugged. "Some."

"Okay," I said. "So what was wrong with your patient?"

"Fatigue."

"That's it?" I said. "Simple fatigue?"

"There was nothing simple about it. His condition was quite debilitating. The man was in his eighties, Mr. Weiss. He was frail."

"My uncle was in perfect health for his age," April said, "the last time I saw him."

"What did I tell you?" Kramer said. "Your uncle was never here, Miss Freid. We are dealing with two different people. Isn't that obvious by now?"

"Did an M.D. refer Davidson here?" I asked.

"No," Kramer said. "He came on his own."

"Isn't that unusual?"

"It happens."

"How'd he pay you? Medicare? Personal check? Private insurance?"

Kramer sighed, turned to his computer, punched a few keys, and peered dolefully at the monitor. "Cash," he said.

"Kind of unusual, too, isn't it?"

He shrugged. "Old people—who knows what they will do next? They themselves often don't know."

"Yeah," I said, "they even look alike."

"Are we done, Mr. Weiss?"

"We're getting there. Davidson married?"

"Widowed."

"Offspring?"

"A daughter."

"Where?"

"Woodside, Queens."

"Call her."

"That would be most awkward, not to say premature. We have yet to determine what occurred."

"We're determining it now. Make the call, Doctor."

"What shall I say, that her father has run away?"

"Or been abducted," I said.

Kramer glared at me. When I didn't go up in smoke, he slowly reached for the phone as if he expected the receiver to snap at him.

"Put on the speaker," I said.

He did and tried the number. It didn't exist. He tried information. There was no Stella Davidson listed in Queens. Kramer called Davidson's number in New York. The phone was picked up by a Mrs. Sheldon. Right number, wrong party. She had never heard of a Paul Davidson.

Kramer hung up the receiver. He looked stunned.

"Still sure he isn't Margoshes?" I asked.

"I am no longer sure of anything," Kramer said.

"That's wisdom," I told him. "Your Davidson have a phone in his room?"

"Yes, all our patients do."

"How are they billed?"

"Like everyone else. We get an itemized phone bill every month and include it in his statement."

"So you've still got Davidson's bills?"

"Of course we have them. This is a well-managed establishment."

"I need a copy."

Kramer glowered at me as if I'd asked for the deed to the joint. He picked up the phone, barked some orders into it, and presently a flunky arrived with the document. I gave it a quick glance, folded it double, and stuck it into my pocket.

"Thanks," I said.

"Are we done *now*?"

I nodded.

He rose. "Good day to you both. I'm sorry about this."

April and I got to our feet.

"Not as sorry as I am," she said. "What kind of a place do you run here?"

"A good one," Kramer shot back.

"You'll let us know if your guy turns up?" I asked.

"Naturally."

I left him my card.

At the main entrance I asked the elderly guard if anything suspicious had occurred last night.

"Ain't nothing suspicious ever happens around here," he said.

"Who works the night shift?"

"Jerry, this month."

Kramer had phoned Jerry in our presence. Jerry reported a quiet, uneventful evening.

"When does Jerry go off duty?" I asked.

"Midnight."

"Who takes over?"

"No one, mister."

"No one?"

"Just lock the doors. Keeps the sick folks in, vandals out. Never had any trouble. This ain't no prison, you know."

I showed him our photo. "This man look familiar?" I asked.

The guard slowly put on his reading glasses, wrinkled his brow, and examined the snapshot. "Looks a little like the guy up in 3J."

I handed him my card. "Call me if he turns up. There'll be some cash in it for you."

"I can always use cash," the guard said, wistfully.

CHAPTER 7

Morris Weiss—1948

"You have married a wonderful cook," Morris Weiss said, pushing his empty plate away. "She is as beautiful as her dishes are delicious. The flanken was beyond comparison. And the cabbage soup and kasha varnishkes, they were in a class by themselves. I congratulate you."

Rose Fineberg blushed; her husband beamed. The trio was seated around the small dining room table, the two men in shirtsleeves. Weiss had loosened his tie. One of the two curtained windows looked out on a fire escape; both looked out at other tenement houses. Patterned green and yellow linoleum was underfoot. An original painting of two ballerinas, which Fineberg had taken in lieu of a fee from one of his clients, hung on the wall. An ornate cabinet containing fancy dishes stood across from the painting. A small violin also hung on the wall, a memento from the days when Fineberg's parents had dreamed of making him another Heifetz.

Rose began clearing the table. She was no taller than Molly Picon, the famed Yiddish actress, but she was prettier. With red hair and green eyes, she looked like a movie star, herself.

"So what's the matter?" she asked. "You didn't mention my vegetables. You don't like them?" It was the old vaudeville joke. Weiss appreciated the effort.

"They melt in the mouth," he assured her.

"You are such a liar," Rose said, smiling broadly.

"It's the truth," Weiss insisted.

"I will vouch for him," Fineberg said. "Like the father of this great country, he does not know, *nebech*, how to tell a lie."

"And he has tried to teach me," Weiss said, jabbing a thumb at his friend.

"A head of wood," Fineberg agreed sadly. "He learns nothing."

"Was I complaining?" Rose said. "Rest a minute, then I'll bring you tea and dessert. You like strudel, Morris?"

"I love strudel."

"He does," Fineberg said. "I will vouch for him again."

"Be quiet," Rose said.

"You baked it yourself?" Weiss said.

"Who else, Grossfield's bakery?" she said with great disdain.

"God forbid," Weiss said.

"See, he knows," she said to her husband, stacking the dishes and, with a toss of her head, carrying them off to the kitchen. Weiss watched her go. In her green flower-print dress, she moved like a dancer.

"So what is it?" Weiss whispered to Fineberg. "The bakery is no good?"

"You and I should do such business, Morris. They are

stuffed with money. Only they overcharge. Two cents if the bread is a day old."

"That much? Have they no pity on their customers?"

"What pity? They have a monopoly, the next bakery is four blocks away. My Rosie is right."

"Your Rosie is an angel."

"You are telling me?"

The radio could be heard from the children's bedroom: raised voices, screams, gunshots, fights replete with grunts, crashing furniture, and pounding fists.

Weiss raised an eyebrow. "Very lively."

"*Boston Blackie*," Fineberg said solemnly. "Next comes *Abbott and Costello,* then *Mr. District Attorney.*"

"How do you know?"

"When you have children, you know."

"It fills their heads with garbage," Weiss said. "Let them better read a good book."

"In school they read. For homework they read. At home, like all their friends, they listen. So why should my sons be outcasts, ah, Morris?"

"You're right, Fineberg, I admit it. I was the same way at their age. Only for me it was the early movies."

"Anyway, it is too late," Fineberg said. "Comic books, gangster movies, westerns, they have already done their job. They will outgrow it, God willing."

"This Boston Blackie," Weiss said, "he's a detective?"

Fineberg nodded. "Every week he solves a crime."

"Get him for Joey."

"It is that bad, Morris?"

Weiss shrugged.

"Better you should tell me now before Sadie gets here."

Weiss told him. About Detective O'Toole and his dire prognosis of Joey's chances. About Kabalsky at City College and his accusations. About his visit to the diner on 125th Street and Broadway, earlier that evening. "This diner," Weiss said, "so far it is worse than useless. Not only are they all blind, deaf, and dumb there, but their coffee is tasteless. Their donuts I wouldn't even touch. I showed them the pictures of Joey, of this Grasser, I described the man with the limp and mustache like a Cossack. You would think at least *him* they would remember. The Negroes wouldn't even answer. The whites would be lucky if they remember their own names."

Fineberg sighed.

"I will, of course, go back," Weiss said. "But maybe these people never were at the diner to begin with."

From the kitchen, they could hear Rose's voice rising over the clatter of dishes being rinsed and stacked, the mayhem on the radio, the sound of traffic on Grand Street three floors below. She was singing Dinah Shore's hit "Buttons and Bows" in a beautiful light soprano voice. The two men stopped talking to listen.

"She really *is* an angel," Weiss said.

"A golden voice," Fineberg agreed. "You think Kabalsky is lying?"

"He is very bitter," Weiss said. "Dostoevsky was wrong, Fineberg, suffering doesn't ennoble a man; it makes him worse. The camps ruined Kabalsky. I am not convinced he knows what he's talking about. It is possible he envies Joey."

"Envies what? That he sits in jail?"

"His youth. That he was born in America. That he still has a mother to worry about him. Kabalsky may begrudge him these blessings."

Fineberg nodded sadly. "So what next?"

Weiss shrugged. "I do more *nudging*," he said. "Something will come up. But I'm still not happy with your Joey."

"So who is?"

"Sadie, maybe?"

"She is his mother. What can you expect?"

"Ah-ha. You're having second thoughts yourself, eh, Fineberg?"

"What thoughts?" He leaned closer, lowered his voice. "I am on his side because Rosie is on Sadie's side. I am stuck. You saw him in jail, you saw what he is."

"I saw. That's why I'm asking. Already this has cost you an extra five dollars."

"For what?"

"O'Toole."

"No!"

"Business, Fineberg. You know this better than I do."

"Two dollars is not enough for him?"

"Good will," Weiss said dryly. "But it could be only the beginning. Make sure you want to go on with this. The money will add up. And who says he's innocent?"

"Boston Blackie, he fights crime for nothing."

"Let him fight."

Rose returned with a pot of tea, lemon slices, and the strudel. Three glasses and a bowl of sugar cubes were already on the table. The trio drank, ate, and joked until some twenty minutes later when the doorbell rang.

Rose hurried to answer the bell. Weiss rose, went to the closet, retrieved his jacket and tightened his tie. Fineberg, still in shirtsleeves, closed the door to the children's bedroom, then turned on the lights in the living room. He and Weiss were seated when Rose walked in with her arm around Sadie Ginzberg.

"Here she is," Rose said, smiling.

Weiss was surprised. He had somehow expected Sadie to be Rose's age, in her twenties. But, of course, he realized now, that couldn't be: Joey was a grown man. This short, matronly woman before him was in her mid-forties. Her disheveled brown hair was streaked with gray. She had a double chin, huge bosom, and round, protruding belly that strained against the girdle under her long polka-dot black dress. She also had on white bobby socks and low-heeled, mannish shoes. *An old-fashioned Yiddish mother*, Weiss thought glumly. Like the ones who visited his office every day. Abandoned by husbands, deserted by sons, robbed by boarders, business partners, landlords. An endless procession of complaints. Sadie hadn't spoken a word but already he knew her inside and out.

He and Fineberg stood up.

"Sadie," Fineberg said, opening his arms wide.

The woman flung herself at the lawyer, almost knocking him off his feet. He patted her shoulder awkwardly. "Everything will be all right. The detective is here."

Weiss sighed quietly.

Sadie Ginzberg pulled back quickly and turned to face him. "You are the detective!"

"Morris Weiss," Weiss said, extending his hand. She grabbed it in both of hers and began kissing it.

"Wonderful man," she wailed. "You will save my Joey. God will bless you!"

"I will do what I can," Weiss said hastily, wrenching his hand free.

"You must do more, more!"

"Calm yourself," Weiss said.

Fineberg dislodged Sadie and steered her to the padded armchair across from the sofa. "Sit. He is here to help."

Sadie remained on her feet, looking wildly around her. "He is my one hope!" she wailed. "My one hope!"

"Sit," Rose said.

"Sit," Weiss said.

"I have no one to turn to but him!"

"I beg you," Fineberg said," seat yourself!"

She sat. Heavily.

"Rosie," Weiss said, "bring her some tea and strudel."

"You want, Sadie?" Rose asked anxiously.

"What is food to me with my Joey in jail?"

"You must eat to keep up your strength," Rose said.

"*Oy vey*," Sadie groaned, looking up beseechingly from one face to another.

"For Joey," Rose said.

Sadie let out a long sigh. "*Nu*, a little maybe. Food has not crossed my lips today."

"Then it's about time," Rose said. "I will fix you something good."

"What appetite do I got? But fix if you want."

"Fix," Weiss said.

"Fix," Fineberg said.

Rose went out to the kitchen. Weiss and Fineberg seated themselves on the overstuffed, flowery sofa. Long flowered drapes covered the windows. An oriental carpet stretched across the floor. A bookcase behind the armchair was filled with works of the three classic Yiddish writers, Mendele Mocher Sforim, I. L. Peretz, and Sholom Aleichem, as well as some of the younger ones, Sholem Asch, Joseph Opatoshu, I. J. Singer. Tolstoi, Dostoevsky, and Thomas Mann were represented in English translations. There were some law books, Darwin's *The Origin of Species*, and Pearl Buck's *The Good Earth*, as well as paperbacks, and copies of the *Reader's Digest*. Weiss often learned about people by simply scanning their bookcase. Fineberg was an intellectual. But this, Weiss already knew.

"So Mrs. Ginzberg," he said, "about your son—"

"He has done nothing! They tell lies!"

"You know this?"

"Who should know better if not his mother? My Joey would not hurt even a fly."

"You see him often?"

"What, I should not see him often? My heart would give out."

"So when did you see him last?"

"Who can remember? Not long ago."

"Last week?"

"No."

"Last month?"

She shook her head.

"Last year, maybe?" Weiss asked hopefully.

"Why do you torture me? My Joey, God forbid, will be sent to prison, and you ask me these questions. Why?"

Weiss nodded. "You are right, Mrs. Ginzberg. So tell me about your son."

"What is to tell? He takes care of his mother. I want for nothing. Other mothers should have such a son. He is a gem."

"He gives you gifts?"

"What a question! He shouldn't give his mother gifts? He knows what I sacrifice for him!"

"You are a widow?"

"Yes, a widow. Joey, he is my whole life. I raise him by myself, with God's help."

"Besides gifts, Mrs. Ginzberg, how does he take care of you?"

"How? My rent he pays. For food he gives me money. For clothes. What doesn't he give me?"

"He puts this money in your hands?"

"He sends me. My son, he works for the City College, such important work, it eats up all his time. Always he is busy."

"And this money, it covers everything?"

"It shouldn't cover? Without my Joey I have nothing."

"All this money, it is from his job at the college, eh?"

"Where else should it be from?"

"A second job, maybe?"

"What second job? From the college my Joey has all he needs and more."

Weiss exchanged glances with Fineberg.

"Before this job," Weiss said, "he did what, Mrs. Ginzberg?"

She shrugged. "Small jobs. Some for not even a week. They were no good. My Joey was always looking to better himself. At the college he is, thank God, appreciated."

"And before that?"

"Before? He was in the army."

From the kitchen Rose called out, "Ready." She marched into the living room. "Come," she said to Sadie, "I will set a place for you at the table. You can talk more when you finish."

"He will wait?" Sadie asked, nodding at Weiss.

"Eat in good health," Weiss said. "I have nowhere else to go." He waited until the women had left the room before turning to his friend. "Rosie and Sadie, they are this close, eh, Fineberg?" He put his thumb and forefinger together.

"I said this?" The lawyer looked uncomfortable. "Sadie is like a mother to my Rosie."

"And Rosie's mother?"

"She is like a mother, too."

"Fineberg," Weiss said, "it is time for clear speaking."

"All right, Morris." The lawyer got to his feet. "My wife, she will tell you everything—in her own words."

"She is now the lawyer in the family?"

"I am training her." Fineberg left to sit with Sadie. Rose appeared a moment later.

"It is all my fault, Morris," she said, seating herself next to Weiss.

"Ah-ha! You killed this Grasser?"

"I mean about Sadie."

Weiss raised an eyebrow, smiled thinly. "You are not best friends?"

"I made Irving say so. I was afraid you would not help her otherwise."

"So who is this woman?"

"She is my mother's best friend."

"Your mother?"

"Sarah. They grew up together in Minsk like sisters. On the same boat they came to America, and for fifteen years they were neighbors on Hester Street. She helped take care of me when I was a baby. What these two women have been through together I cannot even begin to tell you, Morris."

"Sarah and Sadie. They should go into business together."

She laughed. "Be serious. You will not desert her?"

"I desert no one. Send back your husband."

She kissed him on the cheek, left, and was instantly replaced by Fineberg.

"That woman," Fineberg said, "she never stops *kvetching*."

"You brought this on yourself, Fineberg. And on me."

The lawyer spread his hands. "My mother-in-law, she comes here crying into her kerchief. What could I do? My Rosie begged me to hire you."

"Of course. I am the Boston Blackie of the Lower East Side. Only I charge. And for this, plenty. Bring back the woman, she can eat later."

"Sadie!" Fineberg yelled. "Come here a minute."

Sadie Ginzberg rushed in, followed by Rose. "*Oy vey*, what is it? What has happened?"

Weiss was on his feet. He held up Grasser's snapshot. "You know this man?"

She peered at the photo. "No. Who is he?"

"A dead man. Your son, he has a friend with a big mustache who limps?"

"How should I know this?"

"You don't know Joey's friends?"

"When he was a boy I knew. Not now."

"He tells you nothing about his life?"

"What should he tell me? He works hard."

"Mrs. Ginzberg," Weiss said, "I will try to help your son. But he is in big trouble. Do not expect miracles."

"God will make a miracle."

"Good," Morris Weiss said. "Better him than me."

CHAPTER 8

*It is a good idea, when on a case, to bring a gun. I
myself, alas, rarely do so. This has proven at times
to be an embarrassment, not to mention a very
dangerous mistake.*

From the casebooks of Morris Weiss

Max Weiss—The Present

April and I had a cozy lunch at a rustic inn. My client, over
soup and salad, asked me to continue hunting for her uncle.
We shook on it, finished our meal, and hit the road again.

I spotted the car almost immediately—a dark-green
late '90s Buick sedan. It had come out of a side road just
fast enough to catch my attention. But it didn't hang with
us for long, soon fading completely from view. Still, with
my blonde-headed client perched on the seat next to me,

I decided to take no chances. Better paranoid than sorry.

I said, "Come on, I'll show you something nice."

"After this morning, *nice* would be really pleasant."

"Nothing's too good for a client."

I turned right at the first intersection, and we soon found ourselves cruising down a more modest road, a two-laner heading off toward trees and pastures and green hills in the distance.

"The deluxe tour of the fall scenery," I told her.

"You do tours, too?"

"Sure. We're a full-service agency."

Presently, I made another turn, putting us on an even narrower road. Unlike its predecessor, this one had only a few twists and curves. It took only a couple of minutes for the sedan to pop up behind us again. It was keeping its distance, but since the road was all but empty, the green car was a standout.

"We may have company," I reluctantly informed my client.

April took it as a joke and wrinkled her nose at me. "*Where?* Is someone hiding in the backseat?"

"That would be too simple. There's a car following us."

She twisted around to look. "*What* car?"

The Buick drifted into view as the road straightened out again.

"There," I said.

"What's going on, Max?"

"I wish I knew. They've been behind us since lunch and probably even before that."

I dropped into fourth and spooled up the rpms to about 5000. The car behind us kept up.

"Hang on," I said.

I double-clutched into third, floored the pedal, and my little Saab took off as though she had grown wings.

The Buick also accelerated.

"Nuts," I said. "They should have dropped back. Now they've tipped their hand."

"Well," April said, "you could always shoot a couple of holes in their car if they don't behave, couldn't you? That *is* what private eyes do, isn't it?"

"Only in the land of Oz. For one thing, they might shoot back. Besides, I didn't bring my gun."

"You didn't bring your gun?"

"You got it," I said. "Who takes a gun to a rehab center? Reach into the glove compartment. You'll find a pair of binoculars. Swivel around and see if you can read their license plate."

She did as I asked. "I can't make it out," she said. "It's smeared. The numbers are illegible."

"Can you see who's in the car?"

She looked again. "Two men. I can't make out their faces. They're both wearing baseball caps."

"What team?"

"The Yankees."

"My team. How bad can they be?"

I slammed the short-throw shifter back to third, and wound her up to 6500. Our necks snapped back with each shift. I geared down for the turns but otherwise kept her at full throttle. We howled along the roadway. Luckily, no hikers or bikers were on the road, so, I didn't get to bump anyone off. Leaning on the horn and flashing my lights, we passed a few startled drivers. The green sedan steadily dropped back.

A small, four-block hamlet whose name I didn't catch rose up before us. There were jaywalkers and a little traffic.

I mashed the air horn, slowed only a fraction, and sailed on ahead.

The four blocks blazed by. I noticed neither a police nor

a fire department—obviously, a grave oversight. Maybe there was at least a speed trap near by.

Outside of town, I eased up on the pedal, braked hard for a sliding 180-degree turn, then doubled back on a street parallel to the main drag. I was getting tricky.

I hung a left at the third block and recrossed Main Street. The green car was speeding down Main, horn blaring, two blocks beyond us, heading out of town. Only I wasn't there anymore.

I went slowly across to the other street that ran parallel to Main. Here was a mix of blue-collar houses, a grocery store, pizza parlor, and Shell gas station with a four-bay garage.

The Shell station it was.

I drove right past the gas pumps and straight into an empty bay. A black sedan and two pickups were already there in various stages of repair. I opened the car door and smelled oil, gas, and grease, all very comforting. I looked over at April. She was breathing hard.

A stocky, middle-aged guy in overalls came over and asked me what the trouble was. I almost told him, too. Instead I said, "We just need a breather."

"Car overheated?"

"We are."

The guy looked at me. It was time to use irrefutable logic and banish that look. I handed him a twenty. "We just want to park here for a little while."

He inspected me, April, the Saab, and the money. "Sure," he said, "take your time."

"If anyone asks," I told him, "we're not here."

"Not here," he said, as if that made perfect sense. He nodded good-naturedly, pocketed his cash, and walked away.

"Logic never fails," I told April.

"What are we doing here?" my client asked.

"Hiding."

"So the Buick can't find us?"

"Right. We don't know what they want. And that's bad for our side."

"Bad?"

"Sure. Because we might not like what they want. In fact, we might hate it."

"Max, what's going on? This can't be about Uncle Felix."

"Maybe it's about Davidson. Maybe it's about both of them. Or maybe neither. Who knows? One thing's for sure, I'm going to do my best to find out."

We hung around another fifteen minutes. No green Buick came back looking for us.

We drove back to the city.

CHAPTER 9

Morris Weiss—1948

"It's Weiss," Morris Weiss said into the phone.

"Ah, and a fine good morning to you, Mr. Weiss."

"Anything new with this Ginzberg business, Sergeant O'Toole?"

"There has been some movement. Your client Ginzberg—"

"Please," Weiss said in a pained voice. "Fineberg is my client, and Ginzberg is his client."

"Of course. Well, he claims to have been in the army."

"Claims?"

"There is no record of his ever having served in our grand armed forces."

"What did he say about this?"

"Nothing. Johnny Ryan is handling the case. He hasn't braced our lad yet."

"Anything else?"

"Earl Grasser. Now this one did see active duty. He was even decorated. Honorable discharge in '46 with the rank of corporal. Grasser, his neighbors all agree, was a salesman."

"What did he sell?"

"Anything and everything, it seems. But no one is sure exactly what, or even where."

"But he didn't live from thin air alone?"

"He wasn't a pauper, Mr. Weiss. Detective Ryan has just begun making the rounds."

"Give him my regards."

Weiss went to his bedroom closet and pulled out a gray tweed jacket, charcoal-gray slacks, and a red paisley tie. He removed a dark-gray shirt, shorts, and a clean sleeveless undershirt from a chest of drawers and spread them all on his freshly made bed. He was satisfied. Argyle socks and black wing-tipped shoes completed the outfit. He dressed slowly and with care. Then, seating himself on the edge of the bed, he reached for the phone on the bedside table and dialed Fineberg at his storefront office. The lawyer picked up on the first ring.

Weiss identified himself.

"Good morning, Morris," Fineberg said. "You are up early."

"Only lawyers get up early? Listen, Fineberg, your Joey turns out to be even less kosher than he seemed."

"Now he is my Joey? This must be something very bad. What is his new crime?"

"Lying."

"Tell me something I do not already know, Morris."

"Joey was never in the army."

There was a silence. "True, this I did not know. With my own eyes I saw him in uniform. You are sure?"

"Anyone can buy a uniform in America. O'Toole says the army has no record of him."

"Then where was he for four years?"

"A good question. Only put to the wrong man. For an answer you must ask Joey. Now would be a good time to do it."

"Now?"

"Better sooner than later."

"You want I should *schlep* to Center Street in the middle of my workday?"

"Me they wouldn't even let into his cell alone. He's your client. I don't have to tell you how this works."

"You will ruin me."

"Joey will ruin you. This case, Fineberg, was never my idea. Also, ask that woman—the mother."

"There I draw the line."

"Suddenly you are a man of principle, eh?"

"My Rosie will speak to her."

"Excellent. I'll be in touch. Have a good day."

Weiss sat alone at a long table in the City College cafeteria. He had on his full-length trench coat and gray homburg. Spread in front of him was the *Daily Mirror*. He smelled bacon, eggs, coffee, fried potatoes, and corned-beef hash. There was the constant din of voices, the clatter of trays and dishes.

At ten-twenty Weiss looked up and spotted a once-familiar face. He rose, tossed the tabloid into a trash basket, and made his way to the "red" table, far over by the east wall.

A small group was seated there. Some looked like typical undergraduates but for their clothing. Ties and jackets were the custom at the college. These boys wore denim or plaid work shirts and overalls, as if instantly ready to take their places on a picket line or engage in manual labor. The two girls with them were dressed normally. Education majors or girlfriends. City College, Weiss knew, did not allow women to matriculate. Four older men, the GI Bill contingent, wore wrinkled white dress shirts, open at the collar, and creaseless suit pants.

One of the boys had begun tuning a guitar; another was reaching for his banjo case. Weiss hoped he could finish his business here before this crew broke into ardent song.

Stepping up behind one of the white-shirted men, Weiss placed a hand on his shoulder. "Rudy," he said.

Rudy swung half around in his chair and glanced up blankly at Weiss. "Yeah?" he said.

Rudy Tile was trim, medium height, with an angular face and crooked nose. Brown eyes peered out at Weiss from under black bushy eyebrows. Recognition came.

"Sarge?"

Weiss nodded, smiling. "The same."

"Jeez, you gettin' an education here, too?"

Weiss laughed. "Hardly."

"Know it all already, huh?"

"And then some." Weiss grinned.

Rudy turned to the table. "This here is Morry Weiss, we served in Germany together. Small world."

There were a couple of smiles, some nods, and a few indifferent stares.

Rudy got to his feet. The two men shook.

"So what are ya doin' here, Sarge, slummin'?"

"Just passing through."

The guitarist had begun to softly sing "Which Side Are You On?" He was joined by the banjo player.

Weiss said, "Let me borrow you for a short while, Rudy?"

"Sure, what's up?"

"Army talk."

Rudy shrugged, slid into his leather jacket, and reached for a battered briefcase on the floor. He nodded his good-byes to the table, and the two men headed up the main aisle for the door. Behind them, the entire "red" table was singing full voice in four-part harmony.

"They should charge money," Weiss said.

The pair left the building. The sky was gray, overcast. Plumes of black smoke poured from surrounding chimneys, darkening the sky and sending acrid fumes over the neighborhood. An east wind was blowing. Weiss buttoned his trench coat, pulled down his hat brim. He steered Rudy down the block, away from Shepard Hall. A few students could be seen. Otherwise, the street was empty.

"Hey, Sarge, you sure this meetin' was an accident?"

"Accidents happen in automobiles."

"So what's this about?"

"A question first. Are they paying you well, Rudy?"

"Who?"

"The F.B.I."

"You nuts? What the hell for?"

"For informing on your left-wing friends."

"Where'd you hear this crap?"

"I don't have to hear it."

"No?"

"I know you from Germany."

"You always were a card, Sarge."

"And you were always a fixer. Selling army property that winter, when you were a corporal in supply. Wool coats, jackets, pants, caps, sweaters. All very scarce then in Germany. And worth plenty. Also, rubber tires. Though that wasn't in your department. A Sergeant Kleinman was in charge. The pair of you made a deal. You had the customers; he had the goods. You would get rich together. But

before this could happen, Kleinman was caught. He tried
to sell a Jeep, which was a very bad mistake. They had him
dead to rights because the buyer was an undercover C.I.C.
In his statement, Kleinman implicated you. But you had
made only peanuts so far. And your cousin Hanks was a
major at Division Headquarters. So you, Rudy, were
shipped stateside. And the unfortunate Kleinman, he was
shipped to prison. But you were still guilty."

Rudy laughed. "Guilty as hell. So what do you want?"

"An operator. Like you, Rudy. With fingers in every pie.
That's why I kept track of you. In Germany, you knew
everyone, even street pickpockets. That's what I need now."

"A pickpocket?"

"An associate of sorts. For such work the pay is not
bad." The detective reached into a pocket, withdrew his
wallet and handed Rudy a five. "A down payment."

"So what do I gotta do, Sarge, burn down the college?"

"That comes later. For five dollars, the work is less
strenuous."

"What is it?"

"Find a man for me. I don't know his name but I think
he's a student here on the GI Bill."

"Day or night?"

"This you'll have to find out for yourself. Also, there is
a chance he is not a student, but someone who loiters at
the college. Maybe for business reasons."

"What business?"

"I hope you will also find this out."

"Got a description?"

Weiss described the man who had a mustache like a
Cossack and a bad limp. He went on to show Rudy mug
shots of Joey Ginzberg and Earl Grasser. "Grasser is dead;
Ginzberg's in the hoosegow. All three seemed to have
known each other. I want to know what went on between
them."

"You don't want much for a lousy fin, do you?"

"There will be more, Rudy, if you produce."

"That's what I like to hear," Rudy said.

"We have a deal?" Weiss said.

"We got it, Sarge," Rudy said.

Morris Weiss smiled.

"What do you think?" he said.

Ida took his arm.

They were on West Thirty-ninth and Seventh Avenue strolling through the semidarkness toward the lights of Forty-second Street, part of the crowd that had just left the Metropolitan Opera House.

"I have," she said, "seen better."

"You are a tough critic," Weiss said.

They had gone to a performance of *Swan Lake* given by the Ballet Russe de Monte Carlo.

"Maybe," Weiss said, "they are tired from their long trip across the ocean?"

"That, Morris dear, is not an excuse."

"I thought maybe it would do."

"A lot you know."

They both laughed.

"At Madison Square Garden," Weiss said, "they now have the World's Championship Rodeo. Gene Autry and Champion are there." The detective swept his gray fedora off his head and bowed gallantly. "You have only to ask."

Ida laughed. "So, you saw nothing wrong?"

He shrugged. "What's to see? What I know about dancing you could put in a thimble. If they don't fall down on the floor, I am satisfied. Now, if you ask me about serious music, that's another story. As you well know, Idaleh."

"I should," she said. "And look what it's gotten me."

"A cavalier who worships you?"

"A private detective who is always on a case."

"Shhhhh. Not so loud," Weiss said. "Others will want one, too. Also, you must remember what *I* have gotten. A wonderful musician who goes from city to city like a wandering minstrel, and is never home. Not that I complain."

Ida Kaufman, a professional violist, often played in pickup orchestras to make ends meet. But mostly she and her three colleagues struggled to preserve their fledgling string quartet. She was petite, dark, and perky, with large brown eyes and long, glistening black hair that made her look like a gypsy. Tonight she wore a billowy, multicolored dress under her coat.

They had first met at a party after one of her concerts. Weiss had come with a date but had gone home with Ida. He considered it one of his better decisions. They had been seeing each other for more than a year now.

"A nightcap?" Weiss asked.

"Why not?"

The pair stopped for coffee and cake at an automat. They got a table for themselves.

"You know, I was just complaining to Fineberg about this place," Weiss said, taking a bite of chocolate cake. "But the desserts aren't so bad. And you don't have to wait for service."

"And you are a miser." Ida laughed.

"You would rather go to the Stork Club?" Weiss asked. "And make me a pauper?"

Ida smiled and drank her coffee.

"So," she said, "what is this case that keeps you so busy?"

Weiss stopped eating and sighed. "It is a mishmash. The accused, who I am for some reason trying to get off, is a lowlife."

"What is he accused of?"

"A killing."

"You are working for a murderer?"

"Who knows? Everything this lowlife says is a lie. But he may be innocent."

"You have a reason for believing this?"

"I always have a reason," Weiss said, smiling. "Only sometimes the reason is wrong."

"And now?"

"Even a child could come up with a better story than this man. And he is an experienced criminal. That is in his favor."

"I understand nothing," Ida said.

Weiss smiled. "I understand even less," he said, finishing his cake and coffee.

Outside, they flagged down a checkered cab.

Ida lived on East Fifty-second Street off First Avenue. Unlike the detective's flat, it was relatively close by, and, being on the ground floor, rear, there were no stairs to climb.

The cab dropped them off in front of her brownstone.

"It feels like coming home," Weiss said.

"It should," Ida said. "You spend so much time here." She grinned. "Of course, it's always a pleasure having you."

The first thing they did on entering the apartment was fling their hats and overcoats on the sofa and fall into each other's arms, kissing ardently. The second thing they did was hurry hand-in-hand into the small bedroom and strip off the rest of their clothes. They gazed at each other for an instant. Weiss was always amazed to see how beautiful she was. Then, throwing back the quilt, they fell onto the bed and made passionate love together.

Afterward, they lay there, breathless.

"Magic," she whispered to him. "As always."

Weiss smiled and kissed her. "Better than Houdini and Thurston combined," he said.

"Can I get you something, Moisheleh?" she asked, snuggling close to him. "Coffee, tea, juice, maybe?"

"Just you, Idaleh," he whispered in her ear.

"You have already had me."

"That," Weiss said, "was only the appetizer."

"True. This life we live, you know, it could be even better."

"I know," Weiss said, smiling. "Now you will tell me that if only I got a nine-to-five job everything would be fine."

"And you will tell me, Moisheleh, that if I performed only on weekends, we would have more time together."

"We would."

"And again everything would be fine."

They both laughed. She rolled on top of him.

"Maybe," she said, "you will catch a big criminal. And get a reward."

"I have already caught a big criminal. The expense almost ruined me. And there was no reward."

"Don't worry, darling," she said. "We will think of something."

"I look worried?" Morris Weiss said. "We always think of something."

CHAPTER 10

There are times when one case turns out to be another case. This can be very confusing and should be avoided whenever possible. Sometimes, of course, it is not possible.

From the casebooks of Morris Weiss

Max Weiss—The Present

No one seemed to be hanging around April's Lower Manhattan office building. That made sense, even if nothing else did. If the Buick guys knew who we were, why bother chasing us?

"You okay?" I asked April.

"I think so."

I rode up the elevator with my client, checked out her

office, then went down again and reclaimed my car before I got a ticket for double parking.

Back in my office, I called Uncle Morris.

He picked up on the first ring. I could hear kids yelling in the background.

"Where are you?" I asked.

"I am on the beach. A very pleasant place, too. And you?"

"At the office."

"Ah, then we still have an office. Excellent. And we are, I trust, still solvent?"

"Uh-huh," I said.

"That is good to hear. I have only been gone one day. What could happen?"

"I'll tell you," I said. "I've been chased by two guys in a car. The guy I'm looking for turns out to be another guy. Maybe. And both are still missing. Otherwise, everything is just dandy."

"Dandy doesn't sound so bad. We still have a client?"

"Yeah."

"Then I won't worry. Confidentially speaking, wild horses couldn't drag me back to the city. I have just begun working on my tan."

"Bad for the skin," I said.

"At my age, who will notice?"

We said our goodbyes.

I booted up my PC, logged on to the Web, and accessed the Manhattan reverse directory. I pulled Davidson's phone bill out of a pocket and set to work. The reverse directory lists phone numbers first, then names and addresses. Paul Davidson had been in Mannerdale three weeks. During that time he had made one call each week, all to the same number. The number belonged to a Stella Kanufsky. The nonexistent Queens daughter was also named Stella.

I opened my wall safe and took out my Browning automatic. Maybe I was a bit under-gunned these days, when every cop, pusher, looney, and even school kids toted seventeen-round plastic-framed Glocks and Sigsauers or Uzis. But Uncle Morris had done pretty well in his day with the then-revolutionary 1935 Browning high-powered "captain," mainly by shooting straight. Weiss and Weiss believed in tradition.

I opened a box of forty S&W cartridges, loaded up, stuck the ten-round double-stack magazine into my shoulder holster, shrugged into a blue windbreaker, and was on my way.

Stella Kanufsky lived on East Fourth Street between Avenue B and C. I parked around the corner, walked over to the address, a small yellow brick apartment house, and buzzed her. No one buzzed back. I rang a different bell, with the same results. Undaunted, I tried a third time. A man's voice, through the intercom, asked who I was. I said FedEx. The buzzer sounded instantly. No one messes with FedEx.

I stepped into a well-lit, beige hallway. A self-service elevator was to the right, which I ignored. Instead, I hurried to the door at the end of the corridor marked "Staircase." Before the guy came down to find out what had happened to his package, I started climbing stairs. I didn't have far to go. Stella Kanufsky lived on the second floor.

She did not respond when I rang her bell or knocked on the door. I put my ear to the door, expecting to hear dead silence. What I heard instead was something that sounded like sobbing.

I kept my ear pressed against the door long enough to eliminate TV as the source of the sound.

I stepped back and called out, "Mrs. Kanufsky, are you in there?"

That drew a blank.

I tried again. "Mrs. Kanufsky, I need to speak with you, it's urgent."

That got me more of the same.

"Tell me what's wrong," I called. "I can help you."

The senior partner of our agency would have tipped his hat to me. Another good deed in the offing. A few more freebies like this and I'd be out of business.

"Who are you?" a voice called back. It was an old voice, tremulous and hushed.

"My name is Max Weiss. I'm a private detective."

"Weiss? You are Jewish?"

"Sure."

"You are not with them?"

"I'm against them," I said without a moment's hesitation. I only hoped they deserved my enmity.

"Wait."

Soon I heard a click. The door, held firm by a chain lock, opened an inch. An eye gazed up at me. I smiled back at it. The door closed to unfasten the chain, then swung open all the way.

A very small, white-haired elderly woman stood in the doorway. She wore a long yellow dress under a see-through plastic apron.

"I am so upset, I do not know what is going on with me. Please come in."

I followed her into a small living room. Everything looked as though it had been around since the early fifties. My hostess had been around a tad longer. I smelled onions, broiled liver, cabbage.

"Sit, please," she said.

I sat.

Stella chose a hard-backed chair across from me. She dabbed at her eyes with a man's hanky. "They know," she whispered, "where he is."

"Where who is, Mrs. Kanufsky? Your husband?"

"What husband? I am since the war a widow. Mine brother, Leo."

"Leo Kanufsky?"

"Who else?"

"Does the name Paul Davidson mean anything to you?"

"What Davidson? They know where Leo is."

"Who knows?"

"Two men. I open mine door. They show me guns. They hold these guns so close to mine head, I think I am already shot. They make me to tell."

"Who were they?" I asked.

"How should I know this? They did not confide their secrets. Only mine they wanted."

"Why were these men after Leo?"

"This they did not tell me either."

"Did Leo say he was in some kind of trouble?"

She shrugged. "He does not tell me his troubles. He say nothing. Only I should not tell where he is, or it will be bad for him."

"Why was he in Mannerdale, Mrs. Kanufsky?"

"He was nervous, so tired. There they help him."

"When were these men here?"

"Now. Minutes ago they leave. Why you stay here? Go to him. Go."

"Don't worry, I won't let him get hurt. Where is he?"

She looked me straight in the eye and told me.

"Thanks." I had one more question. "Does your brother know a Felix Margoshes?"

"Margoshes?" She shrugged. "This name I have never heard."

CHAPTER 11

Morris Weiss—1948

"Fineberg," Morris Weiss said.

Fineberg looked up from his lunch. "Go, Morris, get something to eat. I have saved a place for you."

Weiss nodded, glanced around the cafeteria. Twelve-thirty, and the lunch crowd was out in full force. The din here was even worse than at City College. But it was a *haymish* din. The Garden Cafeteria was only a few steps from the Forward Building, and staff members of the *Jewish Daily Forward* and its rival, the *Day,* ate here. Along with Yiddish intellectuals, writers, and poets from all over the Lower East Side. Both Weiss and Fineberg were regulars.

Weiss moved toward the steam table, nodding at famil-iar faces as he went. Presently he returned carrying a tray loaded with split pea soup, stuffed peppers, two slices of rye bread, butter, coffee, and peach pie. Fineberg removed his overcoat from the empty chair. Weiss put down his tray, shrugged out of his trench coat, and seated himself.

The lawyer had already finished his borscht and was digging into his blintzes. He looked up. "Tonight, Morris, I am buying two tickets for my Rosie and me to the Yiddish Art Theatre. Maurice Schwartz, he is in *The Voice of Israel*."

"The Yiddish John Barrymore, eh?"

"Better than Barrymore."

Weiss finished his soup. "Schwartz was already an old man ten years ago, yet he still plays young lovers."

"With such talent, let him play who he wants," Fineberg said. "I would take my boys, too, but wild horses could not drag them to a Yiddish play. Them I take to *Abbott and Costello Meet Frankenstein*." He drank his coffee.

"A smart move," Weiss said.

"Morris, I can also buy another pair of tickets for you and Ida. Rose would be very happy if you both joined us. I also wouldn't complain."

The two friends smiled at each other.

"When are you going, Irving?"

"Tomorrow night."

"Ah." Weiss sighed. "Ida and I already have tickets for *Carmen* tomorrow. I am sorry."

"Don't be sorry. We will go another time. Is everything well between you two?"

"Better then well." *And then some*, Weiss thought. He recalled Bessie, the hairdresser. She had come before Ida. Poor Bessie. It was best only to take her dancing. Naomi, a secretary at the Workmen's Circle, was very pretty but preferred Yiddish lectures above all, especially about how to improve the world. He could hardly sit through them. And Molly, the dentist's assistant. If she had any interests besides teeth, he never found out what they were. They were all, fortunately, good in bed. But not as good as Ida.

"What happened with you and Joey?" Weiss asked.

"You will not believe it."

Weiss raised an eyebrow and began eating his stuffed peppers. "How bad can it be?" he finally asked between bites.

"He swears he was in the army."

"So that's good."

"But he lost his papers."

"That's bad."

"Even worse."

"What can be worse?"

"Listen. My Rosie spoke to the mother. She says he wrote to her from basic training. And from Europe came a few letters, too."

"Ah-ha. But she also lost them."

"You are a mind reader, Morris. When she moved from Hester Street to Second Avenue, she saw suddenly they were gone."

"That family," Weiss said, "should be more careful."

"I asked Joey where he served. He said here and there. I asked who his friends were. He said he remembers only first names. Morris, he could not even give me his battalion. I threatened him. I said I would drop the case like a hot coal."

"He was impressed?"

"He said I could do what I want." Fineberg pushed away his empty coffee cup. "What is he, an idiot?"

"Not a genius. But even if suddenly he finds his discharge papers, this would still not explain why the army doesn't have his name. There is here a bigger mystery."

Weiss sighed.

"Fineberg, let me speak openly with you."

"When, Morris, have we not spoken openly with each other?"

"All right, short and simple. With this Joey you will lose your shirt."

"This, Morris, you have already told me. I have many shirts."

"More of your dollars have gone into the pocket of this Rudy, a hooligan."

"Is he worth it?"

Weiss nodded.

"Then I will pay."

"Yesterday you were complaining."

"That was yesterday. Rosie and I talked about this. She is very satisfied with what you are doing."

"Send her my regards." Weiss ate his pie and washed it down with the coffee.

"I will cover all expenses, Morris. My Rosie should have no complaints that I did not do enough."

"And if he's guilty?"

"That is another story."

"I can stop, eh?"

"Guilty is guilty. Your job is done."

"Some job. You are crazy, Fineberg."

"Of course," Fineberg said. "Wait until you marry, Morris, then you will be crazy, too."

Weiss walked the short distance from the cafeteria to his office. He went up four flights of stairs. The door to his office stood open. Cautiously he entered. Rudy was sitting in Weiss's chair, still in the black leather jacket he had worn at the college, his feet up on the desk, reading an office copy of *Look Magazine*. Rudy glanced up and grinned.

Weiss said, "I was just talking about you, Rudy."

"Yeah? Whaddya say?"

"That you were a hooligan."

Rudy laughed.

"You got it right, Sarge," he said.

Weiss smiled.

"You picked my lock, Rudy?"

Rudy lowered his feet, put aside the magazine.

"Sure," he said. "I figure you wanna hear what I got, right? You don't want me coolin' my heels out in the hall."

"True, you are now a valued employee."

Rudy rose to relinquish his seat to Weiss. The detective waved him back. "Sit," he said.

Rudy lowered himself back into the chair.

"You have something for me already?" Weiss said.

"You know me, Sarge. Quick."

"You are a marvel, Rudy. But I don't want you to cut too many classes because of me. Your education is important."

"To hell with my education."

"Always the same Rudy." Weiss hung up his hat and coat. He moved the client's chair to the side of his desk, settled in, and nodded at his guest to begin.

"It's a racket, Sarge, they're peddlin' dope."

"The students are dope fiends?"

"Forget them."

"The professors?"

Rudy shook his head.

"So who is left?"

"The vets."

"Ah-ha. But they are students, too."

"Older. And in a class by themselves, right?"

Weiss nodded. "And what of your left-wing friends?"

"A buncha creeps. All they know is a lotta big words they picked up in books."

"So who, Rudy, are the pushers? Is maybe Joey Ginzberg one?"

"You got the wrong guy, Sarge."

"His mother will be happy."

"Look, I asked around plenty. No one's got a thing on

the guy. I dunno what he does off campus, but on, he's clean as a whistle."

Weiss turned his head slightly toward his office windows as though seeking inspiration from the view. A large billboard in the distance showed a smiling, rosy-cheeked beauty peddling Tip-Top Bread, another, Nash cars. No inspiration was to be found there. He turned back. "And our friend Earl Grasser?"

"Him neither."

"He was an innocent student?"

"Innocent, maybe. Only the guy was never no student."

"So then what was he?"

"The hell knows. He came around sometimes. That's all I got."

"And this leaves us where?"

"With the gimp."

"An unfortunate nickname."

"Yeah, but on the button. So far, Sarge, I ain't had much luck with this guy. No one's seen him for a while. An' get this, no one can even give me his right name."

"He has wrong names?"

Rudy grinned. "He got plenty. All first ones, too. Chuck. Larry. Billy. Listen, no one's ever seen him in a classroom. So what does he do at the college? You figure it out."

"Maybe he too works for the F.B.I.?"

"Yeah, yeah, t' F.B.I."

Weiss smiled. "So who else, Rudy?"

"One other guy was dealin', a Pete Munchanko. This was a couple months ago. He ain't been around since."

"So now for the big question," Weiss said. "Who is the supplier?"

"Look, Sarge, if I knew that right off the bat, so would the cops. I need time on this."

Weiss smiled broadly. "Of course. I think you have

done an excellent piece of work." He reached into a pocket, removed his wallet, and handed Rudy another five. "More to follow."

The two men rose.

"Take care," Weiss said, shaking hands.

As soon as Rudy was on the other side of the door, the detective's smile vanished. Moving fast, he stepped to the closet, pulled off his suit, and threw on a blue denim work shirt and work pants. He stepped into a pair of Adler's Elevator Shoes, which added a full inch to his height, shrugged into a worn brown leather jacket, and donned a green checkered peaked cap that he pulled down low over his forehead. He locked the office door and ran down the four flights of stairs to the street.

Rudy was a full block away, heading west. The detective followed quickly.

When Rudy stepped into a phone booth Weiss was only a few yards behind him. He turned into a candy store where he could easily watch his quarry through the storefront window.

He spent five cents on a cigar and three cents for a *New York Times*. He stuck the unlit cigar in his mouth, again adjusted the brim of his cap, and folded the paper under his arm. Studying his reflection in the window, he saw a cigar-chomping stranger.

When Rudy left the phone booth, Weiss was behind him.

The pair trekked by a number of small shops and markets, all with Yiddish lettering on their storefronts. *A Yiddish country*, Weiss thought. *But how long will it last? Already first-generation Jews—like Fineberg's sons— were American to the bone.*

Rudy hit East Broadway and headed down into the IND subway station.

Weiss ran to catch up.

An uptown train pulled in and both men boarded. Each sat at different ends of the car. The detective hid behind his copy of the *Times*, occasionally peering out at the back of Rudy's head. He had a pretty good idea where his man was going. They changed trains twice before reaching the City College stop at 135th Street and Broadway.

Weiss walked uphill to Convent Avenue and took up a position opposite Shepard Hall. Leaning against a parked car, hands in jacket pockets, he waited patiently.

It was dark by the time Rudy emerged through the wide double doors, part of the crowd of students streaming out into the night.

Rudy crossed the street, turned west. Weiss tagged along, but at a good distance. The neighborhood here was colored. Any closer and Weiss would be a standout if Rudy glanced back.

Broadway was crowded. The show windows of a diner, ice cream parlor, and grocery store lit up the corner. A framed autographed picture of Sugar Ray Robinson, the welterweight champ, hung in a bar window. Rudy did not linger. He continued west, then turned north at Riverside Drive.

Weiss turned with him.

They were on a deserted semi-residential block. Weiss, standing in the shadow of a corner building, saw Rudy stop mid-block and lean up against a lamppost.

Some godforsaken place, he thought; *only in the river itself would it be worse.*

Rudy lit a cigarette. He looked twice at his watch during the next ten minutes.

A black Cadillac Coupe cruised down the block and pulled to a stop next to him.

Three men climbed out.

The tallest was in his forties and wore a black, loose-fitting overcoat and black snap-brim hat. He was thin to the point of emaciation. A hook nose and sunken cheeks looked out of a long, sallow face. A shorter, burly man in a worn gray herringbone coat and gray peaked cap was on his left. He had a wide, thick-featured face and massive shoulders. He was the one to watch out for, Weiss thought. The third, the car's driver, was the youngest of the lot, a slender man in a brown suburban coat, tan porkpie hat, and dark glasses.

Weiss gazed at the three men, then removed a pen and notepad from his pocket and jotted down the Cadillac's license plate number.

The three strolled over to Rudy. He and the tall man engaged in a brief animated conversation. Then the man hit Rudy in the face.

Rudy stepped back, apparently more surprised than hurt.

Gray Cap swung a long looping right to the side of Rudy's jaw.

Weiss winced. Rudy fell to the pavement.

The tall man kicked him in the ribs, dug a blackjack out of a coat pocket.

Weiss regretted not having brought his gun. He sighed, stepped out from the shadow of the building, and began walking toward the men under the lamppost. Even in his elevator shoes he knew he was not an imposing figure. He counted on that.

All three had now turned to look at him. Rudy, on the ground, glazed eyes open, did not bother.

"What's going on here?" Weiss demanded, sounding comical even to himself.

"Get lost," Gray Cap snarled.

"Why have you hit this man?" Weiss shouted back. As if it were a perfectly sane question to ask under these circumstances.

Gray Cap stepped forward, his hands balled into fists

at his sides—definitely the wrong place for them to be.

"You deaf?" he said.

Weiss, very fast, hit him three times with a combination of straight shots to the jaw. Gray Cap bounced off the lamppost, but instead of falling down came back with a slashing right of his own. The detective blocked the blow with a forearm, found himself rocked back, nearly knocked off his feet.

He danced away as Gray Cap threw another right. *Hits like a sledgehammer*, he thought, *but a one-armed fighter, thank God*.

Weiss slid under the right and planted a left squarely on Gray Cap's chin.

He slipped another right.

A short, jarring uppercut straightened Gray Cap to his full height. Weiss hammered his head with right/left combinations. Gray Cap turned as if to casually stroll away and fell flat on his face.

Black Suit began to raise his blackjack, more in self-defense than aggression. Weiss moved in with a left jab followed by a right cross with plenty of hip action.

Black Suit shuddered and fell backward to the pavement.

Dark Glasses had seen enough.

His right hand went inside his coat. Weiss threw himself at the man, pinning his arm, and slammed him in the side of the head with two quick looping rights. He stepped back and shot a straight left to finish the job.

The man reeled against the big car and hung there motionless as if impaled.

The detective sighed. This was the first time he'd fought in elevator shoes. And hopefully, the last.

Weiss yanked the gun, an army model Colt .45 automatic, from the man's holster. Stepping back, he surveyed the three fallen men. They lay perfectly still, heedless of his presence. He shrugged, put the gun in his jacket pocket, and looked down at Rudy.

"Sarge," Rudy said in some wonder, "that you?"

"The same."

He held out a hand and helped Rudy to his feet.

"I shoulda been straight with you, Sarge."

"It's never too late."

"You're taller."

"I often grow on people."

"You followed me."

"That is what detectives do."

"An' you beat up them big guys."

"Of course. I am the Heifetz of pugilism."

Together, the pair disappeared around the corner.

CHAPTER 12

When faced with danger, it is better to take evasive action than risk, God forbid, injury or an untimely death. This I learned in the army as a young man. It is still true.

From the casebooks of Morris Weiss

Max Weiss—The Present

It was a short ride.

I parked and sat in my car, staring out the window. Street lamps were lit now, but the darkness couldn't obscure the neighborhood. It still looked like something the dog had dug up and then rejected.

The Brooklyn Bridge loomed to my right over the decaying tenements. Where I was, the pavement had crumbled. No pedestrians were showing their faces. Only a

handful of sorry-looking cars were parked here. A green
Buick was not among them.

I climbed out of my Saab, unzipped my windbreaker so
I could get at my gun, and headed for the address Kanufsky's sister had given me. A cold, damp wind had started to
blow off the East River. The old man sure picked a great
hideout. If the guys from the Buick didn't get him, the ele-
ments would. At least it wasn't pouring rain.

The house had been painted once, but most of the
paint had flaked off by now. I looked up and saw lights in
three windows. People actually lived here. That encour-
aged me. I pushed open the door and stepped into a dim
hallway. Dim was better than nothing.

I went up the staircase. The banister swung away
from me as if disgusted by my touch. Crooked stairs with
worn marble treads creaked with each step I took. Aside
from that and the wind howling against the walls, there
were no sounds in the building, as if the people who in-
habited these flats were too feeble to stir themselves. The
smell of rotting wood and mold hovered over me.

I reached the third floor. A large gray rat at the far end
of the hallway peered at me with small malevolent red
eyes, then scampered away. I thought of calling it back.
I could use the company. Of course, if I found Kanufsky
I wouldn't be alone. I wasn't all that sure it would be an
improvement.

His flat was at the rear of the building. I was headed
in that direction when the wind suddenly flung his door
open and banged it shut. I stood stock still waiting for something more to happen. When it didn't, I started breathing
again and continued on my way. A few more steps brought
me to the door.

I pushed it open, and stepped into the flat.

The plaster on all four walls was cracked and peeling.
A cot, a small table, and a hard-backed chair were the

only furnishings. A man's gray jacket hung over the chair. The window directly facing me was wide open, which accounted for the slamming door. But what accounted for the open window?

I called Kanufsky's name. No one answered. A glance into the bathroom and tiny kitchen showed that they were empty. Aside from the jacket there were no signs that anyone was living here. I went over to the window and looked out. Out front where I'd parked, was an area destined for demolition. Back here the steel frames of new buildings were rising.

I turned from the window and went to inspect the gray jacket. I found nothing in any of the pockets.

While I was mulling over what to do next, I heard something outside. It could have been someone yelling for help. Or just the wind.

I went to the open window and stuck my head out. Only darkness. I was turning away when I heard it again, a faint and wavering voice.

I leaned far out and tried to see beyond the first structure. Nothing. Then, for an instant, I seemed to see a running man in a white shirt. He was gone before I was sure he was really there. I couldn't tell what he was running from. Then I saw a pair of guys, and they were running, too. Maybe after him or away from something.

My best bet, I figured, was to call the cops. If nothing else, there'd be two of them besides me. All I needed was a phone.

Then I heard what sounded like a firecracker—but a shot fit the scenario better. I thought of Kanufsky. I thought of two guys in a green Buick. I thought of crawling out the open window, taking the fire escape down, and becoming a potential target myself. So much for that thought.

Then I was out of there, heading down the stairs, two at a time. The safe way wasn't all that safe. The stairs popped out of their moorings, tipping sideways as if eager to shrug me off. They almost succeeded, too. I almost broke my neck getting down.

Outside, I raced around the corner, ran through an alley, jumped a short wooden fence, and there I was, metal skeletons looming above me, the row of tenements to my back, and more steel structures up ahead.

I seemed to be alone.

Maybe the pair I'd seen had taken off? Maybe the shot I'd heard had connected and the white-shirted guy was lying here somewhere right now. Who else could that be but Kanufsky?

I made a megaphone of my hands and bawled into it. "Kanufsky! Your sister sent me. I'm here to help you. Follow my voice."

I repeated the message once. Then I got out of there. I headed into the thicket of steel columns, bars, girders, and wooden planks. Crouching low, gun in hand, I waited.

I heard them before I saw them, the wind carrying their voices up and away, so I only caught a few isolated words. Two men materialized a few yards away from me. I could barely make them out in the darkness.

"Hey," one of them called, "we want to talk to you, fella."

Who doesn't these days?

"Listen," the guy called again, "no one's gonna get hurt."

Right, unless I lost my cool and shot them.

"Come on out," the other guy called, as if all I needed was a bit more coaxing and we'd all be slapping each other on the back and cracking jokes.

They stood motionless, waiting for my response. After a while they got tired of waiting.

"Listen," the first guy finally yelled again, "you don't know what's goin' on here."

That was putting it mildly.

"Keep out of it," the other one called. "We won't tell you twice."

They turned and in an instant I couldn't see them at all. I waited a beat, then stood up. I hurried to my car and drove away.

The front door was open this time when I got to the house on East Fourth Street. Again, I went up the stairs. Kanufsky's door was also standing open. I pulled out my Browning and went looking. Neither brother nor sister was in the flat. Ditto the bad guys. I frisked the place from top to bottom but came up empty. It was that kind of day.

CHAPTER 13

Morris Weiss—1948

The checkered cab dropped Morris Weiss and Rudy off on Broadway and 116th Street, across from Columbia University. Only a short trip from Harlem.

"Your friends," Weiss said, "will not come looking for us here."

"Some great friends."

The pair entered the Chock Full o' Nuts coffee shop, which was right on the southwest corner. They seated themselves at the far side of the counter, facing the door and plate glass window, so they would see anyone entering the shop. At this time of night the place was empty.

"Take what you want," Weiss said. "I'm paying."

"Big spender."

"Rudy, I have already done you two favors today,"

Weiss said. "Paid you for false information and saved you from a bad beating. You want more?"

"Skip it."

"Very sensible."

Weiss ordered coffee. Rudy ordered coffee and two glazed donuts, a specialty of the house.

"How'd you know to follow me?" he asked.

Weiss smiled. "Have you ever heard of Emmanuel Lasker?"

Rudy shook his head.

"Years ago, he was the world chess champion. Lasker always played the man, not the board."

"Meaning what?"

"Meaning I expected you to pull a fast one."

"Bullshit."

"Listen," Weiss said, "you gave me only the name of a dead man, one I already knew. An operator like you, Rudy, would be the first to know what is going on at the college. Yet you claimed ignorance. And you showed up at my office much too fast."

"So what?"

"So this. In Germany, you made a practice of ingratiating yourself with both sides, then selling out one to the other. But first, of course, you collected from both. When I again gave you money, I felt you were ready for your usual double cross. But it looks to me as if the other side wasn't buying, either, eh, Rudy?"

"Dumb bastards."

"What can you expect from hoodlums? They are unreliable."

"This Pete Munchanko—"

"Ah, the pusher no one can find."

"He ain't no pusher, no more. He's muscle. He was the ape in the gray coat."

"Play with fire, Rudy—"

"Don't say it, Sarge. We still got a deal?"

"If you can behave yourself."

Weiss drank his coffee. The *Herald Tribune* truck, he saw, was delivering the early-bird edition of the paper to the corner newsstand. Tomorrow's *News* and *Mirror* were already there. The lights of Columbia University were dull smudges in the dense fog.

"So talk," Weiss said.

Rudy swallowed the last of his donuts. "The gimpy guy is Tommy Blake. He's the pusher. Got shot up in the war. He's here on the GI Bill."

"Blake, he works alone?"

"Yeah. Sometimes some other guys show up. But he's the main one."

"And the supplier?"

"Harry Lang. The tall guy in black."

"He is the boss?"

"No way."

"So who is?"

"A guy I ain't run down yet."

"Ah-ha."

"Look, Sarge, it ain't none of your damn business, but you was dead right. I got me a swell deal with the Feds. Mostly, they want me to keep tabs on the reds. But they don't mind if I bring in somethin' extra. So I been pokin' my nose in all kinda places."

"And that's why you befriended Blake?"

"Yeah, that's why."

"And Joey Ginzberg?"

"Never knew the guy."

"So where, Rudy, does he fit in?"

"He gotta have some angle, or he wouldn't be in the clink now. But like I said, I ain't got nothin' on him."

"You are telling me the truth?"

"Swear, Sarge. Honest to God."

"Where does this Blake live?"

"In Hell's Kitchen."

"You have an address for me?"

Rudy gave him the address.

"Thank you, Rudy. I never lost confidence in you."

Rudy gave him a look.

"Well." Weiss smiled. "Maybe a little bit."

CHAPTER 14

My nephew, Max, is actually as generous and big-hearted as I am, but he simply hates to admit it. Anyone listening to him complain would think he works only for the money.

From the casebooks of Morris Weiss

Max Weiss—The Present

The phone woke me. One thirty-five A.M.

"Yeah?" I grumbled into the receiver.

"This is Mr. Weiss?" A woman's voice.

"Unfortunately."

"You are the detective?"

"If this is business, lady, call my office, I'm off duty."

"Please, it is me, Stella Kanufsky."

That prodded me fully awake.

"Where are you, Ms. Kanufsky?"

"In building. I do not know where. Leo come and take me."

"Is he there?"

"No."

"Where is he?"

"To that place he went back. The sanitarium."

"Mannerdale?"

"Yes. Where before he was."

This was getting worse and worse.

"Why?" I asked.

"He must find there something."

Of course. "Find what, Ms. Kanufsky?"

"How should I know this? I ask. He does not tell. Always it is like this."

"So why have you called me?"

"For Leo. For him I call."

"What does he want?"

"He say I must get help if he does not call in two hours. Already it is three. You see?"

Only too well. "Call the police, Ms. Kanufsky."

"He say get the detective."

"He said that?"

"Yes, only you."

"Ms. Kanufsky," I said, "you still don't know a Dr. Margoshes?"

"Who Margoshes? What Margoshes?"

"A scholar at the Jewish Heritage Foundation."

"How should I know such a person?"

"What about Leo?"

"Maybe. About him I cannot say."

"Okay. What does your brother do for a living, Ms. Kanufsky?"

"In Poland he teach. Such a pleasure is his English. Here he sell fruits and vegetables. This is important?"

"I think so. He has a store?"

"No more. Now he collect Social Security."

"But he's got some money put away."

"What money?"

"He paid for Mannerdale with cash, Ms. Kanufsky."

"He has Medicare. Why should he pay with cash?"

"Good question."

"No more questions. Hurry, please. Or they find him again. This time it not go so easy."

"Lady, it's not so easy now."

I asked for and got the number of the phone from which she was calling.

And then I was off and running for Mannerdale again.

but beyond twenty feet, it was mostly luck if you hit anything. Still, men like Tommy Blake paid attention to big guns.

He went up three steps, opened the front door, whose lock was broken, and began climbing stairs. A small yellow lightbulb dangled from the ceiling on each floor. The house smelled of damp wood, cabbage, and bleach. Voices could be heard from behind the closed doors. A man and woman talking. A baby crying. Children playing and laughing. All very ordinary. Certainly not a den of dope dealers. Weiss heard a radio announcer introducing *Suspense*, the voice of Nelson Eddy, the singer, coming out of a radio speaker on another floor. He almost felt as if he were intruding.

The young woman in 5A who answered his knock had short brown hair, freckles across the bridge of her nose, a round face. She wore a faded pink house dress and was barefoot. She barely came up to Weiss's chin. Were it not for a sullen downturn of her full lips—replete with dangling cigarette—she might have been quite pretty. Weiss considered making a joke to see if he could change her mood but thought better of it.

"Mrs. Blake?"

"Who wants to know?"

Her expression was now belligerent, not an improvement.

"My name is Morris Weiss," Weiss said. "I would like to speak to your husband."

"You and everyone else. What's the beef?"

"There is no beef, Mrs. Blake. This is not about him but some people he knows."

"Sure. Tell me another one and you'll have me rolling in the aisles. Who are you? You don't look like a cop."

"I'm not." Weiss showed her his license. "I am a private detective."

CHAPTER 15

Morris Weiss—1948

Weiss stood under a street lamp on West Twenty-eigh
Street and gazed up at the five-story tenement houses t
seemed to be leaning against each other for support in
middle of the block. Early evening. Fog had rolled
from the waterfront, which was only a block away, co
ing all of Chelsea. Somewhere on the Hudson fogh
sounded their familiar dirge. The whole neighborh
was gray and seemed to sag under the weight of the
No one was out on the street except Weiss.

He shrugged. At least in his worn jacket and pe
cap he looked like a denizen of these parts. The extra
he'd gained from the elevator shoes wouldn't hurt e
The gun he'd picked up in the tussle, however, w
biggest asset. He didn't care for the Colt .45; it was
and not well balanced. The massive bullets were sto

"Jeez, what next? We've had every kind of snoop here during the last coupla weeks."

"What has happened?"

She stepped back from the doorway. "Better come in before the neighbors get an earful. They got enough to gossip about already. And quit calling me Mrs. Blake. That's my mother-in-law. I'm Cora."

"A pleasure to meet you, Cora."

Weiss removed his cap and stepped into the sparsely furnished flat. A bathtub with crow's feet was over to the side, next to a small stove and a tarnished sink. A sagging brown sofa with the usual crocheted doilies protecting each arm, a chipped wooden table, and three chairs were on the other side of the room. The floor was bare wood.

Weiss seated himself on the sofa, Cora across from him on one of the hard-backed wooden chairs.

"Your husband is not here?" Weiss asked.

"The creep hasn't been here for three weeks."

"What happened?"

"The bum powdered out."

Weiss wanted to know why.

"That's a swell question. It's what I've been asking myself, too."

"He said nothing?"

"Not a word. Cleaned out the bank account, packed a suitcase, and just beat it."

The detective leaned forward. "Was he in trouble of any sort?"

"Go ask him," she said. "If you can find him."

"Actually," Weiss said, smiling, "my specialty is finding missing husbands."

"I hope I never see that louse again."

"There have been people looking for him?"

"Yeah. And you should see some of those mugs. They'd scare Boris Karloff."

"What did they want?"

"Same as you. And I gave them the same answer. He's gone. I don't know where, why, or how. All we had in the bank was a lousy forty bucks. How far's he gonna get on that?"

"Cora," Weiss said, "these men, they left names?"

"You kidding?"

"Were they maybe from the college?"

"More likely the penitentiary."

"And the police?"

"I called them," she said, "to report the bastard gone."

Weiss regarded the woman closely. So far, he could have saved himself the trip up the stairs.

"Did you meet any of his college friends?"

"He never brought them home."

"Did he at least speak of them?"

"No. Tommy didn't speak much about anything. Look, we got hitched young. Too young to know better. Then Tommy went off to fight in the war and came back a cripple. It changed everything. It changed him. You get it?"

Weiss nodded. "I understand. He was a full-time student?"

"Yeah. That's what he said. But you coulda fooled me. If it weren't for the textbooks he brought home, I'd never've guessed."

"He had no other job?"

"What could he do? Sell papers on street corners?"

"Push dope, maybe."

"You're nuts."

"You know an Earl Grasser?"

"No."

"What about Pete Munchanko, or Harry Lang?"

"Uh-uh."

"Your husband was said to peddle dope at the college. Mr. Lang is reputed to be his supplier."

"That's crazy."

Weiss shrugged. "Your husband is missing, Cora. And Earl Grasser is dead. A man named Joey Ginzberg is being held for his murder. Maybe you have heard of him?"

"No. I haven't heard of any of those bums. And I don't care what you say. Tommy is no pusher."

Weiss raised an eyebrow. *Her husband, it seemed, had gone up a few notches in her eyes. Or had he?*

"Then who were those men asking for him, the ones who look like gangsters?"

"How should I know? Tommy liked to gamble. Maybe he owed them money?"

"Maybe." Weiss rose to his feet. "Thank you for your time, Cora."

"Sure. If you drop by again, better make it after six. I wait on tables from eight to five these days, in a hash house, The Allegro. I thought I was hard up before. Just look at me now. It's a laugh a minute."

"I am sorry," Weiss said. He nodded toward the wall. "That is your husband's honorable discharge?"

"Yeah. He was real proud of that. But he left it behind."

"And the photograph underneath?"

"Him and his army buddies."

Weiss walked over, looked at the framed photo. "Which is your husband?"

"That one." Cora pointed to a round-shouldered man in uniform.

"And the one next to him?"

She shrugged.

"That is Earl Grasser," Weiss said.

"The dead guy?"

"The same." Weiss handed her his card. "Should you hear from your husband, please call me."

"Sure."

Weiss put on his cap and left.

CHAPTER 16

On-the-job training is a good way to acquire the tricks of the trade. Better yet, is from a wise teacher who knows the ropes inside and out. Need I say who this is?

From the casebooks of Morris Weiss

Max Weiss—The Present

I didn't drive right up to the Mannerdale. I parked the Saab up the road and hiked back on foot.

The lights, I saw, were on in a couple of second-story windows. Kanufsky's old room was up on the third floor where all the windows were dark. So far, everything looked normal enough. Except maybe for me.

I dodged the cameras aimed at the front lawn and

made my way to the back of the building. I used my pick-lock and quietly let myself in.

Dead quiet. That suited me fine.

First I went up the back staircase to the third floor and checked 3J. It was empty. Kanufsky hadn't returned to catch forty winks or rip up the floorboards. Maybe he hadn't returned at all.

I went down the length of the third-floor corridor, opening doors at random and shining my penlight around. No surprises. The rooms were either empty or held sleeping patients. Thankfully, no one awoke.

I went down to the second floor and repeated the operation again. I found nothing.

Finally I was standing in front of Dr. Kramer's door. Dim light shone from under the sill. Was the guy still up? Or was this my elusive friend Kanufsky?

I turned the knob and quietly let myself in.

The lights were all on, but no one was around. Ditto for Kramer's private quarters, which I tried a moment later.

The last reasonable places left to look were the recreation area, the kitchen, and dining room downstairs. Especially if I stretched the word *reasonable*.

I used the front staircase, climbed down to the ground floor, and turned left.

The recreation area was dark, the TVs off, the chairs empty. I hurried to the cafeteria next door. The fading odors of food and disinfectant made my stomach do flip-flops. No one was around here either.

Now what? Wake the staff? Head for home? Find an empty bed and curl up til morning? I'd had worse ideas.

"Mr. Weiss," a voice whispered.

I didn't actually jump out of my skin, but I came close.

"Where are you?" I whispered.

"Shhhh. Here, here," the voice whispered back.

"Here" seemed to be a large, lidded trash can in the next aisle.

"Come out," I said, "where I can see you."

The lid jiggled and a small disheveled white-haired man began to climb out. At least it wasn't Kramer. I couldn't have stood that. I could hardly stand this.

"You're Kanufsky," I said. It came out sounding like an accusation.

"Yes, yes," he said, finally managing to get out of the receptacle. He wasn't any taller than his sister. "And you are, thank God, the detective."

"Yeah," I said. "The name's Weiss."

"I called my sister at home. And she described you perfectly. I waited for you, Mr. Weiss. A Jewish detective, he is one in a million. Wait for him, I said to myself. He will help you. Yes, always I believe in the higher powers. And now they have brought you here."

"With your sister's help," I said. "What are you doing in that can?"

"Hiding."

"From what?"

"From them, Mr. Weiss. They are here." Kanufsky climbed out of the can. "More is not necessary to say. We understand each other with a wink. Is that not so?"

"Not even on good days, Kanufsky. Spell it out."

"They are the ones who chase after me. The evil ones. Now you see?"

"Just barely."

He took a deep breath. "They have the doctor, Mr. Weiss, they have him."

"Who, Kramer?"

"Yes. They hold him. Here." He pointed to the floor. "Down there."

"The basement?"

"Yes, yes, there. I have left certain papers behind. Papers of great value. They want them. They believe Dr. Kramer knows their location. In this they are wrong."

"What are these papers?"

"Please, Mr. Weiss. The doctor is in their hands. They make him search. Come, come, you will save him. I have complete confidence in you."

"Misplaced confidence," I told him. But I was already talking to his back. He had begun trotting toward the exit sign. I hurried after him.

A narrow staircase led us down. This time I had the Browning in my hand.

We hit the basement. Concrete lay underfoot. We slowly moved out.

Each step took us into greater darkness. I didn't use my light. Just in case someone was actually here, unlikely as that was beginning to seem.

We came to a wall. I felt my way along it. We had either reached the end of the line, or a door was here somewhere. I found no door. The wall ended. I took a step beyond it. And came to a sudden halt. Kanufsky stumbled against me. I moved back to the cover of the wall, then peered around it.

Five concrete stairs led down to a second level. A bright overhead light spotlighted a boiler, a furnace, a cluster of water pipes, and four figures on the packed earth floor below. The one on his knees in pajamas, bathrobe, and slippers was reaching for a red gym bag, one of many bags, both large and small, stacked before him. The other three hovered silently above him. The guy on his knees was the good doctor. He looked a bit peeved, but who could blame him?

"You see?" Kanufsky whispered. "What did I tell you? Was I not speaking the truth?"

He was right, too. Now I had him, what were probably

three Buick guys, instead of two, and Kramer as a bonus. Everyone I'd been hunting for, and then some. But what the hell was I going to do with them all?

As if reading my mind, Kanufsky whispered, "Shoot them! Shoot them!"

"How about I just tell them to put up their hands?" I said. "Will that do?"

"You are a fool!" Kanufsky said.

He sprang by me. And suddenly he was in the open. I made an instinctive grab to pull him back. Too late. One leap and the little guy was down on the next level.

I couldn't believe my eyes. I stood there waiting for the hallucination to vanish and Kanufsky to appear at my side again.

The three men with Kramer didn't have such problems. No hallucinations plagued them. As Kanufsky idiotically ran forward, one of the three yanked a black automatic out of his belt. My Browning was already pointed. I fired. Lord knows what part of him I hit. He went down hard.

Then the real shooting began.

But it wasn't me or the two guys left standing. It was the old duffer who'd been guarding the front door during my first visit. In the shadowy light, he looked disheveled and battered, as if he'd just had a losing tussle with our guests. He was on his feet coming forward, a long-barreled heavy-caliber revolver in his shaking hand. He was screaming curses in a hoarse voice and letting fly a barrage of bullets in our direction. So far he had only hit the water pipes, which had begun spraying water furiously onto the floor. Any one of us could be next. And he wouldn't last long there either.

I shot out the light. It seemed the humane thing to do. Darkness.

I heard shots for another few seconds. Then, only the sound of rushing water.

I stayed put behind the wall and stuck my penlight out into the open, shining the beam on the lower level.

Kramer sat on the floor, water splashing over him, a bewildered expression on his face. He looked like I felt.

The watchman, across the way, had sat down on the concrete, too. He was muttering to himself and cradling the gun in his lap. He didn't seem any the worse for wear.

Everyone else was gone.

And the red bag was gone with them.

CHAPTER 17

Morris Weiss—1948

"It's been a long time, Morry," Rabbi Kaufman said.

Morris Weiss shrugged. "What could I do? After the war they sent me home. You, Rabbi, they must have liked better." The two shook hands. "It is good to see you again," Weiss said. "You look like a million dollars."

"Maybe like fifty dollars."

"You are being too modest, Rabbi. Let us compromise and make it a full hundred."

"Like always, Morry, you drive a hard bargain."

Kaufman was a large, heavyset man in his early forties. He had a round, jovial face, under a short army haircut. The rabbi did not sport a long black beard or even wear a yarmulka. Kaufman was a Conservative rabbi and the Jewish chaplain at Fort Dix. He was decked out in dress greens and the brassware of a major in the U.S. Army.

"I still think of you as my spiritual leader," Weiss said.

"Then you are in big trouble."

"You're telling me," Weiss said, grinning.

The two men seated themselves on the sofa. An American flag hung on the wall behind the rabbi's desk. A small bookcase, containing religious tomes, Norman Mailer's *The Naked and the Dead*, and S. J. Perleman's *Westward Ha!*, along with an array of other popular books, was over to the left. Weiss admired the rabbi's taste in literature, but nothing could offset the sterility of an army base, not even good books. On the right, two windows looked out at Fort Dix. Weiss's gaze lingered for an instant on the flat grounds and endless rows of small buildings, many of them still makeshift.

When he was here last, the country was at war. A sense of mission and urgency had prevailed, one that Weiss shared. Still, what he best remembered were pinups of Betty Grable and Veronica Lake everywhere. "Praise the Lord and Pass the Ammunition" was being played on the radio and jukeboxes. Weiss liked Irving Berlin's "This Is the Army" better because it tickled his funny bone. He was still in his early twenties then. Odd, he didn't feel a day older now.

"So," Weiss said, "you are going to be a thirty-year man?"

The rabbi shrugged.

"At this stage in my life, Morry, what else can I do?"

"You could," Weiss said, "take early retirement and find yourself a congregation."

"True. But here I have a captive audience." Kaufman grinned broadly. "To avoid duty on Friday nights and *Shabbos*, they flock to my chapel. And on the holidays, Morry, there's only standing room. Naturally, I attribute this to my great appeal."

"Naturally," Weiss said.

Both men laughed.

"You know," Weiss said, "I was bar mitzvahed."

"I always assumed so."

"Both my parents were secularists. The closest they ever came to a religious service was going to Yiddish Socialist meetings on Friday night. There my father also played cards. But they wanted me to know the other side, too. So I was bar mitzvahed. My mother said a *shul* was the best place to make business deals. About business and about *shuls*, of course, she knew absolutely nothing. So here at the base and there at the yeshiva were the only times I ever attended services."

"I am honored," the rabbi said.

Weiss nodded. "So you see, you are my spiritual leader."

"You've come for spiritual guidance, Morry?"

"I will spare you, Rabbi."

"You are a true friend."

"There is something you can do for me."

"Of course. I didn't think you came all this way just to relive your past glories as a recruit. So what is this something?"

"You know I'm a private detective."

"Who could forget? You were the Dick Tracy of the chapel."

"More like Sherlock Holmes, Rabbi. Dick Tracy is a policeman."

"True. You solved three crimes."

"Two. The missing wine and the stolen silverware. The *siddurs* were merely misplaced. The wine, Rabbi, was a lost cause; it was already drunk by the time I collared the culprit. The silverware I found in a recruit's locker before he could pawn it. Today he is probably a bank president."

"I remember," Kaufman said.

"Well, I'm again on a case. Now I'm working for a

lawyer whose client is accused of murder. Both he and the victim are veterans, Rabbi. As is another man who is somehow involved. How, I don't know yet."

"They're all Jewish?"

"One, the alleged perpetrator, Joey Ginzberg."

"He's a New York boy?"

"Him and the other two."

"So they all took their basic training here."

"No doubt."

"The Jewish one, he went to chapel?"

"Not likely."

"Then how can I help you, Morry?"

"You would not know Joey. But maybe there are others who will." Weiss leaned back on the sofa, crossed one leg over the other, and held up three fingers. "Joey Ginzberg. Earl Grasser. Tommy Blake. There is some connection between all three. The last two have discharge papers. Joey says he was in the army, his mother says so, too. People have seen him in uniform. He was gone for the duration of the war. But the army says they have no service records."

"You think he was in the army?"

Weiss nodded. "What I would like, Rabbi, is your help in getting his service record and those of the other two."

"And if Joey Ginzberg has no records?"

"If you can, find out why."

Kaufman wrote down the names.

"About Earl Grasser," Weiss said, "I have more."

"This is the victim?"

"Yes. The police got hold of his service record."

"And gave it to you?"

Weiss grinned. "We are chummy," he said, and handed the rabbi a handwritten sheet of paper.

Kaufman studied it. "Drafted in '42," he read, "did basic here, was assigned to an infantry support unit, saw active duty in the '43 Salerno landing in Italy under

General Mark Clark, a good man, remained with the unit until he was transferred to special services in July '44, honorably discharged in March of '45. Well, it's a good record, Morry. What did he do in civilian life?"

"He was a salesman."

"Sometimes the army is the high point of a man's life. What did he sell?"

"Whatever he could."

The rabbi nodded. "You have any idea why he was killed?"

"That is what I'm trying to find out."

Kaufman sighed. "Well, I have friends everywhere. Some are in high places."

"I know. You have generals?"

"I have sergeants and lieutenants who work for generals."

"Even better."

"It's always a pleasure, Morry, to help you. After all we've been through together."

Weiss raised an eyebrow. "What have we been through?"

The rabbi grinned. "Many hours of fine conversation."

"I cannot deny it. Thank you, Rabbi. If you ever have a problem, you know where to come."

"No question about it. I will make some calls, Morry. Where can I reach you this afternoon?"

"After two I will be in my office."

"You will hear from me, one way or another."

"Excellent," Weiss said.

The phone rang.

Instantly, Morris Weiss was awake, one hand reaching for the receiver, the other for the switch on the bedside lamp.

"Yes?" he said.

"It's me, Zach," an excited voice said.

The Lake boy, Weiss thought, one of the locals he had asked to keep an eye on his office.

"Someone's up there, Mr. Weiss."

"You are sure?"

"I saw a light in your window."

"Maybe I left my desk lamp on."

"It looked more like a flashlight. And it was moving around. That's what tipped me off there was something fishy going on."

"Excellent point," Weiss said.

"I got a reward coming, right?"

"Of course. I will see to it in a very few days. Only do not make a habit of staying up late," Weiss said. "Something like this happens once in a blue moon. There are better ways to make a few dollars."

"I ca. t think of any," the boy said.

Weiss sighed. Already he felt responsible for steering him in the wrong direction. Maybe he'll grow up to be a private detective, Weiss thought. Or, more probably, a crook.

Weiss dressed hurriedly, stuck his Browning in a coat pocket, and ran out the door. He wondered if this was a random break-in, or if someone was looking for a specific item, maybe something to do with this Ginzberg business. Either way, they were out of luck. He kept little of importance in the office. Of course, he was out of luck, too. This would cost him part of a night's sleep.

Muffled voices came from behind the door. He could make out few words. But there seemed to be only two men speaking. Better than a crowd, Weiss thought. The Browning in his hand, he pushed open the door.

Two men, their backs to him, were on their knees, working on his floor safe by flashlight. The file cabinet drawers were all pulled open.

"Gentlemen," Weiss said from the doorway, "you are wasting your time. Even the bank in this neighborhood has no money."

Both men stiffened, turned to look at him, then rose hurriedly to their feet.

Weiss shook his head.

"Rudy," he said, "I expected better from you."

Rudy shrugged. "It wasn't my idea, Sarge."

"Then whose was it? His?"

"Yeah, as a matter of fact," Rudy said, grinning. For some reason the ex-soldier seemed to be enjoying himself.

Weiss took a step into his office.

"So, Rudy, who is your accomplice?"

"Ask him, Sarge. Go on, he'll tell you."

Weiss turned his attention to the other man. He was stocky, of medium height, with a prominent nose and large ears, and wearing a black hat and gray overcoat. The man stared at him unblinkingly, accusingly almost, as if it were the detective who had been caught committing a crime and not he.

The old game, Weiss thought. Another *schlepper* trying to bluff his way out of a pickle. Weiss did not appreciate the look. It irritated him.

"You do this for a living, mister?" he asked. "Believe me, you're in the wrong line of work."

"And you, my friend, are in trouble."

"*I'm* in trouble?"

"Big trouble."

"Who is he?" Weiss asked. "Someone from a lunatic asylum?"

Rudy seemed delighted by the question. "He's my boss," he said.

"He directs your criminal activities?"

"Always the card, Sarge."

"Tell him who I am," the man said.

Rudy jerked a thumb at his companion. "He's a Fed."

Weiss said, "You don't say?"

"My name is George Fletcher," the man said. "I'm a special agent of the F.B.I."

"Show me," Weiss said.

Very slowly, Fletcher moved a hand to his coat pocket, withdrew a wallet with thumb and forefinger, and flipped it open. "Satisfied?"

"Hardly," Weiss said. "Unless you have a search warrant, Fletcher, you are still breaking the law. You have one, of course?"

"Let's just call this an informal visit," Fletcher said.

"Let's not," Weiss said. "Let us have a judge decide what this is."

"You wouldn't want that," Fletcher said quickly.

"Why not? It seems the sensible thing to do."

"This is about your family, Weiss."

"My family?"

"Your brother and his wife."

"What about them?" Weiss said.

"Joined the Communist Party in '36."

"You don't say?"

Rudy grinned. "Watch out, Sarge, this guy's got something on everyone."

"They were fighting Fascism," Weiss said. "No one else was at the time."

"Yes," Fletcher said, "they were a bit early, weren't they?"

Weiss shook his head.

"It was never too early to come out against Hitler," he said.

"We call them premature anti-Fascists," Fletcher said.

" 'We'?"

"The Bureau."

"If there had been more like them—" Weiss began, then cut himself short. "My brother and sister-in-law are both dead."

"We know that."

"Then you didn't expect to find them hiding in my files or safe," Weiss said. "So what is all this about?"

"You," Fletcher said.

"Go on," Weiss said.

"How about you first put down your gun?" Fletcher said.

Weiss reflected on the possibility of the F.B.I. agent actually shooting him, decided it wasn't too likely, and put the Browning back in his coat pocket. Striding to his desk, he seated himself and turned on his desk lamp. He swiveled his chair so he was facing his visitors and crossed one leg over a knee.

"You were saying?" he said.

"We're looking into subversives," Fletcher said.

"You consider me a subversive?"

Fletcher shrugged. "Your brother was a red."

"I am a registered Democrat," Weiss said indignantly.

"But you know plenty of reds, don't you? Some have even been your clients."

"I do not ask my clients about their political beliefs."

"Sure you don't." Fletcher grinned. "I bet they speak their minds right in front of you."

"What does that have to do with anything?"

"Weiss, you could be very helpful to the Bureau."

"How?"

"We need informers."

"That is why you're here?"

Fletcher nodded.

"Get out," Weiss said quietly.

"See, Sarge," Rudy said, "a hundred percent Fed."

"And you with him!"

Fletcher said, "You don't want to buck the government, Weiss. That would be stupid."

Weiss drew his gun. "We will see what is stupid. You have broken into my office. That gives you maybe three seconds to get out before I shoot you."

Both men headed for the door.

Fletcher turned.

"I'll be back," he said.

"Go to hell," Weiss told him.

CHAPTER 18

Interrogating suspects does not always lead to enlightenment. That is why it is good to have a backup plan. Unfortunately, such plans are often in short supply.

From the casebooks of Morris Weiss

Max Weiss—The Present

"It was *you* who shot out the light?" Kramer said.

I admitted it.

"I thought it was old Benny."

"Old Benny, just then, was the problem. I was the solution."

Kramer glared at me. "I must disagree, Mr. Weiss. You should have shot *them*."

"You wanted me to gun them all down? As in carnage?"

"Those men," Kramer said, "were dangerous."

"Not as dangerous as your Benny. He could have killed us all."

"He was trying to help me."

"So was I."

We were camped in the doctor's office. His staff had come running down to the basement at the sound of gunshots. All they found were Kramer, Benny, and me, ankle deep in water. They turned off the water, put in an emergency call to the plumber, and led old Benny away, still jabbering. Kramer had them go through the building. No intruders turned up.

The doctor reached into a desk drawer, produced a bottle of Johnnie Walker Red. A pair of shot glasses followed. I waved mine away.

"Never touch the stuff before eight A.M.," I said.

"As you wish. This has been a most trying night."

Filling his shot glass, he downed its contents in a single gulp, sighed, and then returned bottle and glasses to their drawer and his attention to me.

"Who in heaven's name are they?" he asked.

"I haven't a clue, Doctor."

"They made me search my own facility. It was an outrage."

"At least you knew the territory. What were they looking for?"

"Some sort of bag."

"That would be Kanufsky's."

"What?"

"Davidson to you. Only his real name's Kanufsky."

"I beg your pardon."

"Your patient was using an alias," I said. "You see him earlier tonight?"

"Tonight?"

"He was here."

"I had no idea."

"Guy gets around. He led me to the basement, kept saying you were in trouble."

"He was in the basement with you?"

"You were facing the wrong way, Doctor."

"What in God's name was he doing here?"

"Came for his bag."

"What were you doing here?"

"Came for Kanufsky."

"Why?"

"His sister sent me."

"He has a sister?"

"Yeah," I said. "She didn't want him getting hurt."

"I understand none of this."

"Who does?"

"Surely the sister does."

"I doubt it. She says Kanufsky doesn't tell her a thing."

"Then we are still at sea."

"Something like that," I said. "What happened, Dr. Kramer?"

"They woke me at gunpoint. Your Kanufsky, when he first came here as a patient, wished to safeguard one of his belongings. I told him to put it in our safe. But he adamantly refused. It ended up in the basement. We have a number of items stored there. He insisted on taking it down himself. I had no idea where he put it. They demanded that I search through everything."

"It was in the red bag you had in your hands."

"He told you?"

"He didn't have to. The bag was gone when the lights came on, and so was Kanufsky. He took it and ran away."

"I profoundly regret," Kramer said, "ever having taken that man as a patient."

"What are you going to do now?"

"Do? What can I do?"

"Call the cops."

He stared at me. "Are you insane? This facility caters to the ill, people who require quiet and peace of mind. Can you imagine what would happen if word of this ever got out? It would be a catastrophe."

"My lips," I told him, "are sealed."

Kramer nodded. "I appreciate that. Are you planning to go after him?"

"Kanufsky? I'll try his sister. But frankly I'm not too hopeful."

"What then?"

"Drop it," I said. "And go back to earning a living."

"But what if Kanufsky was dragged off by these men?"

"It's a possibility. But the old guy's pretty slippery. And don't forget, I shot one of them. I think they had their hands full just getting out of here."

"So that is that."

"Yeah," I agreed, "that's that, Doctor. Definitely."

"I lied," I told Boris Minsky, pouring him another cup of coffee.

"You are not dropping the case?"

"What case? A few more like it and we'll both be selling pencils on street corners. But it's a loose end and that bothers me."

"What," he said, "do you propose?"

"Putting you on the job."

Minsky smiled, reached for another prune danish, and said, "A sound decision."

I had gotten home just before dawn, managed to grab a few hours' shut-eye, took a quick shower, and then phoned Minsky, whom I invited over to my place for a late breakfast. He had probably eaten two breakfasts by then, but Minsky was not one to turn down a meal. While we ate, I had filled him in on the night's doings.

"But why lie to the doctor?" he asked.

"Because I'm not so sure he's telling me everything he knows. Kanufsky was a strange kind of patient. No doctor's records, no insurance, no Medicare, and no questions asked when he paid with cash."

"That is rather unusual."

"Calls for an ace investigator. Good thing you're around, or I'd have to do it myself."

Minsky smiled. "And in the meantime, dear boy, what are your plans?"

"Go after Margoshes," I said. "And I know just the place to start—the Jewish Heritage Foundation. He's worked there his whole life, Boris. They'll have a soft spot for the guy. I'm sure they'll lean over backward to help."

"If you say so, Maxwell."

CHAPTER 19

Morris Weiss—1948

Morris Weiss said, "I knew him in Germany."

"From the army?" Ida said.

"Where else?"

"You were friends?"

"More like business acquaintances," Weiss said. "He was very helpful in turning up scarce items."

Ida laughed. "What? Guns? Bullets? Bombs?"

Weiss smiled at her. "Those weren't scarce."

They were in Katz's Delicatessen on the corner of Houston and Orchard Streets. Weiss had gone to one of Ida's chamber music evenings. She and her group had played Beethoven, Brahms, and, as an encore, a medley of Yiddish folk songs. The performance had occurred in a very large living room packed full of people, some of them

Yiddish writers. *If it wasn't in Carnegie*, Weiss thought, *at least it was haymish. And the group had collected over sixty dollars. Not bad for a few hours' work.*

Now they were grabbing a bite before going off to his flat.

"Then what did Rudy find for you?" Ida said.

"Nylon stockings."

Ida looked at him.

"You have a hidden nylon stockings fetish?" she said.

"Not so hidden when you wear them, darling."

"That's better."

They both laughed.

"These," Weiss said, "were for my lady friends. They couldn't do without them."

"Lady friends?" Ida said, feigning outrage. "That is even worse."

Weiss grinned. "If I had only known you would come into my life, Idaleh, I would have ignored them all."

"This I would have liked to see," she said. "During the war, you know, I couldn't do without my nylons either. But I made do."

"Because you had no Rudy," Weiss said. "Also he found whole boxes of chocolates. Canned goods, too." Weiss sighed and rolled his eyes. "They were priceless."

Ida leaned across the table and kissed him. "You are priceless."

"Ah," he said, "but not as priceless as a can of spam in those days."

Ida laughed. "Did your Rudy have a price?"

"Of course. Or he would not have been Rudy. But it was a reasonable price. So I was glad to pay."

"Moisheleh, you were a rich man then?"

"He didn't want money."

Weiss poured the last of his Dr. Brown Cel-Ray soda into his glass and took a bite of his turkey on rye.

Ida was having a bowl of chicken soup with kreplach and matzo balls.

"What he wanted," Weiss said, "was for me to forget what I had found out about some of his other dealings. These were, of course, not so kosher. But this was, thank God, not my responsibility. Or, who knows, I might have lost the stockings."

"A catastrophe."

"True. When I got out of the army I kept track of him. I thought he might be useful to me."

"And is he?"

"Up to a point. He gives information, but not all of it is true. I could maybe live with that. But he is also an FBI informer."

"And that is bad?"

"It is not good," Weiss said. "Now he is informing on me."

Ida looked genuinely shocked. "What have you done, Moisheleh?"

"Nothing."

"So?"

"My older brother Ben and his wife, Sonya, were party members."

"Really?"

"Absolutely. They joined in the mid-thirties. At that time," Weiss said, "it looked like the Soviet Union was the only country standing up to Nazi Germany. The Yiddish press was the first to report what Hitler had planned for the Jews. This information did not make a ripple in the American press. But some Yiddish-speaking Jews became party members because of it."

"Your Ben and Sonya were among them, of course."

"Yes."

"And in '39?" Ida said. "What happened then?"

Weiss sighed. "They stayed."

Ida shook her head. It was hard to tell whether in disgust or dismay.

"By then," Weiss said, "it had become a sort of religion with them. Comrade Stalin, they once told me, never makes a mistake." Weiss shrugged. "With a record like that, how could they leave? Even the Yankees never did that well. And they had Babe Ruth."

"So how long," Ida asked, "did they stay members?"

"Too long. Through the Hitler-Stalin pact," Weiss said. "And right through the Second World War, when being a party member became almost respectable again. At least in some circles."

"And then?"

"Wait, darling."

Weiss rose, went to the counter, and returned with two cups of coffee and two slices of cherry pie.

He reseated himself.

"For a serious topic like this," he said, smiling, "I must keep my strength up."

"Not to mention mine," Ida said, smiling back.

Weiss took a bite of pie, a sip of coffee, and said, "They both died in a car crash a few months after the war ended."

"I'm sorry."

Weiss nodded.

"Probably an accident," he said.

"You're not sure?"

Weiss shrugged. "Maybe they were spies."

"Spies?"

"They were open party members," Weiss said. "So what kind of spies would they make?"

"Bad ones," Ida said.

"Of course. Still, as a detective, Idaleh, I can tell you, nothing is for sure. If they were spies, maybe they fell out of favor with their Moscow bosses? Or maybe the Americans found out and arranged an accident. It could even be they were double agents."

"Stop, you are giving me a headache."

"I'm giving me a headache," Weiss said. "Well, out of the blue, Rudy broke into my office last night with this F.B.I. agent, a Mr. Fletcher."

"Why?"

"They were looking for names of Communists."

"In your office?"

Weiss shrugged.

"Also, I think," he said, "they were ready to drag my family's name through the mud."

Ida shook her head in dismay.

"They had gone crazy," Weiss said. "How else can you explain it?"

"And then?"

"This Fletcher wanted that I should become an informer, too, just like Rudy."

"What did you do?"

"I took out my gun and said I would shoot him if he did not leave."

"And?"

Weiss smiled sweetly. "He left."

The pair sat in silence for a moment.

"He will be back," Ida said, "won't he, Moisheleh?"

Weiss nodded. "Sooner or later."

"And then what?"

"Then I will be ready for him," Morris Weiss said.

Weiss sat at his desk, a copy of the *Sun* spread out before him. He was halfway through Grantland Rice's sports column when the door opened. It was ten minutes past two on the following day.

"Morris Weiss?"

Weiss nodded and folded the paper. "Come in," he said.

A tall, gangly young man stepped into the office. He had a long pale face, large nose, slight pot belly, and round shoulders. His black hair was in a GI crew cut that somehow looked totally out of place, as did his wrinkled army uniform. He peered at Weiss through thick, black-framed glasses.

"You are a client?" Weiss asked, nodding his visitor to a chair.

"I am an emissary." They shook hands and the soldier sat. "Boris Minsky at your service. The Major, Rabbi Kaufman, sends you his most ardent regards."

Weiss smiled. "I was expecting a phone call. Instead I have a live body. You have come all the way from Fort Dix to see me?"

"Thank God, I have seen the last of that dreadful place. I come from Centre Street, the Army Public Information Office."

"Ah-ha. I see you are a T-4."

"It is my rank, not who I am."

"Of course."

"Until next month," Minsky said, "when I am finally to be relieved of this odious obligation."

"And then?"

"New York University. To enhance my education."

Weiss smiled. "A good move. So, your army specialty is what, Minsky?"

"I write for them."

"Very nice. You are a reporter?"

"As I said, I am with the Public Information Office. I respond to written inquiries from the public."

"I am sure the public is gratified."

"The public, my dear sir, is an ass."

Weiss nodded. Already he was beginning to feel sorry for this gangly, awkward soldier. He seemed unfit for the military. And Weiss did not see him faring much better in civilian life. Luckily, it was not his problem.

"The rabbi," Weiss said, "got you a pass?"

Minsky shrugged. "What pass? He is there, and I am here."

"You are not, God forbid, AWOL?"

Minsky curled his lip.

"They would not notice if I were," he said.

"You are so superfluous?"

"They give me the letters. From civilians who have nothing better to do. I answer them. Most are imbecilic. I do my job quickly. Then I go. No one has yet taken notice."

"Good, good. I wouldn't want you on my conscience. I hear a slight accent, Minsky."

"It is Russian, acquired from my parents who had the wisdom to flee the Worker's Paradise at the first opportunity."

"Ah, so you are American-born?"

"It was my great good fortune to be born in Sea Gate in Brooklyn. At home we spoke only Russian, of course, the language of Pushkin, Lermontov, Chekov, Tolstoi, and Dostoevsky."

"You forgot Turgenev," Weiss said.

"Merely for the sake of brevity."

Weiss leaned back in his chair, clasped his hands in his lap, and smiled good-naturedly. "And your parents, they spoke Yiddish too?"

"Never. They considered it a loathsome jargon."

Weiss lost his smile and sat up straight. "It's their loss."

"I, personally," Minsky said, "keep an open mind."

"That's good of you," Weiss said icily. "So what do you have for me, Minsky?"

The soldier reached into a pocket, withdrew two sheets of paper. "On your behalf, I called the National Personnel Administration Office in St. Louis, Missouri; it is where all service records are stored."

"Thank you," Weiss said.

"They were most helpful. The data you gave Rabbi Kaufman concerning Corporal Earl Grasser was correct. Thomas Blake is also quite well-documented. On January 22, 1944, the Allies landed some fifty thousand sea-borne troops at Anzio in Italy. Your Mr. Blake bore the rank of corporal, and acquitted himself nobly. He received two commendations for bravery under fire. As for Joseph Ginzberg, he does not appear to have served in the armed forces. At least there is no record of him." Minsky put the sheets of paper on the desk.

"That's it?" Weiss asked. "All you have got for me?"

"Hardly. Both Corporal Blake and Corporal Grasser were removed from their respective units in July of 1944 and transferred to something called Special Services."

"Really?" Weiss said. "They entertained the troops?"

"It is senseless, Mr. Weiss, that these two should be attached to a unit of Hollywood celebrity entertainers. Nor could I see experienced combat veterans being taken from their units to act as mere prop men. So I requested more details."

"And?"

"The information was classified."

Weiss raised an eyebrow. "That is very peculiar. What did you do, Minsky?"

"I called Colonel Minsky."

"Of course," Weiss said, "who else? And this Colonel Minsky is?"

"My uncle, Sasha. The army knows him as Steven."

"Ah-ha. It is very good that you have such a nice uncle, eh?"

"It is a nightmare. Were it not for him I should never have enlisted. He promised me many great things."

"He didn't deliver?"

"Only if you consider the Information Office a great thing."

"Did he at least solve our problem?"

"In a manner of speaking. He called his friend the major who then called his friend the lieutenant colonel and so on. Until the general was reached. The general has clearance. And is in the right office in Washington. *He* solved your problem. In part."

"So," Weiss said, "what part did he solve?"

"There was a secret mission. Six soldiers were chosen from various European divisions. Earl Grasser, Gerry Sykes, Ben Robinson, Leon Asher, Thomas Blake, and Gordon Keller."

"Why them?"

Minsky shrugged.

"Who was the commanding officer?"

"A Colonel Milton Rutledge, since deceased."

"What was the mission?"

Minsky allowed himself a slight smile. "That, my dear Mr. Weiss, is the part that remains unsolved."

"The general also couldn't find out?"

"It appears someone has tampered with the records. The nature of the mission, its execution, and aftermath— these items have been removed from the files. And with them the answers that you seek."

"The army is investigating?"

"What is there to investigate? Too much time has passed. And what is to be gained if these files are finally located? Sasha believes it is no more than a clerical error. For the army the case is closed."

"So you have reached a dead end?"

Minsky gazed at Weiss imperiously. "That is not my way. Gerry Sykes was second in command—a second lieutenant. According to his records, before the war, Sykes had worked for Prudential Life Insurance. I checked there first. He was no longer employed by them. There was no listing for a Gerry Sykes in any of the directories of the five boroughs. His parents had lived in Brooklyn; their number was in his files. The woman who answered my call told me Mr. and Mrs. Sykes were both deceased. From her I obtained the numbers of two elderly tenants still in the building. A Mr. Kipnes said that Gerry Sykes now resided in Jersey City. Kipnes did not have an address, but was fairly certain that Sykes was now a claims adjuster for Magnum Life Insurance here in Manhattan. I called their switchboard. Your Mr. Sykes was on the premises. With him you have no need of army records. He can tell you exactly what transpired. And your problem will be solved, will it not?"

Weiss nodded. "That would be nice. But your Mr. Sykes might hesitate to discuss classified information with an outsider."

"That is true." Minsky reached into a pocket, handed Weiss a card. "Should there be any difficulties, tell Mr. Sykes to call this number."

Weiss glanced at the card. "Your uncle Sasha?"

"Have no fear. I will put in a good word for you."

"My thanks," Weiss said. He regarded his visitor. Maybe the soldier wasn't as useless as he had first seemed. "When you are discharged from the service, Minsky, come and see me. Maybe I can help you make an extra dollar."

"You need an assistant?"

"A part-time secret agent," Weiss said with a straight face.

Minsky did not smile. "If it does not conflict with

my studies, I will be glad to spy for you. On whom are we spying?"

"Bad people."

"Then it is socially useful work."

"Of course."

The soldier rose to go. Weiss also got to his feet.

"It has been a pleasure," he said. "Give my regards to the rabbi."

"Consider it done."

CHAPTER 20

I myself am a full-fledged citizen of the Yiddish world, Max only a sometime visitor. Maybe it's better that way.

From the casebooks of Morris Weiss

Max Weiss—The Present

"Margoshes?" Dr. Shavinsky yelled. "A hothead!"

"No," Ms. Fogal said coolly. "Overly strong-willed, perhaps." And gave him the evil eye.

"He was *impossible*," Shavinsky shouted, utterly impervious to the eyeball assault.

"Improbable," Fogal shot back, not missing a beat.

Great. There went my soft-spot theory. If these guys were Margoshes fans, they were doing a fine job of hiding it.

I held up my hand like a traffic cop and nodded hopefully at the third party, the latecomer who had just waltzed in through the door. Maybe he could restore some sanity.

"Well," Halkin said, "frankly, I enjoyed working with the old buzzard."

"Old buzzard?" I asked.

He grinned broadly. "Merely a term of endearment." And laughed heartily.

So much for restoring sanity. They were all nuts.

I was in Shavinsky's office on the ground floor of the Jewish Heritage Foundation. These three were supposed to be my Margoshes experts. They were supposed to make my life easier, not tougher. Obviously, they didn't know that.

Dr. Theodore Shavinsky, the Foundation's director was a short, stocky, bald guy in his early seventies, decked out in a brown tweed jacket. He looked normal, only he wasn't acting normal. Leonard Halkin, the Foundation archivist, a slender, sandy-haired guy of medium height in a loose tan sweater, didn't look crazy, but in this place looks meant nothing. Sara Fogal, the Foundation librarian, was a small, mid-sixtyish woman with short-cropped gray hair and rimless glasses, in a blue skirt and jacket with a black flower print scarf thrown rakishly over one shoulder. She also seemed to have all her marbles. Until the conversation got around to Margoshes. Then all bets were off.

Shavinsky was seated behind his desk. His two colleagues and I sat in armchairs facing him. Through the ground-floor windows I could see the corner of Madison Avenue and East Seventy-seventh Street, full of swanky shops and tall buildings. There were lots of pedestrians on the street. They were beginning to look crazy, too.

Shavinsky turned to Halkin. "You are young," he said.

"Thank you. But I am forty-five," Halkin said.

"For Margoshes," Shavinsky said, "you were a mere youngster."

"Felix saw you as his successor," Fogal said.

"I *am* his successor," Halkin said. "Or haven't you noticed?" He laughed at his own joke and looked gaily around at his colleagues. They sat stony-faced. Halkin stopped laughing.

Shavinsky grimaced. "With peers he was a demon."

"With you, maybe, Theo, he was a demon," Fogal said, "not with everyone."

"With everyone," Shavinsky insisted. "Only not women."

"Let's see," I broke in. "For a demon, Margoshes wasn't half bad. Have I got that right?"

Three heads shook in immediate disagreement. All three, I saw, were staring expectantly at me, as though it were now *my* turn to either malign or defend the missing archivist. And I didn't even know the guy.

"So," I said, "none of you has any idea where Dr. Margoshes might have gone?"

"Believe me, young man, he would not have told us," Shavinsky said.

"How about you?" I asked Halkin. "You got along with him."

Halkin smiled. "We spoke about rare Yiddish manuscripts, Mr. Weiss, about the collected papers of Yiddish poets, diaries written by victims and survivors of the Holocaust, copies of ancient Yiddish periodicals. All shoptalk. Endlessly fascinating, but still shoptalk. I never knew what he did on weekends. Or who his outside friends were. I didn't even know where he lived until last month. And I have worked side by side with him for over a decade."

I turned to Ms. Fogal. "Ms. Fogal," I said.

"Dr. Fogal," she said. "Felix was always the gentleman

with me, the cavalier. He would bow when he saw me in the building, and tip his hat if we passed on the street. He helped me with the library, and I, of course, helped him with the archives. Scholars often came to us both with their problems." She smiled primly. "About his personal life, I never asked, and he never offered."

Not bad. They were starting to sound almost sane. I didn't let the opportunity go to waste. "Was Margoshes working on anything special before he left?" I asked.

"What wasn't he working on?" Fogal said. "He had dozens of his own projects. He published in each issue of our *Research Bulletin*. He helped scores of scholars with their projects. Felix was tireless."

"How about an ideal retirement spot?" I asked. "He ever mention one?"

Shavinsky laughed. "The only place he would retire to was his own archives. There they would feed him three meals a day and leave him in peace with his research."

"Work was his life," Fogal said.

"Sure," I said. "But he did retire, didn't he?"

Shavinsky shrugged. "He was eighty, what could he do? It was time to make room for our young friend here." The director nodded toward Halkin, who shifted uneasily in his chair.

"No one forced him out," Halkin said quickly. "He was slated to be our Archivist Emeritus. We expected him to be here almost every day."

"What happened?"

"He never showed up."

"You try to reach him?"

"Not at first. I was sure he was off on vacation, his first real one in forty years."

"Fifty," Shavinsky said.

"Weeks went by and we didn't hear from him," Halkin

said. "I called him at home but his phone had been disconnected."

"What did you think?"

"I was baffled," Halkin said.

"All of us," Fogal said, "were baffled."

"So what did you do then?"

"What should we do?" Shavinsky said, throwing up his hands. "He was not obliged to give us reports of his activities. This is a free country."

"Well, I checked around," Halkin said, "on my own."

"*Mazeltov*," Shavinsky said. "Now you are a detective, too."

Halkin shrugged. "I was worried. I called Yeshiva University here. I faxed Jerusalem University and Oxford. All three have Yiddish programs, Mr. Weiss, and quite extensive archives. There is also a worldwide network of scholars, most of whom knew Margoshes personally. They can be reached through E-mail."

"Any leads?"

"Nothing," Halkin said. "Absolutely nothing."

I asked if the name Leo Kanufsky meant anything to anyone. I was rewarded by three shrugs almost in unison. It reminded me of the Marx Brothers. That's all I needed. I said my goodbyes and left.

I worked my way through the building, pestering everyone I could get hold of. The younger staff members all assured me that Dr. Margoshes was not only tops in his field, but a grand old guy who gladly went out of his way to help others. Senior staffers split down the middle. The ladies thought him gallant. The men, depending on their age, saw him as either prickly or downright hostile. Regardless of age, they all agreed on one thing: Margoshes

had neglected to say goodbye. And, of course, no one had
the least idea where he might be, although a pretty librarian reported that the archivist once said he was looking
forward to a long rest. Hopefully, he didn't mean the
grave. Raising the possibility that the "old buzzard" had
simply gone off to sun himself in Bermuda or someplace
and not bothered to tell anyone. I mentioned Kanufsky,
too. I even described him. No one had ever heard of him.

CHAPTER 21

Morris Weiss—1948

Morris Weiss crossed at the intersection, turning west on Forty-second Street. A blinking marquee offered "Dancing." A billboard touted Schenley Whiskey. The New Amsterdam movie house featured a double bill for a quarter: *Flying Serpent* and *Strangler Swamp*. *The land of plenty*, Weiss thought.

A few blocks down, he turned in at the green McGraw-Hill building. The open cage elevator rattled as it carried him up. The uniformed operator let him off on the tenth floor. The Magnum Insurance Company was directly across from the elevator.

Weiss pushed open the door, entered a small wood-paneled reception room, and asked the receptionist for Gerry Sykes.

* * *

"No," Sykes said emphatically.

Weiss shrugged, settled back in his padded green side chair. He was in a small pale-green windowless office with a pair of gray steel filing cabinets, an oak desk, a black phone, and a Royal typewriter.

"You gotta have a screw loose, chum," Sykes said. "Even if I knew what you were talking about, I wouldn't admit it. Not in a million years."

Weiss looked genuinely puzzled. "Why not?"

"Classified."

"The war is long over, Mr. Sykes. Whatever happened is not anymore a matter of strategical importance to anyone."

"Listen, once you take an oath, it's for life."

"Even if you are not a soldier anymore?"

"Yeah."

"Then why," Weiss asked, "did you agree to see me?"

"I figured you were gonna ask about an insurance claim, not some old cloak-and-dagger crap. It's dead history, chum. Forget it."

Sykes was a short, stocky man with slicked-back dark blond hair, a round face, and upturned nose. He had on a wide-shouldered pinstriped business suit, with a three-pointed white handkerchief sticking out of his breast pocket, a white shirt, and a wide striped tie held in place by a silver tie bar, engraved "G.S." in old English type.

The modern businessman, Weiss thought, *in his battle fatigues*.

"Look," Sykes said, "I wouldn't've even seen you if I'd known what this was about."

"Then it's a good thing I did not tell you. A man's life is at stake here."

"That's your business, not mine." Sykes took out a pack

of Fatimas and lit up, neglecting to offer one to Weiss. The detective didn't mind.

"Maybe," Weiss said, "the army doesn't see it in such a way."

"The army?"

"How do you think I found you?"

"They gave you my name?"

"And address."

"That's crazy. It's a breach of security."

Weiss nodded toward the phone on Sykes's desk. "Call them," he said. He slid a piece of paper across the desk.

Sykes looked at Weiss, then at the paper. "This guy's a full-bird colonel."

"What did you expect, a private?"

"Is this a gag?"

"It's no joke, Mr. Sykes. There is more involved here than my case. The army has a stake in this, too. They would be very pleased if you would give me your full co-operation."

"I don't get it. Everything I got, they got in spades, along with plenty more. Why come to me?"

"Because the army no longer has this information in its possession."

"They lost it?"

"Either that or it was stolen."

Sykes ground out his cigarette butt in a large glass ashtray.

"Stolen?" he said. "Why would anyone do that?"

"An excellent question," Weiss said. "And you, Mr. Sykes, may have the answer, even if you don't know it." Weiss gestured toward the phone again. "Colonel Steven Minsky would like to speak with you. Call him—or he will call you. That would not be good."

"Hey, I'm a civilian now."

"But also a patriot. You and the Colonel are both on the same side. Call him."

Sykes stared at Weiss, then looked toward the door as if hoping it might offer a tactical diversion of some sort. Reluctantly, he reached for the phone, slowly dialed the number. Identifying himself, he asked to speak to Colonel Minsky. There was a pause as Sykes clutched the receiver and glared at Weiss. Then the colonel came on the line. Immediately, a change was apparent in the claims adjuster's demeanor.

"Sir," he said stiffly, as though once again on active duty. "There's a man here who says—what, sir? Yes, sir, of course, sir, but sir, I just want to—"

Sykes was suddenly silent as he listened to the voice on the other side of the line.

Some voice that must be, Weiss thought. *This Sykes takes orders well, even if he pretends not to. Soon Minsky will have him saluting me. There must be more to his nephew, Boris, than meets the eye, or none of this would be happening.*

"Yes, sir," Sykes said one last time, his face perspiring. He held the phone out to Weiss. "He wants to talk to you."

Weiss took the receiver. "Colonel," he said.

"How did I do?" Minsky asked in a stage whisper.

"First rate."

Minsky chuckled. "He's docile, uh?"

"Absolutely."

"Good, good," Minsky said with obvious satisfaction. "My nephew thinks the world of you."

"And I of him."

"Glad to hear it. The kid said you offered him a job."

"Part-time."

"Fine. Help pay his tuition. Let me know how this turns out."

"I will, Colonel."

"Personally," Minsky said, "I think the file you want just got buried in the wrong place. Happens all the time here. But who would believe it? The U.S. Army just won a war, we're known for our efficiency. Sooner or later it'll turn up. Meanwhile, good hunting, Mr. Weiss."

"Thank you." Weiss hung up.

Sykes was busy swiping at his face with his pocket hanky. "That's one tough-bird colonel," he said.

"What did he say to you?"

"Pretty much what you did. Said the files on our mission had been looted."

"Looted, eh?"

"Said I should help you in any way I can."

"That's good."

"Okay, I got my orders right from the top. No sweat. Whaddya wanna know?"

Weiss smiled. "Everything."

"That'll take some doing. Let's get outta here. There's a Schrafft's next block."

Weiss plucked his hat and coat from the coatrack. Sykes removed a long gray coat and fedora from the closet. They left.

The restaurant wasn't busy at this time of day.

The two men took seats by the window. The late-afternoon crowd on Eighth Avenue streamed by, women in veiled hats and gloves, men in broad-shouldered full-length overcoats.

Weiss examined the menu.

Braised beef à la mode was the special, with rice, gravy, carrots, peas, and mashed potatoes, all for a dollar thirty.

Weiss wasn't even tempted. Schrafft's was a good place for elderly ladies to congregate, and, during business hours, for businessmen to grab a quick bite. But no one in his right mind would want to eat an early dinner here. Or even a late one. It was mediocre chain-restaurant fare, not home cooking like at Ratner's on Delancey Street. He regretted not having steered his guest to the Chase cafeteria near Broadway. Even there the food was better.

A pink-uniformed, white-capped waitress approached the table. Weiss ordered the house specialty, a grilled cheese sandwich. Sykes went for the grilled cheese and ham sandwich. Both ordered coffee.

"Right from the start," Sykes said, "the whole thing looked screwy."

"Why?"

"The guys making up my team, for one thing."

"You didn't like them?"

"Whaddya mean like? I didn't even know them."

"How is that possible, Mr. Sykes?"

"Yeah, it's one for the books, all right. I was with the Rainbow Division, stationed in the south of France. This was in the last months of the war. Everyone knew the Nazis were done for, especially them.

"I got me a sweet job as Company Supply Officer. It's a no-hassle job. My boss, the captain, is off playing golf all day. I got me a staff of fifteen doing the work. I got it made. No more foxholes, no more mud, no more ducking bullets. That's all behind me. Suddenly, outta nowhere, I'm yanked outta my office, handed combat fatigues, a carbine, a duffel full of gear I haven't laid eyes on since they pulled me outta the trenches, and hustled on a C-47—all in the space of two hours. I almost shit. No one briefs me or nothing. I got sealed orders. The pilot's a nice guy. He tells me I'm going to Yugoslavia. Yugoslavia?

It's just a name to me. I don't get it. We land, and a donkey takes me the rest of the way."

"And that is where, Mr. Sykes?"

"Get this. With Tito's partisans somewhere in the mountains, I don't even know where. Some help I'm gonna be. I'm outta shape. All I been doing for exercise is walking to and from my office. My skills are shuffling papers and sharpening pencils. They gotta be crazy sending me there.

"The Croats, some guy who hardly speaks English tells me, aren't far away. The Croats are Nazis; Tito is a Commie. Now I got a scorecard, only I don't know the game. I unseal my orders. They don't tell me much. There's an American light colonel with Tito's partisans, some kinda advisor. I'm to report to him. Guy's name is Rutledge. Only I don't get to meet him yet. I sit around cooling my heels. No one speaks English worth a damn. I don't learn a thing. Just when I'm beginning to crawl outta my skin, I get some company. One by one, GIs start showing up. They're some crew. None of them's seen combat in months. They can't figure any of this either. They're all noncoms, so as Second Looey, I'm the big cheese til we see this colonel. I take down their names."

The food came. Sykes dug into his sandwich, made short work of it. Weiss took a bite of his, chewed thoughtfully, then asked, "These names, you have them still?"

Sykes tapped his skull with a forefinger and grinned. "Yep."

"I congratulate you on your memory, Mr. Sykes."

"My memory stinks. The names stuck on accounta' what happened."

Weiss nodded, removed a small notebook and pen from the inside breast pocket of his jacket. "Can you give them to me now, Mr. Sykes, before we go on?"

"Why not? That's what all this is about, isn't it? These guys."

Weiss smiled. "I'm hoping to find out."

"Okay. Corporals Ben Robinson, Thomas Blake, Earl Grasser, Leon Asher, Sergeant Gordon Keller, and me. That's the lot, for what it's worth."

"A good deal, I think. Is there maybe anything else you can give me about them?"

"Yeah. Like me, they were Rainbow Division. But all from different outfits."

"What else?"

"Nothing. We talked. No one knows beans. All we can do is guess. So that's how we spend the time. Me, I still figure they got the wrong guy. I expect any minute I'm gonna be kicked back to my company."

Weiss took another bite of his sandwich, wiped his lips with his napkin. "What happened next, Mr. Sykes?"

"What happened? We finally get to see this Colonel Rutledge. It's a pitch-black night. The cold goes right through my field jacket. I feel lousy. But at least I'm gonna get some answers now.

"First we hike down a small road through the woods, the locals up front with the flashlights, us GIs bringing up the rear. We get to a clearing and there's this command tent. And inside, there's the colonel."

Weiss finished his sandwich, picked up his coffee cup, saw it was empty, and motioned to the waitress. "What did he look like?"

"The colonel? He was a squirt. A little fat guy with a big chin and nose, large head, and not much hair. But the guy's a light colonel so that makes him nine feet tall.

"He congratulates us, tells us we're about to serve our country in a big way, and we should feel real proud. Then he gives us the lowdown. We were brought together for this one mission. It's gonna be a snap. When it's over, we go back to our units and forget all about what happened here. And that's an order."

"And this mission was?"

"Safe conduct through Allied lines for a bigwig Nazi."

"Who was he?"

"Ludwig von Richtler."

Weiss shrugged.

"Don't sweat it. No one's ever heard of this guy."

"He was a general?"

"I never knew."

"So what, Mr. Sykes, made him so important?"

"The colonel didn't bother briefing us on that one. After I got back to my base in France, I asked around. I had some pals in Army Intelligence. They told me all the Allies were falling over themselves trying to recruit Nazis. Yeah, according to my pals, these bums were being offered new identities, big jobs, and plenty of cabbage. No one cared they were murderers."

"So this Nazi knew something important?"

"Or had some kinda skill we needed. I never found out which. Well, the natives fix us up with some pup tents and we spend the night there. Next morning we're off to a village down the road. One of the partisan guys takes us. It's a hike, but we get there on time. A couple shacks, a couple stores, a beat-up Duzenhalf truck, a couple bikes, no pavement even, just dirt. How can people live like that? Suddenly, I spot the Nazi. The guy's in full regular army gray uniform. He's just stepped out from one of the shacks. He's just standing there. Probably, the bum oughta be in a prison camp. Instead, we're rolling out the red carpet for him. The guy starts walking toward us. Some of my guys go to meet him. And that's when the shit hits the fan. The damn truck explodes. The guy goes up like a clappa thunder. When the smoke clears, Robinson's dead, Blake's wounded, and von Richtler's gone.

And that, chum, believe it or not, is the story, all I got. I was debriefed when I got back to France. I told them what I told you. I don't know about the other guys. The records musta all landed in Washington. Now you say they've been swiped. So that makes you maybe the one outside party to know the whole rotten story. Good luck, chum. I hope it buys you something. All it ever got me was a headache."

From the darkness, Weiss said, "Good evening, Rudy."

"What?"

Weiss snapped on the light. "Over here," he said.

"Jeez, Sarge," Rudy said, "what the hell you doing here?"

"Visiting."

"You scared the shit outta me."

"That was my plan, Rudy."

"What plan?"

"To make you more pliable."

"Cut the crap. How'd you get in here?"

Weiss smiled. "The same way you got into my office. I picked the lock."

They were in Rudy's Yorkville flat on East Eighty-sixth Street between Second and Third Avenues. It was ten-thirty at night. Weiss wore a long black wool coat with a dark-blue muffler and blue fedora. Rudy had on a brown leather jacket and gray peaked cap. There were two rooms here, a kitchen and a bedroom. The kitchen was painted a bright yellow.

"How'd you find me?" Rudy said. "My name ain't even in the phone book."

"But it is at the college."

"They gave it to you?"

"No. They gave it to my friend O'Toole, who is a policeman. He gave it to me."

Rudy was still standing in the doorway, as though bolted to the floor.

"Look, Sarge, like I said, all that was Fletcher's idea, not mine. The guy never let on he was going to bring your family into it, or I woulda tipped you for sure."

Weiss nodded, a pleasant smile on his face.

"Come in, Rudy, sit down. You don't look comfortable standing there."

"No hard feelings?"

"None," the detective assured him. "We are, after all, colleagues."

When Rudy still hesitated, Weiss stepped over, took him by the arm, and led him to the small kitchen table.

"I want you to feel at home here," he said with a straight face.

Weiss pulled out a chair, put an arm on Rudy's shoulder, and gently eased him down. Still in hat and coat, Weiss took the chair across from him.

"Don't worry," he said. "We still have our deal. You are still a trusted associate."

"You sure, Sarge?"

Weiss shrugged. "Why shouldn't I be sure?"

"So how come," Rudy said, "you're even here?"

"To ask for your help."

"You still digging for dirt at the college?"

"Not that."

"Then what?"

"I am glad you asked, Rudy. This agent of yours," Weiss said. "I want him off my back. That is why I am here."

"Gee whiz, Sarge, why don't you ask for something easy, like having him knocked off. The guy's a Fed. You don't know what he can do."

"You tell me, Rudy."

"He can ruin me."

Weiss glanced around the almost bare flat. To him it looked as if somebody had already ruined Rudy. Probably Rudy himself. *The F.B.I. must be paying him something,* Weiss thought. *And God knows who else. What does he do with the money? Gamble, maybe? Spend it on women? He certainly doesn't spend it on rent.*

Weiss sat back in his chair, interlocked his fingers on the tabletop, and said, "I will not have my family dragged through the mud."

"Now I get it, Sarge. You want me to get hold of J. Edgar Hoover and read him the riot act. Sure thing." Rudy laughed nervously.

Too bad, Weiss thought, *he is regaining his courage.*

Outside, a long chain of German restaurants and bars stretched along the avenue. Weiss could hear music coming from a German dance hall on Lexington Avenue. Before the war this neighborhood was the home of the pro-Nazi German Bund. Hollywood even made a movie about it: *The House on Ninety-second Street.*

"What I want," Weiss said, "is for you to find out everything you can about this man that might put him at a disadvantage. And give it to me."

"How'm I gonna do that?"

Weiss shrugged. "You will find a way. It is what you do."

"You're crazy. I ain't messing with no Feds."

"Rudy," Weiss said, "you are crazy if you don't. Remember the crooked deals you made in the army? Remember your confederate, the unfortunate Sergeant Kleinman who was serving time while you were walking around a free man? He was very angry about that, I am told. He gets out of prison next month. Of course he doesn't know where to find you, and neither do his friends. But I do.

You should think about that, Rudy. Kleinman himself is not a violent man. But some of his friends are *very* violent."

"You'd finger me?"

"Worse than that, Rudy," Weiss said. "I'd help them beat you to a pulp."

CHAPTER 22

In my youth, both the lowlifes and their victims always spoke Yiddish. Today, the crimes are almost the same, but the language is different. This, it seems to me, is not much of an improvement.

From the casebooks of Morris Weiss

Max Weiss—The Present

I cast an eye over the faded redbrick apartment house. Margoshes had lived here since the sixties, first with his wife, then, after she passed away, alone. It was a narrow building on Claremont Avenue, a block away from Upper Broadway and only a stone's throw from Columbia University, where he had once taught courses.

I stepped up and rang the super's bell. And presently

found myself addressing a tall, white-haired black man in blue denim shirt and jeans, who said his name was Jackson.

I showed him my license, which seemed to impress him. To tell the truth, having one impressed me, too. I asked him about Margoshes.

"Yeah, he's gone," Jackson said. "Ain't got a clue where to. But I know where his furniture went, if that'll help."

"It'll help," I told him.

He gave me a name and address on Union Square. I gave him a ten. We shook hands, and I headed for the nearest subway station.

Union Square was where the radicals used to hang out before I was born. It's where the Labor Day parades kicked off on May Day, red banners flying. It's where left-wingers harangued the crowd, Paul Robeson sang spirituals, and the Almanac Singers belted out union songs.

Today, chintzy discount outfits and a cut-rate department store are there, catering to the masses who wouldn't know a red banner from a Yankee pennant. A Virgin Record store and United Artists multiplex cinema are on the southeast corner. An upscale high-rise complex, with an A&P supermarket and small shops on its ground floor, is on the east side of the Square. Klein's Department Store—where my sainted grandmother upheld the Weiss honor by battling hordes of ladies for the bargains on its racks and tables—once occupied the spot. There are plenty of ghosts haunting that square.

Kierston Storage was on the eighth floor of an old building west of Union Square Park. I walked into a tiny office with a yellowed map of the five boroughs on its

wall, and a framed, brown-tinted photograph of Franklin
D. Roosevelt.

"Yes?"

I showed the elderly woman seated at the table my license. She brushed it aside with an angry wave of her hand.

"Don't try to impress me with that," she told me. "You
have no legal standing."

She wore rimless spectacles, a mid-calf shirtwaist
with silver-dollar-sized buttons running down the front,
and too much makeup on her sharp-featured face. Her
gray hair was tied back in a severe bun.

"Sure. Never said I did." I smiled at her. She glowered
back at me. I put the smile away for a more worthy candidate.

"What do you want?" she demanded.

"Just some information."

She shook her head, her mouth a tight line.

"How about a nice tip for your help?" I said.

"I am not an employee," she told me icily. "I am Kierston, I own this business. And I am not in the habit of ac-
cepting tips."

"Give me a break, Ms. Kierston. You don't even know
what I'm asking about."

"Something slimy," she said. "That's all you people
ever want. The objects stored in my warehouse are private
property. I can tell you nothing about them. If you wish ac-
cess to them, you must obtain a court order."

"That's not what I want," I protested.

"So what is it?"

"Not much. I just need the address of one of your
clients."

"I cannot help you. We do not give out that sort of information. If you have no further business, I suggest you
leave."

If she'd been trying to win me over, she'd blown it.

"You work every day, Ms. Kierston?" I asked.

"What business is that of yours?"

I handed her the archivist's snapshot. "You might have seen this man three months ago," I said. "His furniture is in your warehouse. He's missing."

She glanced at the photo. "What do you mean 'missing'?" she snapped at me.

"He can't be found," I said. "He's disappeared, vanished, melted into thin air."

"Nonsense!"

"You know where he is?"

"Of course. In Europe."

"Europe?"

She waved the snapshot at me. "This is Dr. Felix Margoshes, is it not?"

"Yes."

"Then he's in Europe. I trust you do not begrudge him his retirement?"

"Me? Never. He didn't say where in Europe, did he?"

"Everywhere."

"Did he leave an address where he can be reached?"

"He did not. He does not wish to be disturbed. This is his free time."

"How long is he planning to be gone?"

"He is paid up with us for two years. He said he should have left his job long ago."

"At the Jewish Heritage Foundation?"

"Where else? That is where he worked, is it not? As chief archivist."

"Right. He say anything else to you?"

"He said he was tired and overworked. He said he had been pestered long enough, that most of the questions he was asked were stupid. He told me he had been looking forward to this trip a long time. He deserves his rest. Why can't you leave him alone?"

"You liked him, didn't you?"

"Of course I did. He was a real gentleman—unlike some I could mention."

CHAPTER 23

Morris Weiss—1948

"Boris?"

"Yes?"

"Good evening. This is Morris Weiss."

"How are you, sir?"

"Very fine. I hope I'm not disturbing you, Boris."

"Not in the least. I am merely leafing through Gibbon's *The Decline and Fall of the Roman Empire*, a wonderful diversion. Such literature keeps one mentally fit. Even in these dire surroundings of toil and servitude."

"You mean the army?"

"What else? Was Uncle Sasha of any use to you?"

"Of great use, Boris. I thank you."

"I am delighted to hear that. Did you find the information you sought, Mr. Weiss?"

"I did. And please, call me Morris."

"I do not wish to appear forward."

"It's all right. You are about to become a valued associate of mine, Boris."

"I am?"

"Absolutely. A fee is also included. And my associates are my friends. So I am now Morris and not Mr. Weiss."

"That is very kind of you, sir."

"This is business, not kindness. And no more sirs. I was an enlisted man. And, in any case, you are almost finished with the army."

"Thank God."

"Boris, I need your help again."

"It is my privilege. What do you want done?"

"Another records search."

"That is a simple matter."

"I hope so. Corporals Ben Robinson, Leon Asher, Earl Grasser, Thomas Blake, and Sergeant Gordon Keller. Please see what you can find out about them."

"These are the men from the secret mission?"

"Yes. All from the Rainbow Division, autumn 1945."

"What precisely do you wish to know?"

"Anything and everything."

"I will do my best."

"That goes without saying. There are two others I am also interested in. They will be harder."

"I thrive on challenges."

"I'm sure. A German officer, Ludwig von Richtler. For some reason he was to be given the kid-glove treatment, escorted through Allied lines to one of our intelligence units. Whatever this man knew or did, we did not want him to fall into Allied hands. We wanted him for ourselves. But this von Richtler never reached his safe haven. A truck blew up as he was walking toward his American escorts."

"He survived the blast?"

"He vanished, Boris, in a puff of smoke."

"Strange."

"Not to say unlikely. The other is the commander of the mission, a Lieutenant Colonel Rutledge."

"I remember him from my last search. He died in combat a month later."

"I want to know everything there is to know about this man."

"I understand."

"And one last thing."

"Yes?"

"I want you to say my first name."

"Your first name?"

"Say 'Morris.'"

Minsky hesitated. "Morris," he finally said.

"There. How was it?"

"Very hard."

"Don't worry," Weiss said. "It will grow easier with time."

Morris Weiss entered his office.

"How ya doin', Sarge?"

Rudy sat behind the desk, his feet up on the desktop, his hands clasped behind his neck, in a typical Rudy pose.

Weiss shook his head. "Picked the lock again?" he said.

Rudy grinned. "Just returning the favor, Sarge."

"Rudy, you are a menace to society."

"Wait til you hear what I've done for you."

Weiss pulled up the client's chair and seated himself.

"Done for me or to me?"

"I solved your problem, Sarge, that's what I did."

"That is very kind of you, Rudy," Weiss said. "Which problem are you talking about?"

"Fletcher."

"You have found a way to call him off?" Weiss said. "The man must have a truly checkered past. His type usually does."

"Uh-uh," Rudy said. "Guy's a damn straight arrow. I couldn't even get him for jaywalking."

"So, what did you do?"

Rudy smiled. "I got him kicked upstairs."

"The Bureau has given him a promotion?"

"Not the Bureau. I got him a new job with another outfit."

"Really?" Weiss said. "And just like that he quit the F.B.I.?"

"Sure," Rudy said. "Why not? Pays three times the dough. And it's got a swell future, too."

"What is this wondrous job, Rudy? Maybe I should apply myself?"

Rudy took his feet off the desk, and sat up straight. He shook his head.

"You wouldn't like it, Sarge," he said.

"Why not? It sounds good."

"It's hunting commies."

"What is this outfit?" Weiss said sharply. "It has a name?"

"They're working on it. Something like Red Menace. Or Citizen's Alert."

"Very catchy," Weiss said coldly. "How will this so-called promotion protect my family?"

"Simple. This new outfit is out to peg real big shots. Actors, say, in movies and radio. Reporters, editors from really big newspapers. Even some congressmen. Your brother and his wife don't rate the attention. What's the payoff? Besides, they're dead. See? You got nothing to worry about, Sarge."

"That is gratifying to know. And you, Rudy, plan to remain an F.B.I. informer?"

"Not me. I'm going with Fletcher to the new outfit. That's where the action's gonna be. You just wait and see."

CHAPTER 24

Well-placed friends and acquaintances are important. As a rule, they cost less than paid informers. The latter, however, have their advantages, too. Often they take up far less of the detective's valuable time and do an even better job.

From the casebooks of Morris Weiss

Max Weiss—The Present

I drove to Tribeca, spent a good ten minutes hunting for a parking spot, found none, and left the car and another buck with the attendant. In my office, the air was stale and musty. I opened a window and stood looking down on the street below. Some stores, two restaurants, and a card shop. My search of Margoshes's apartment that afternoon, after leaving the Foundation, had been a dud. Also, the neighbors and the super knew nothing about the scholar in their midst. I sat down at my desk, scrolled through the address file on my small PDA and made a call.

Zachary Lake worked for one of the larger out-of-state credit bureaus. I had never met the man, but we had transacted a good deal of mutually rewarding business over the phone. Uncle Morris had landed him years ago. He was one of the neighborhood kids who did small jobs for the agency when it was still located on the Lower East Side. Fortunately, Lake never discriminated between the cash I or my uncle Morris mailed to his home address. He was always delighted to hear from either one of us.

The gentleman in question was still at his desk when I called. We never bothered exchanging small talk, though the senior Weiss had been heard to inquire after his wife and children. For all I know, he may actually have met them somewhere along the line.

I told Lake what I wanted. He promised to call back within the hour. I phoned April, my client, and arranged to meet her for dinner at Niko's, an uptown Mediterranean grill and bistro on Broadway and Seventy-sixth Street. The food was good, and the location was only a couple of blocks from my apartment.

Twenty minutes later, Lake phoned with the information I'd asked for. I locked up the office, reclaimed my car, and drove uptown.

"It's a tough call," I said.

"What makes it so tough?" April asked.

"Money," I said. "What else?"

April was working away at her shrimp tourkolimano. She looked composed and competent in her Chanel suit. She paused long enough to ask, "Why?"

I took a sip of ouzo and another bite of my yuvetsi—a

casserole of tender lamb, crushed plum tomatoes, cheese, peas, and carrots that they cooked and served in a clay pot.

"To go on with this investigation," I said, "will probably cost you."

April nodded. We both continued to eat. Big Nick, who not only owned this place but also the burger and pizza joint a few doors over, was strolling around making sure that everything was shipshape. Our single-minded devotion to his fare must have pleased him—he smiled as he passed our table. Or maybe he was calculating the take. Niko's was packed. And it wasn't even eight o'clock yet.

"How much?" April finally asked.

"Depends," I said, finishing my dish. April was only a moment behind me. The way we'd both wolfed down our food, I figured she'd skipped lunch, too. We consulted the menu again, and ordered a plate of honey-soaked baklava, pieces of pistachio Kataif, and strong, fragrant Greek coffee.

"I've got money," April said. "I can dip into my savings."

"Sure, but there's just the chance that Uncle Felix, dubbed 'the old buzzard' by even his closest colleagues, doesn't give a hoot for you or anyone else, just now. He may simply have packed his bags and gone off somewhere to have some fun. He told a girl at the Foundation he was looking forward to that. Then there's this Kanufsky guy. But I don't know if he's actually connected to your uncle's disappearance."

I took a last sip of the heavily sugared coffee, put down my cup, and continued. "I have a contact at one of the credit bureaus. Your uncle left a nice plastic trail. He spent a couple of weeks in Saratoga Springs. He a racing fan?"

"My uncle? Never."

"How about classical music?"

She nodded. "Yes, he's addicted to it."

"Okay, the concert season there was still in full swing in mid-August. Plenty of nice hotels and restaurants, too. A great place to unwind."

"I can't imagine my uncle going there."

"But he did."

"And then what? Where did he go after that?"

"Anywhere."

"Your plastic trail?"

"It dries up after Saratoga Springs. If he really didn't want to be found, he could simply switch to cash and that would do it. As I said, it's a tough call. Your uncle may be on the run, or basking in the sun somewhere. Either way could cost you a great deal of money."

"I don't care. I want you to go on."

"To Saratoga Springs?"

"He's the only uncle I have. I don't want to bother him if he wants to be left alone. I just want to know that he's safe and well."

I nodded. "Seems like a reasonable thing to want. I'll get on it first thing tomorrow morning."

"Thank you."

"Thank *you*. I like Saratoga Springs. And if your uncle does, too, maybe he'll still be there."

Uncle Morris called that night.

"You are making progress on the case?" he asked.

"I'm going to Saratoga Springs," I told him.

"A fine place. Even when there is no racing at the track. The missing uncle is there?"

"He left a paper trail."

"Ah, then you have spoken with the indispensable Mr. Lake. How is he?"

"Still indispensable."

"Excellent. When you find the uncle, please give him my regards."

"Sure. Why?"

"We uncles must stick together."

"I should have guessed."

"And my best to Boris, of course."

"Of course. How's Ida?"

"Still giving her master class at the university. I am allowed to see her between students."

"Your wife was always a generous woman, Uncle."

"To a fault. Some of the scholarships for her course, you know, come out of her own pocket. Which actually is mine, too. It should keep me slaving at the agency for another twenty years, at least. Good night, Max."

"Good night, Uncle Morris," I said. "And my love to Aunt Ida."

CHAPTER 25

Morris Weiss—1948

The phone rang.

Morris Weiss put down his copy of the *Jewish Daily Forward* and reached for the receiver on his desk. "Weiss," he said.

"It is I, Boris Minsky."

"Hello, Boris."

"I bring news," Minsky said. "You requested a background search of five enlisted men, one colonel, and a German officer."

"My very words."

"I have completed the task."

"I am impressed."

"It was not difficult. Shall we commence?"

"By all means."

"First I have Corporal Benjamin Robinson."

"Blown up by a truck, I believe."

"Yes. In the line of duty."

"Too bad. And before the army this Robinson was what?"

"A student at James Monroe High School in the Bronx."

"A mere boy."

"He enlisted at seventeen."

Weiss sighed.

"There is no record," Minsky said, "of criminal activity."

"How did you find this out?"

"The police are always willing to cooperate with a representative of the armed forces."

"Of course. The uniforms stick together. Who is next?"

"Earl Grasser," Minsky said. "Raised in the state orphanage in Rockland County, and in two foster homes. Social Services has nothing derogatory to say about him. There was no discernible involvement in criminal activities as an adult."

"What did he do for a living?"

"He worked at the Gimbels department store, first as a stock boy, then in the men's clothing department."

"He also enlisted in the army?"

"He was drafted. After his discharge Mr. Grasser was temporarily a salesman at Abraham and Straus in Brooklyn."

"He was fired?"

"On the contrary. He had a commendable sales record but chose to go out on his own. It is, after all, the American way to riches. Mr. Grasser purchased various job lots that he then sold at flea markets, fairs, and even door to door. Apparently, there were also periods when he did no work at all."

"And how did you happen to come by all this, Boris?"

"The tabloids ran stories on Mr. Grasser's demise. Some neighbors were quoted. A few were listed in the telephone directory. They were most helpful after I told them the army was taking an interest in the murder of one of its veterans."

"Grasser was well liked?"

"So it appears."

"And what," Weiss asked, "of Thomas Blake?"

"He graduated from a parochial high school, Saint Paul's, in Brooklyn, with good grades. Both parents are still alive. He worked in his father's candy store while taking night courses at Brooklyn College until he was drafted. You know the rest."

"Excellent, Boris. I will make it my business to send you a nice check."

"It is not necessary."

"I insist."

"You are most kind," Minsky said. "Gordon Keller before the war resided in Brooklyn. Mr. Keller comes from a broken home. He never knew his father, who deserted the family. The mother was a seamstress. Her attempts to support the boy and his sister were admirable, but ultimately futile."

"The life of a seamstress is never easy."

"Mrs. Keller made it harder. She was a drunk, and for that reason unable to hold a steady job. The son took to the streets at an early age. By turns he was a numbers runner, a bookie's assistant, and a pimp."

"Very industrious for one so young," Weiss said. "He graduated to better things, no doubt?"

"Oh, yes. Mr. Keller was quite ambitious. At eighteen he joined a gang that offered protection to neighborhood storekeepers for a moderate or exorbitant sum depending on the nature of the enterprise. There were payoffs to the local precinct and beatings for storekeepers who refused their generous offer."

"He has an arrest record?"

"None as an adult."

"The police told you this?"

"Only in the most general terms. For the rest I was obliged to enlist the aid of Uncle Vladimir. He is a Brooklyn councilman and has exceptional sources at the precinct level. They did not hesitate to enlighten him."

"Your choice in uncles is commendable. Were you able to find Keller's current address?"

"I was not."

"Boris, a man of your resources?"

"Mr. Keller is unknown at his prewar address. He is not in the phone book. He has no driver's license. He is not in the Army Reserve. Nor is there a death certificate that I could locate."

"This sister, did you try to find her?"

"Naturally. Linda Keller is also gone. Perhaps Miss Keller wed and is therefore living under another name."

"The bane of the detective business. The mother?"

"Long dead."

"Who is next?"

"Leon Asher, who is even more elusive than your Gordon Keller. He gave the army a prewar address on Manhattan's West Side. I spoke to the landlord. No Leon Asher ever lived there. Mr. Asher was supposedly an usher at the Roxy. There is no record of his ever having worked there. In short, all we know of him is his service record, which was undistinguished."

"Yet he was chosen for this secret mission. Boris, can you find out if these five soldiers were in the same training company at Fort Dix?"

"I have already done that. A copy of the company roster is before me at this very moment."

"You are a wonder."

"It was an obvious step. They were. But never at the same time."

"And Gerry Sykes?"

"He was not among them."

"And no Joey Ginzberg, of course?"

"None."

"What of our two officers, the American and the German?"

"About the German I was able to learn nothing. He was serving in the wrong army, and ours has no record of him."

"And the fat colonel?"

"Milton Rutledge ran a small import business."

"What did he import?"

"Fabrics. From the Near East. The war put an end to that."

"He enlisted?"

"He was already a captain in the Army Reserve, having taken R.O.T.C. at Princeton."

"A business major?"

"Linguistics. He knew six languages."

"A nice number."

"My uncle Yuri knows twelve."

"Your uncles are a national treasure."

"They certainly think so."

"How did the colonel die?"

"A land mine."

"Where?"

"The outskirts of Berlin."

"When?"

"One month to the day after the secret mission."

"He was alone?"

"The colonel was part of the Allied invasion forces."

"He was in good company. Thank you, Boris."

"It was my pleasure . . . Morris."

* * *

"Mr. Sykes?"

"Speaking."

"This is Morris Weiss."

"How you doing, chum?"

"Fine."

"Got more questions, I bet."

"Just one."

"Okay, shoot."

"The five enlisted men on your secret mission—"

"What about them?"

"They knew each other?"

"Not a chance."

"You are sure?"

"Yeah, positive. Look, those guys were all in shock. Like me. They didn't have a clue to what was going on. Hell, they'd've fallen into each others arms if they were any kind of friends."

"You were there all the time?"

"Sure."

"But you slept in your pup tent."

"So what?"

"Where did they sleep?"

"In their pup tents. Jeez."

"Alone?"

"Yeah, alone. Whaddya think?"

"Thank you, Mr. Sykes."

"Detective Sergeant O'Toole, please," Weiss said.

The desk sergeant asked him to hold.

Weiss reached for the *Forward*. The lead story in the Yiddish daily was the assassination of Count Folke Bernadotte in the Israeli-held area of Jerusalem. The story had been making headlines around the world for two days. The United Nations' mediator had been gunned down by Jewish irregulars, members of a splinter group that had broken off from the extremist Stern Gang. The splinter group was even more extreme, although Weiss found that hard to imagine. Both groups had vowed that all of Palestine would remain permanently in Jewish hands. Weiss shook his head in dismay.

"O'Toole speaking," a familiar voice said in his ear.

Weiss put aside the *Forward*. "It's Weiss," he said.

"Mr. Weiss, and how are you this fine day?"

"Excellent, Detective O'Toole."

"Well, lad, the fight grows near. My bet is still on Zale. Only the great Stanley Ketchel did what Zale has done, regain the Middleweight crown. From Billy Papke it was, in 1908."

Weiss laughed. "I see you are a devotee of *Ring Magazine*, Detective O'Toole."

"It is a passion," O'Toole said. "Now, Mr. Weiss, that license plate number—"

"You ran it, eh?"

"If the coppers can't, who can?"

"And?"

"Joyce Griller." O'Toole gave him an address in the East Nineties on Third Avenue, under the El.

Weiss told him the story of the secret mission and recited the names of the five GIs involved.

"But your lad, Joey Ginzberg, isn't part of this lot."

"Earl Grasser is. To free Joey I have only to find his killer."

"Ginzberg's story, Mr. Weiss, is still not convincing."

"I will speak to him by and by. His story will improve," Weiss said. "This Tommy Blake may be known to some of your fellow officers."

"What did he do?"

"He disappeared. He packed his clothes and emptied his bank account."

"Well, when they take leave on their own it's not police business."

"True. But his wife, Cora, reported him missing anyway. This Cora works at the Allegro Diner in Hell's Kitchen in the Thirties." Weiss gave him the address. "What I need is for one of your fine colleagues to approach her."

"Don't worry. I'll find you a good man. What do I have him tell the wife?"

"That you are on the trail of the husband. And expect to have good news for her soon. Then tell her we think Blake's disappearance is somehow connected to a man called Gordon Keller."

"And what, Mr. Weiss, will that accomplish?"

"Who knows?"

"When do you want this done?"

"Give me three hours."

"Boris, it's Morris Weiss again."

"An unexpected pleasure. What is it Morris . . . more business?"

"Precisely."

"What would you have me do?"

"It's outside work. Can you be spared?"

"For how long?"

"The rest of the day," Weiss said. "And maybe well into the night."

"It is possible."

"You will not be missed?"

"I have never been missed yet. I shall have some of my fellow sufferers cover for me should the need arise."

"Excellent. There is a Joyce Griller I want you to watch tonight." Weiss gave him the address.

"What has she done?"

"Nothing that I know of. But her husband or boyfriend is somehow involved in this Grasser business. You will need a car. Watch Griller's door and if a man leaves, follow him."

CHAPTER 26

I have spent many happy summers in Saratoga Springs. If I still had all the money I lost at the track there, I would not be renting this office now, I'd own the whole building.

From the casebooks of Morris Weiss

Max Weiss—The Present

I made it to Saratoga Springs by 10:30 A.M. A three-and-a-half-hour run. The sun had risen in a blue, almost cloudless sky, and the trees still had most of their leaves, which were now a mix of greens, reds, and yellows.

During summer Saratoga Springs is jumping. There's the world-famous racetrack, where you can drop a bundle without batting an eye, the Saratoga Performing Arts Center, known as SPAC, where the Philadelphia Orchestra and

New York City Ballet turn up to perform, landmark hotels and plenty of restaurants, natural mineral baths, the SPAC swimming pool, where some of the ballet stars hang out in their off hours, and Congress Park, where you can picnic on the grass, watch the ducks in the pond, or sample free mineral water from the fountains. The town is a summer playground. It says so in the chamber of commerce brochures. And for once, a chamber of commerce was telling the truth.

Only this wasn't summer.

The streets were mostly empty, along with the stores. Conventions picked up the slack, but none seemed to be around now.

I parked down the block from the Adelphi Hotel and went into Compton's Diner. There were only two other customers around. I ordered a late breakfast and gazed out through the plate glass window at Broadway while I worked my way through fried eggs, home fries, and toast.

After I finished my second cup of coffee, I paid my bill, flashed my Margoshes snapshot at the waiter, busboy, and the lady at the cash register, and drew three blank stares, two shrugs, and one uh-uh. I left.

My missing scholar had been here while the racing season was still in full swing, making him all but invisible. The town was too crowded for anyone to notice one old guy—there were thousands floating around. But his credit card statement, which had him eating twice at Compton's last month, also showed him staying well into the off-season when the town was far less crowded. Sooner or later I'd come across his trail. And if he'd merely switched from plastic to cash, I might actually bump into him myself.

I drove the few blocks to the Holiday Inn, another name on the credit card statement, and showed my license to the pretty blonde behind the registration desk. She furrowed her brow. Next, I showed her my snapshot. That got me a stare.

"Well?" I asked.

"This old guy's a crook?"

"Far from it. He's a highly respected academic."

"Well, I don't know him," she said. "I just started working here last week. How come you're looking for him?"

"His niece thinks he's missing."

"She's not sure?"

"He may just be misplaced."

"Old age," the blonde said, "I'm really looking forward to it." She consulted her computer and nodded. "He was here, all right."

"I always get my man."

"Maybe not. He checked out on September eighth."

"These old academics," I said, "are getting sneaky. When did he check in?"

"August the twenty-first," she said.

"Any other tidbits in that machine?"

"Sorry, that's all I have."

"More than enough," I said. "Thanks."

I checked in myself, went up to a room on the third floor, unpacked, showered, and changed into a black T-shirt, black jeans, and a blue windbreaker. The hotel had a restaurant called Bookmakers. Its head waiter remembered the old man who had stayed beyond the season. But they had swapped only small talk. One waitress had chatted about New York museums with him, another had directed him to the best buys in town, such as they were during the overpriced racing season: the Army-Navy store on upper Broadway, Putnam Market, also on Broadway, and the Lincoln Baths in Spa State Park. I spoke to all the staff I could dig up on the day shift. Some recalled Margoshes, others didn't. My missing scholar had confided to a few that he was here on a well-earned holiday. But exactly how he spent his days no one could say for sure.

I left the hotel and strolled toward the center of town.

The Lincoln Baths closed after August, so I was out of luck there. The people at the Putnam Market had never heard of him. Although his credit card statement had him buying a sweater in the Army-Navy store, the guy who ran it didn't remember him.

I checked out the Springwater Inn on Union and Nelson Avenues. He had eaten there often and paid with his credit card. Some of the staff knew who he was. He had told one that he was here on a busman's holiday. The Saratoga Springs library was on Henry Street. A nice place to go, I figured, if you were interested in doing research. Not a single librarian recalled ever laying eyes on him. I examined the shelves full of popular books, and saw my mistake. This was a *public* library. For a scholar like Margoshes, it would have as much appeal as a comic-book stand.

I retraced my steps to Broadway, stopped at Scallions for a midday snack, and then began hiking north toward the Skidmore campus and the largest research library within miles.

Instead of shops and street lamps, trees now lined the walkway. Manor houses, manicured lawns, and town houses became the main attractions. And some attractions they were. All were showcase houses. But half the mansions stood vacant until the racing season began. Then nightly parties made the rafters shake.

I turned in at Skidmore and followed a sign to the library.

Business was brisk inside. Students were busy furthering their education. Or at least trying to. I got in line, a standout among all these youngsters. An eighty-year-old guy waiting in these lines would have stood out even more.

The kid behind the counter was a student himself. I showed him my snapshot.

He shrugged.

"I'm just part-time," he said.

The line behind me had grown.

I moved along the counter and became last man in another line.

The girl receiving books didn't know anything either.

"I don't work summers," she said.

"Who does?"

"Not at this desk. Try one of our permanent librarians." She gave me directions. I followed them, turned down a corridor and came to an open door.

The woman sitting behind the small desk was in her early sixties, gray-haired, short, and well preserved. Her face, almost wrinkle free, radiated warmth and good humor. She probably knew about books, too. But did she know about Margoshes?

"Hi," I said, smiling, "my name's Max Weiss. I need help. Have I come to the right place?"

"You certainly have," she said, returning the smile. Her voice was mellow, low, and musical. It was the kind of voice that never grows old.

"I'm looking for a Dr. Margoshes who—" I was in the process of pulling out my snapshot when she cut me short.

"Felix?" Her smile became absolutely radiant. "Are you a friend of his?"

Suddenly, I was feeling very good.

"In a way," I said. "I know his niece."

"How nice," she said, rising and extending a small hand. "I'm Mona Simon. Just Mona, please."

"Max," I said.

We shook on it, and I seated myself in the hard-backed chair by the side of her desk.

Her eyes beaming, she said, "Felix is such a pleasant man, isn't he?"

"Actually," I admitted, "I've never met Dr. Margoshes."

"Oh?"

"But I look forward to that pleasure."

"Such a gentleman," Mona said in a dreamy voice. "You will enjoy the experience, I'm sure."

Maybe I would. As long as I wasn't a competing male scholar, he'd probably let me live.

I smiled at her. "I've heard so much about him, I actually feel I know him. For instance, I bet he took you to a SPAC concert."

"Why, yes. How did you know?"

"Keen insight." I'd been briefed about his love of music by my client. But we investigators like to play our cards close to the vest.

"Not keen enough," she laughed. "It was two."

"Concerts?"

"And dinner, of course, in the Georgian Room at the Gideon Putnam."

"Nice place."

She actually blushed. "I miss him."

"I bet." She sounded so wistful I was starting to miss him myself. "Left town, did he?"

"More than a month ago."

"Back to the big city?"

"Oh, no, Felix is traveling."

That got my adrenaline pumping. I leaned closer. "Mona, did he happen to leave a mailing address by any chance?"

She sighed. "I wish he had. No, Felix's itinerary was still up in the air when he left."

"Did he, at least, say in which direction he was headed?"

"Europe."

"A vacation?" I asked.

"He's celebrating."

"Alone?"

"Yes. Something to do with a pet project," she said. "Why are you looking for him, Max?"

I leaned back in my chair and folded my arms across my chest. "I'm a private detective, Mona. It's my job to look for people. Felix left without saying goodbye to his niece."

She looked surprised. "That is what this is all about? He didn't say goodbye to his niece?"

"His niece," I said, "is very concerned about his well-being. Was he worried about anything?"

"Yes, he was afraid the Philadelphia orchestra might not have enough rehearsal time out here."

"Yeah, I can understand that. Anything else?"

"Not a thing."

"Right." I stood up. "You've been a pal, Mona."

She rose, too. "I'm glad, Max. I've enjoyed this. I have no doubt that you'll find him. Next time you come to Saratoga, I expect you to stop by and say hello."

I gave her a final smile and started to turn toward the door when a thought hit me.

"By the way," I said, "what was Dr. Margoshes doing here at the library?"

"He was going through the Treister archive."

"The what?"

"Kelman Treister donated all of his papers to this library."

"He was a scholar?"

"He is a very successful businessman. On three continents."

Mona reclaimed her chair. I sat down again, too.

"He is also," she continued, "a renowned philanthropist who's given millions to some very worthy Jewish causes."

"Well," I said, "I can see how that might rate an archive or two."

"At least. And he's endowed a chair in Jewish Studies here. His foundation helps refugees all over the world."

"Still, why would Dr. Margoshes be interested in him now?"

"Well, the philanthropy aspect alone, Max, might be of interest to a Jewish scholar. Along with the foundation. Not to mention his business empire, which financed both. I suspect it's ideal material for a series of original monographs. And it's all gone untapped."

"Makes sense. A real busman's holiday for our scholar."

"Felix loves his work. For him it's simply fun."

"Nothing like fun," I said. "Too bad Mr. Treister isn't around to lend a hand and have some of it himself."

"But he is."

"You're kidding."

"He lives just up the road in the really big brick place with the white shutters and columns."

"Goes to show. I figured he must have been long gone if you have his papers."

"Oh, no, Max. The archives are of historical importance, and Mr. Treister is a very generous man. Besides, that phase of his life is long over. Others run his foundation now, and he's been semiretired for years."

"You think Dr. Margoshes went to see him?"

She nodded thoughtfully. "It's certainly possible, though Kelman Treister isn't the easiest man to see. He's a notorious soft touch, and people have tried to take advantage of his generosity. His staff is always on the alert. But Felix had the right credentials."

"Well, he's the guy I should tackle next. Can you wangle me an introduction, Mona?"

"I wish I could. I've only met him twice. And those were ceremonial occasions. There were hundreds present. We merely shook hands and exchanged a few pleasantries. He would never remember me."

"Anyone else at the college know him?"

"Our chief librarian, Dr. Wooster, helped on the archives project. But that was all business. Dr. Wooster is a timid soul. I'm afraid he was rather intimidated by Mr. Treister and his wealth. You could try him, but I don't think you would have much success."

"Anyone else?"

"Our president, of course. But he might prove as hard for you to reach as Mr. Treister himself. You're not exactly a potential source of money for the college."

"You're right. I'll just have to wing it."

"Good luck, Max."

CHAPTER 27

Morris Weiss—1948

Weiss sat quietly in his Packard.

Mostly, he had no great love for machinery. But this car was extraordinary—a black 1940 supereight 180 sedan. The chrome that gleamed off the dashboard and ivory steering wheel somehow always cheered him. Heavy gray wool upholstery with dark-gray trim surrounded him. It was built like a tank with a 160 horsepower that hummed almost silently underway. He had picked it up from the widow of a marine captain who died in Okinawa. Weiss had his mustering-out pay, and she needed the money. He only used it when public transportation or taxis were inconvenient. He and the Packard had become true friends.

Hat brim pulled low, arms folded across the steering wheel, Weiss fixed his gaze on the Allegro Diner across the street. A single musical note in red neon flashed mutely on and off above the plate glass window.

It was late afternoon and business was slow in the diner. He could see Cora Blake and a redheaded woman serving what few customers there were. The portly counterman was busy studying a tabloid that Weiss could easily identify even at this distance: *The Racing News*. Already, he missed the track, though he'd dropped a big twenty there only last week.

Weiss had been waiting a half-hour when he caught sight of Detective Danny Flynn ambling up the block. He had a nodding acquaintance with the detective and knew only good things about him. Except for the few times Flynn had lost his temper and beaten a suspect senseless.

Flynn entered the diner and spoke to the counterman, who nodded toward Cora.

Weiss sat up as he approached her.

Flynn took Cora aside and the pair huddled by an empty table in deep conversation. Flynn had often been accused of kissing the Blarney stone, which, Weiss thought, made him perfect for this job. After a good five minutes, the detective smiled, turned, and left the diner.

Weiss waited, hoping that Cora would make her excuses to the manager and leave too.

But she went right back to waiting on tables as if nothing had happened.

Maybe the woman has been telling the truth, Weiss thought. Then, she would simply go about her business—exactly what she was doing.

A few minutes past five, Cora left the Allegro wearing a heavy red wool coat with a glass-eyed fox collar, a small veiled black hat, and high-heeled shoes that Weiss imagined clicked with every step. Even after an eight-hour stint on her feet, her gait was perky. Weiss admired that.

She didn't hail a cab but crossed the street at a trot and

headed west. *Ah-ha,* Weiss thought, *now maybe we'll learn a thing or two.* He gave her a good head start, then slowly eased the big sedan away from the curb and followed her.

Shabby tenements huddled on both sides of the street as the car worked its way westward. Teenagers with pinched faces, in peaked caps and leather jackets, loitered on the sidewalks, sat smoking on stoops, and clustered around a lone candy store, whose back room, Weiss suspected, had hatched many a misdemeanor and felony.

A few blocks more of this and he knew exactly where she was going: home.

What was wrong with this woman? Flynn's visit should have lit a fire under her. But she seemed to be taking her own sweet time.

His gut feeling was that the five GIs who had hidden their friendship from Sykes in Yugoslavia had a secret postwar history, too. And that Cora knew far more about it than she let on. When Flynn dropped Keller's name, it should have been a bombshell, one that sent her running for a face-to-face meeting with her "missing" husband. But she had done nothing. Weiss had been wrong before. Maybe he was accusing an innocent woman?

Cora turned in at her building and vanished through the front door.

The detective parked a half-dozen houses farther up the block. The building was visible in his rearview mirror. He sat back and waited as dusk darkened the city.

Young toughs eyed him as they swaggered by on the pavement. But no one approached his car. Weiss could have been a plainclothes cop on a stakeout. No one wanted to needlessly tangle with the police, not even the hard cases here.

Cora Blake reappeared some ten minutes later.

She hurried by the detective's car without a sideways

glance, heading west toward the waterfront. Weiss watched as she all but disappeared in the thick blanket of fog that had rolled in from the waterfront. He climbed out of his car just as the woman turned a corner.

Weiss ran to the end of the block, swung around the same corner, but could barely make out his quarry up ahead.

Then she wasn't there at all.

That's all I need, he thought, *to lose her now*.

The detective put on a burst of speed that brought him to the spot where he had last seen Cora Blake.

He stood before a vacant tenement. The building adjacent to it was a warehouse. A narrow alley cut between the buildings.

Let's see, Weiss thought, *if she's really a magician.*

First he tried the front door of the tenement: locked. The wide double doors of the warehouse were padlocked and unbudgeable.

That left the alley.

Moving cautiously, he felt his way between the two brick walls. *I should have brought a flashlight,* Weiss thought, *but I would need a thousand heads to think of everything*.

A side door of the tenement, no more than a dim outline in the wall, appeared locked. He stuck out a hand, turned the knob, and the door obediently opened.

Weiss smiled. His luck was still running good.

He stepped inside. A floorboard creaked under him. He stood perfectly still, then began to move down a dark hallway. Hands touching both walls, he shuffled along just as he had some twelve years ago in a Coney Island fun house on a double date. No monsters leaped at him from hidden recesses this time. At least, not yet.

He went up a flight of stairs.

Soon, Weiss was standing in an empty space that might once have been a living room.

Muffled voices were audible from somewhere in the rear of the house. *Very accommodating of them*, Weiss thought. Slowly, inching forward into another room, he could make out a sink, four-footed stove, and an icebox. He moved toward a door to the left of the icebox and put his ear against it.

"Don't be a fool," Cora Blake was saying.

"Who asked you?" a man demanded.

Blake, no doubt, the detective thought. *Again I have reunited a family.*

"They'll kill us both!" Cora shrieked.

"The hell with you," Blake said. "And them, too."

"For chrissake," Cora said, "use your head, give them what they want! Gordon said he'd give you part of the action."

"Sure thing, Gordon *said*."

"He's your friend."

"Whatta great friend that Keller's been," Blake said. "He'd cut my heart out for a plugged nickel."

"You're wrong."

"A lot you know," Blake said. "I'm gonna put the squeeze on that bastard. But first I'm gonna make him sweat plenty."

"How?" Cora said. "You going to scare him with your crutch?"

"Shut your mouth!"

"You always were a loser, Tommy."

"Get the hell outta here!"

"They'll find you!"

"You better keep your trap shut! You hear?"

"Bastard!"

"Stupid bitch!"

Lowlifes, Weiss thought. *For them it is already too late.*

He heard the clicking of high heels fading away.

Weiss pushed open the door.

"She's right," he said.

"Wha—" Blake's head veered toward Weiss as his hand darted for his small nickel-plated revolver on the table. A woman's gun.

"Don't," Weiss said, stepping into the room.

Blake saw the big automatic in the detective's hand.

He grew very still.

"Good," Weiss said.

He went around the seated man, took the gun from the small table, and stuck it into his coat pocket. "Your hands. Fold them in your lap."

Blake did as he was told.

He was a man of medium height and build. His shoulders were round, hair long and unkempt, eyes red-rimmed. He looked as though he hadn't shaved in over a week. He sat in an old easy chair, dressed in wrinkled gray pants and a faded plaid shirt, a pair of crutches resting against the side of his chair. His left trouser leg was folded back at the knee and pinned in place. Light came from a single floor lamp whose cord stretched across the floorboards and out of the room. Canned goods were piled on a table. A cot, covered by a thin blanket, was over by the far wall. A pair of empty whiskey bottles lay on the floor.

Blake said, "Keller sent you, uh?"

"I have nothing to do with him," Weiss said. "You are quite safe."

"What's this safe stuff? You've got a gun pointed at my head. Who the hell are you?"

"My name is Morris Weiss. I'm a private detective."

"Whaddya want?"

"I have a story for you," Weiss said. "About your wife."

"What story?"

Weiss put his own gun into his coat pocket and stood looking down at the seated man.

"She has sold you out," Weiss said.

"Listen, pal—"

"A policeman spoke to her this afternoon."

"Yeah?"

"He told her that Keller was involved in your disappearance."

"You mean that he snatched me?"

"Yes," Weiss said. "That's what I mean."

"Bullshit."

"He told her," Weiss said, "that the police were very close to finding you."

Blake seemed genuinely puzzled.

"Why would the cops be looking for me?" he said.

"They aren't. He lied. It is really quite simple, Mr. Blake. I needed to speak with you. And now, thanks to your wife, we are having this discussion."

"Speak about what?"

"Keller."

Blake shrugged. "I hardly know the guy."

"Come now, Mr. Blake. You and Keller were both part of a secret mission in Yugoslavia during the last days of the war."

"Says who?"

"It is how you lost your leg—when a truck exploded."

"I stepped on a mine."

"There were five of you: Robinson, Grasser, Keller, Asher, and yourself."

"You're outta your mind. I don't gotta tell you shit."

"That is not good, Mr. Blake," Weiss said. "If you do not speak to me right now I will take you directly to Keller. You can talk to him instead."

Blake reached for a crutch and pushed himself upright in the chair.

"Hey, mister, tell me, what's in it for you? You got some kinda angle I should know about before I spill my guts like you want?"

"I am working for Joey Ginzberg's lawyer."

"Who?"

"The man accused of killing Earl Grasser."

"What a crock! That was Keller."

"He had a motive?"

Blake nodded thoughtfully.

"That's what you wanna know? Sure, why not? Dope. Dope and dough. That's what it was all about right from the start, dope."

"Thank you, Mr. Blake. But could you be a little more precise?"

Blake shrugged. "Grasser wanted a bigger cut of the take. He got pushy. So Keller had him taken care of. That's the long and short of it. You got it now?"

"Your friend Keller runs a dope ring. And Grasser worked for him."

"Yeah. You got it."

"And you?"

"Me? Whaddya think? That's where the money is. Gotta bring in some dough for the little lady and me, right? Can't live like pigs all our lives." He laughed.

"You must be a rich man then, Mr. Blake."

"Yeah, I'm rollin' in it. Just take a look." He laughed again. "See, I wanted a raise."

"I'm sure you deserved one."

"You bet."

"I appreciate your confiding in me, Mr. Blake."

"Yeah? Well, don't get slaphappy about it, pal. What I'm giving you ain't worth shit. You tell the cops, it's your word against mine."

Weiss smiled. "Or your word against Keller's."

"Nah, you ain't gonna rat me out to that bastard. Not

you, mister. He's the guy croaked Earl. He's the guy you want, not me. And now you got a crack at him. Because of what I gave you. Don't say I never did nothin' for you."

"God forbid. What happened in Yugoslavia? Or is that too personal?"

He shrugged. "Dope. That's how Keller got into the racket. That's how it began. The Kraut was bringing in dope."

"Your colonel arranged this?"

"That little prick? It was all Keller. The guy was a staff sergeant. He knew the brass, had his pick of the guys who were right for the job."

"And he picked you?"

"Yeah," Blake said, "me and the other four guys. He knew us."

"From Fort Dix?"

"From before."

Weiss pulled up an old kitchen chair with his foot, swung it around, seated himself, and put his arms on the backrest. "Tell me, Mr. Blake, how did he know von Richtler?"

"The Kraut? Beats me."

"And in the end he also got to the German's dope, despite the explosion."

"Yeah, everything got screwed, but somehow he got it. Cost me my leg, mister. But it cost that damn Nazi a lot more."

"What did it cost him?"

"His life," Blake said.

"He was killed?"

"Blown to smithereens."

"They never found the body?"

"Who went lookin' for it? My buddies were busy scraping Robinson off the ground. They had their hands full. No one gave a shit about some damn Nazi."

Weiss rested his chin on his forearms and smiled thinly at Blake.

"Yes, I see," he said. "So how did Keller manage to pick up this dope right under the nose of Lieutenant Sykes?"

"Whaddya talkin' about?"

"Only three of you were left standing," Weiss said. "Keller, Grasser, and Asher. And you, Mr. Blake, had to be rushed back to where you could get medical attention."

Blake's face twisted in rage.

"I told you what happened. You think you know better—"

Weiss, however, was no longer listening. Suddenly, he was up on his feet, his automatic back in his hand. He put a finger to his lips and nodded toward the doorway. "Listen," he whispered.

Blake's eyes widened. His hand groped for both his crutches as if hoping to make a run for it. His neck tensed as he strained to hear the sounds of intruders.

There were none.

Blake cupped the back of his ear in his palm, turned to Weiss, and shrugged elaborately.

Weiss shook his head, ran a finger across his throat, and pointed it significantly at Blake. He reached over and pulled the lamp's wire. The plug in the kitchen slipped from its socket.

The room went dark.

"What the—" Blake began.

"Shut up!" Weiss whispered.

He hesitated only an instant, then yanked out Blake's gun from his other pocket and thrust it into the man's hand.

Again, Weiss heard the sound. This time he identified it for what it was: a loose floorboard like the one he had himself encountered earlier.

"They're here," he whispered. "Behind the chair. Now!"

The detective didn't wait for a reply. Grasping Blake by his shirt-front, he hurled him to the floor.

The kitchen door banged open.

Flashlights sent beams of light cutting through the darkness.

Weiss flung himself to the ground as three shots rang out.

Flat on his stomach, Weiss instantly squeezed off two rounds toward the open doorway.

Blake, behind the chair, worked his little gun furiously.

More shots sounded.

By then Weiss had crawled across the darkened floor, through the main doorway, and out into the hall. Climbing to his feet, he ran down a flight of stairs and found himself in the front part of the house. The door leading to the street was wide open, its lock hanging loose.

Weiss stepped into the night air and took a deep breath.

A burly man near the head of the alley was smoking a cigarette. He swung around to face the detective. A short black tube emerged from under his coat. Weiss shot him twice. The man fell to the pavement.

Weiss leaped forward, scooped up the sawed-off 12-gauge shotgun, and ran down the alley.

Again he entered the house through the side door and ran up the stairs. When he came to the kitchen it was empty.

He fumbled for the light plug and stuck it back into the socket.

Light went on in the next room.

Weiss entered.

A man whom the detective did not know lay stretched out near the wall. Tommy Blake, on his back on the cracked linoleum, lay on the floor in a puddle of his own blood, two large-caliber entry wounds in his side.

Weiss hurried to him. "Blake," he said.

Blake opened his eyes.

"Don't move," Weiss said.

"You had it right . . . bitch sold me out."

"I'll get help."

"Too late, pal. Lean closer. I got somethin' for you. . . ."

CHAPTER 28

All things being equal, it is better to be a million-aire than not be a millionaire. But when are all things equal?

From the casebooks of Morris Weiss

Max Weiss—The Present

Our millionaire, Kelman Treister, had a triple-decker house, set far back from the road amid old specimen trees, immaculate landscaping, and a billiard-table lawn. I gave it the once-over, debating with myself whether to just barge in and introduce myself, or play it cool and get a legitimate introduction first. Cool carried the day.

* * *

Back in my room at the Holiday Inn, I stretched out
on the bed, propped up my head against a pillow, and
called Dr. Shavinsky at the Jewish Heritage Foundation.

"I've got a problem," I told him.

"Who doesn't? If it has to do with Yiddish scholarship,
you have come to the right place, young man." He laughed.

"It's about Dr. Margoshes."

He stopped laughing. "Ah, our lost colleague. What
more can I tell you, Mr. Weiss?"

"For starters," I said, "do you know a Kelman Treister?"

"Treister? Of course. Who hasn't heard of him in the
Jewish world?"

"Me for one."

"You are not a professional Jew, Mr. Weiss. Those of
us in the Jewish business depend on men like Kelman
Treister. And he has, in fact, been most generous to this
institution. What does he have to do with Margoshes?"

"Plenty. Margoshes spent a good deal of time recently
at Skidmore College, going through the Treister archives."

"I see. Some of those documents," Shavinsky said,
"originally came from our archives. We donated them. Perhaps our missing scholar was homesick." Shavinsky had
himself another laugh. I waited until he was done.

"A librarian here," I said, "thinks Margoshes plans to
write some scholarly papers about Treister and is off to
Europe for more research."

"What did I tell you? Yet another research project. It
will never end. Your librarian is certainly right. He is chasing around the world hunting for more material. It is what
he has always done. Why should he bother telling us mere
mortals of his plans?"

"What I need now, Dr. Shavinsky, is an introduction to
Treister. He just may be able to clear everything up."

"That is all you need? I wish you luck, young man.
The Pope would be easier to see."

"I thought you knew him," I said, trying to suppress a twinge of irritation. As the senior partner of our agency has often pointed out, one needed a bit of self-restraint and patience to work the Yiddish side of the street.

"I myself met Kelman Treister only once," Shavinsky said. "It was here at the Foundation. Before the war, Mr. Weiss, our European center was in Vilna, now called Vilnius; it is the capital of Lithuania. When the Nazis invaded, our staff hurriedly buried our archives. Many of our scholars subsequently perished, but most of our archives survived. Soon after the war we obtained permission to reclaim our property. Our center is here now. So it was necessary to bring everything over, and then to begin the very difficult task of cataloging it. The cost was tremendous, and quite beyond our budget. Mr. Treister stepped in and helped finance the project; he was a godsend."

"So you know him?"

"I do not know him. I wrote to him of our problem, and he sent a check."

"That's it?"

"Of course not. I had the pleasure of thanking him at a reception given in his honor. Then we chatted briefly. But before you make a regular romance out of this, let me tell you, this was so long ago that I am not certain he would even remember my name. I am told that these days he surrounds himself only with friends. In short, my introduction may very well be worth less than nothing."

"Still, I'd like you to give it a try."

"Wait. Perhaps I can find someone with better credentials. Where are you now?"

"Saratoga Springs."

"Do not lose all your money at the racetrack, young man."

"The track is closed, Dr. Shavinsky."

"Just as well. Give me your number," he said. "I will call back within the hour."

The phone rang some ten minutes later.

"Mr. Weiss?"

"You got him."

"This is Leonard Halkin, the Foundation archivist. We met in Dr. Shavinsky's office a few days ago."

"Yes, Mr. Halkin."

"Call me Leonard, please. All the old hands here insist on being addressed formally, as if they never left Europe. It's really too much."

"Sure, Leonard. You have a Treister contact for me?"

"I *am* a Treister contact."

"You?"

"At your service."

"I thought you had to be an old crony or at least a fellow tycoon."

He chuckled. "I'm neither, Mr. Weiss."

"Max," I said. "So, how did you get a foot in the door?"

"It just happened. When we donated our Treister collection to the Skidmore archives, Dr. Margoshes put me in charge of the operation. Research was always his first love. He usually left operational details to me. I took the collection to Skidmore. To my amazement, Mr. Treister himself showed up. We spent long hours poring over these documents together as they were being recatalogued. He was a great help. We became friends. We still are, I trust."

"I'm stunned."

He laughed. "Let me call Mr. Treister and see what I can do. Don't go away."

"I'm not budging."

I lay back on the bed and did some more waiting. Bach's Goldberg's Variations on the radio helped me wait; in fact, it made it a real pleasure.

The phone rang. I lifted the receiver and Halkin's

voice said, "Done!" He sounded elated, as if he'd come up with big bucks for his archives, or won a bundle in the state lottery.

"He'll see me?"

"Tomorrow night."

"You told him what this is about?"

Halkin hesitated. "Not quite. I told him a friend of mine needed to speak with him on an urgent matter. He said any friend of mine was always welcome."

"Sounds good."

"He's having a small gathering, Max. He invited me, too. We can go together. I'll drive up tomorrow afternoon. If I can be of service to the cause, so much the better."

We arranged to meet at the Holiday Inn late the next day. I took the night off and went out to inspect the local amusements at close quarters.

CHAPTER 29

Morris Weiss—1948

The fog had grown thicker.

Weiss made his way through the transformed streets, which now appeared almost ghostlike. He stopped only once to phone the police anonymously about the two bodies in the waterfront house. Then he hurried on to Cora Blake's tenement.

He gazed up at the five-story structure, shrugged stoically, and entered. He had been in far worse places. At least it was an honest working-class building—more or less.

This time there was no smell of cooking, no voices raised behind closed doors. It was as though the fog had swept the house clean of its tenants.

He was halfway to the fifth floor when he heard the

scream. The hair on the back of his neck stood straight up. He hauled out his Browning and ran up the remaining stairs to the top floor, trying to make no noise at all.

The door to 5C was half open.

He could see Cora Blake being beaten by two men. One held her from behind while the other punched her in the face and body. A third man, black-haired, thick-lipped, heavyset, stood apart, watching intently. He had on an immaculate camel hair topcoat, and a white silk scarf. A wide-brimmed hat dangled from two fingers.

The boss, Weiss thought. *A real beauty*.

The detective moved fast, kicked open the door and took a quick step into the flat, his gun leveled before him.

"Back from the woman!" he yelled.

The boss dropped his hat, made a grab for the gun buried under his coat.

Weiss sent a bullet flying past his left ear.

The boss froze. Along with his helpmates.

"The next one," Weiss said, "doesn't miss. Your hands, up in the air—all of you!"

Two pairs of hands instantly went up, letting go of Cora. She swayed but remained upright.

The boss hesitated, then raised his hands halfway.

"You!" Weiss yelled. "Yours, too! Fast!"

The boss stared at him. Then raised his hands all the way.

They learn, Weiss thought, *but slowly*.

"Behind your heads!" he yelled. "All of you!"

The boss, his face slightly flushed, said, "I won't forget this."

"Good," Weiss said. "Maybe you will also remember not to mistreat women." *Even cheap ones like this Cora*, he thought.

"Face the wall," he commanded.

Stepping behind them, Weiss patted down each one, removing their guns with his left hand—two S&W .38 specials and a Berretta for the boss. He tossed them in a far corner.

Weiss prodded the boss in a shoulder blade with his gun. "You, turn around."

The boss faced Weiss. "This is between me and her," he said. "Private business. What's it to you?"

"More than you think," the detective said. "She knows nothing."

"Then who does, you?"

"Very good. Your name, please."

The thick lips sneered.

From the couch, Cora said, "He's Gordon Keller."

"Shut up," Keller said.

"Why should I?" Cora said, coming to life.

"Shoot your mouth off, you'll get what's coming to you," Keller said. "Mind if I put my hands down, sport?"

"Yes, I mind."

"He sells dope to kids," Cora said.

"That's a dirty lie," Keller snapped.

"He's a dealer, for chrissakes," Cora said. "Tommy knows. Tommy's got plenty on him—"

"Sure," Keller said, "shoot your yap off. See what it gets you."

To Keller Weiss said, "Keep your mouth shut." To Cora he said, "What does your husband know?"

"It's not what he knows. It's what he's got."

"And that is?"

"Hey," Keller said. "You don't want to lay it all out for this guy. Tom and me go way back. We can settled this between ourselves."

"You are hardly in a position," Weiss said, "to tell her what to do."

The woman looked from one to the other. Her eyes came to rest on the detective. "I don't know what it is, honest. It's something he got hold of. Whatever it is, the big shot here don't like Tommy having it. He's scared. That's why he made a place for Tommy in the outfit."

"You are saying he blackmailed our friend here?"

"She's raving," Keller said. "No one does that to me."

"Tommy's got him over a barrel," Cora said. "You just wait and see what he does to him."

Weiss bit his lip. This was not the time, he thought, to tell her that she was a widow. He said, "You are sure, Cora, you are giving me everything?"

"Yes."

Weiss turned to Keller. "Where were you during the last hour?"

"You got a badge to show me?"

"Very soon you will be with men who have badges if you do not answer me."

"Look—" Keller began.

"Yeah, look at him now," Cora burst out. "Big Mr. Tough Guy. He's a real puncher when it comes to women. What are you going to do now, Mr. Tough Guy? Why don't you show us?"

"I'll show you plenty."

Weiss said, "Call the police, Cora."

"Sure," Keller said, "call them. You figure out what you're gonna tell them?"

"We will begin with assault," Weiss said.

"That's a laugh. How you gonna make it stick?"

"Look at her face."

"Yeah, she fell down and hurt herself."

"I'll tell the truth," Cora said.

"We know where you live, Cora." Keller smiled. "Your friend isn't always going to be here."

"Then there is the dope, eh?" Weiss said.

"Prove it."

"Not to mention murder."

"Yeah? Who've I killed?"

Weiss sighed. It was time to play the card. "Her husband."

Cora stared at him. *"What?"*

Keller said, "You're crazy."

"And there is poor Grasser. You also were in business with him. He too is now dead."

"What about it?"

"I will tell you—" Weiss began.

Cora screamed.

A thug with a long ashen face came hurtling through the doorway, a very large gun in his shaking hand. He fired repeatedly, sending bullets into the wall.

Weiss fired back as he dove to the floor.

The gunman, carried forward by his own momentum, crumpled to the floor.

Weiss, in one swift motion, hurled himself behind the couch.

He glanced around, breathing hard.

The two thugs, he saw, had already scrambled for their guns and tossed Keller his. Now they had all taken cover.

Not good, Weiss thought. He seemed to be fighting off the same bunch of hooligans all night, as though in a bad dream. Shoot one and another takes his place. There was no end to it. At least, thank God, they were all incompetent.

Before he could decide what to do next, Weiss heard the sound of shattering glass behind him. Gunfire erupted over his head and seemed to fill the room.

Weiss tried to make himself very small.

If I survive this, he vowed, *I will find another line of work.*

Presently, there was silence.

After an instant, Weiss peered out from behind the couch.

The room was empty. Even the ashen-faced gunman Weiss had shot was gone. He took a deep breath. *How nice. They have cleaned up after themselves again.*

He glanced over his shoulder.

A lone figure stood motionless on the fire escape, two guns in his hands. It was his benefactor whose gunfire had suddenly cleared the room of adversaries.

Weiss got to his feet, stepped over chunks of plaster, went to the window, and opened it.

"Watch for broken glass," he said.

The man eased himself off the fire escape and into the room.

"You are full of surprises, Boris," Weiss said, brushing plaster dust off his coat. "Or have I already said that?"

"It is always good to hear."

"Thank you," Weiss said gravely.

"It is nothing," Boris Minsky said. "Uncle Pavel taught me the art when I was younger."

"Of shooting at walls?"

"At targets. These are his pistols. They are of Russian manufacture. I have always acquitted myself well with them."

"You could have nicked one of those hooligans for me."

"Surely you do not expect me to shoot at people?"

"God forbid."

Cora entered from the hallway. "Hey, what was that about Tommy?"

Weiss turned to her. "I am so sorry. Your husband is dead, Cora."

"What are you tryin' to pull? Where do you get off talkin' like that? I just saw the bum an hour ago. He was as alive as you."

"That was an hour ago."

"How the hell would you know, smart guy?"

"I followed you into the building," Weiss said, "when you were calling on him."

"You what?"

"I was in the next room, the kitchen, when you two had your disagreement."

Cora's face turned red. "You dirty bastard you! You followed me? You listened in? What's the big idea? You're no better than that rat Keller."

Weiss smiled thinly. "A little better, maybe. I didn't kill your husband. Keller, I think, did."

"You *think*?"

Weiss shrugged.

"What a great detective you are!"

Minsky said, "Three of those men were in the building when your husband died."

"How would you know?"

"I was there, too. But outside." Minsky turned to Weiss. "I took a Jeep from the motor pool, drove to Joyce Griller's home in Yorkville and waited. When a man left, I was behind him. He led me here, where he met the other three. They followed this woman into the house by the river and then back here again. From the street I saw the light go on on the top floor. I assumed it was her. I used a garbage can to help me reach the first rung of the fire escape. The rest you saw."

"Very good work," Weiss said. To Cora he said, "Your husband told me that he had a package."

"He was full of shit."

"And," Weiss said, "its whereabouts."

"The creep told *you*, a stranger, where he hid the stuff and not *me*? Even Tommy wasn't that dumb."

"He was dying. There was no one else to tell."

"That little creep," Cora wailed. "He left me high and dry. All I ever got from him was grief. And now he's gone."

The woman turned her fury on Weiss. "Listen, Mr. Detective, anything Tommy told you about is mine. You get that? It belongs to me! And I want it!"

Weiss smiled. "You want to blackmail Keller yourself?"

"Don't you worry your head about what I want, you just fork it over."

"First we must find it. Where is your bathroom?"

"That way. You won't find a thing. I already looked a hundred times."

"We will see."

All three hurried down the hallway, squeezed into the small bathroom.

Weiss pointed to the medicine cabinet above the sink. "There," he said.

"You're crazy," Cora said.

Weiss took out his wallet and gave her two dollars.

"What's this for?"

"Damages."

Gripping the cabinet with both hands, Weiss twisted it away from the wall.

"Hey!" Cora yelled.

Weiss laid the cabinet down in the sink, pulled his gun from his coat pocket, and proceeded to batter the plaster where the cabinet had been. It flew apart like eggshells, revealing a large hole. Weiss returned the gun to his pocket, stuck his hand in the hole, and pulled out a small album.

Cora stared at it. "What the hell's that?"

"Photographs."

"Give them to me."

She made a grab for the album.

Weiss held it out of her reach.

"It's mine!"

Weiss stuck the album in his coat pocket. "All in good time," he said.

"Now!" she shrieked.

"Come, Boris," Weiss said.

Together, the two men hurried from the apartment.

CHAPTER 30

*It does not take a private detective to find someone
at a very large party. But sometimes it can certainly help.*

From the casebooks of Morris Weiss

Max Weiss—The Present

Next morning I drove out to the Wilton Mall and bought
some suitable clothes for Treister's party.

Leonard Halkin showed up around five. I was loung-
ing outdoors in a deck chair when he drove up in a bright
yellow Toyota Corolla. I waved and walked over. He was
in a navy blue blazer, charcoal-gray flannel trousers and a
striped red tie.

"Glad you could make it, Leonard," I said.

Halkin pumped my hand and began thanking me

profusely, as though I'd gotten him the invitation to Treister's gathering, and not the other way around. "This could mean a lot to me," he said.

"Finding your ex-boss?"

"That, too, of course."

"So what else?"

"A gift to my archives, Max."

"Manuscripts?"

Halkin grinned. "Money."

"Leonard, you're going to put the bite on our host?"

"Look, we're a nonprofit organization. It's tax deductible. I'd never forgive myself if I passed up this opportunity."

"Right," I said. "Do me a favor. Talk to him after I'm done asking my questions."

"Why?"

"I don't want to be thrown out," I said, "before I've had a crack at the old guy myself."

"Count on me, Max."

"I intend to."

I must have spent my suit money wisely. The butler didn't bat an eye when he opened the front door and Halkin gave him our names.

We followed the slightly stooped, black-tie-clad figure past a wide staircase and along a brightly lit marble hallway, the sounds of merriment growing louder as we walked. I had already viewed the vehicles parked in the driveway and for a quarter-mile up and down the road.

"Small party, uh, Leonard?"

"That's what I was told," he said uneasily. "I hope it's not too crowded. I need a long talk with him."

We reached the end of the corridor and paused at a wide, arched doorway. The butler bowed toward a mob scene in what looked like a huge ballroom with glittering crystal chandeliers and light-colored French boiserie paneling.

At least a couple of hundred people were busy milling around, many of them young or middle-aged. Our host was supposed to hang out only with old cronies. Maybe these were cronies-in-training.

"Recognize anyone?" I asked Halkin over the din.

"Not a soul. This is awful. How will we ever find him?"

"Relax, Leonard, I'm a detective."

I stepped into the crowd, Halkin at my heels, and was immediately lost in a sea of chattering people. I was jostled by arms, elbows, and shoulders. Guests laughed and shouted. Tuxedo-clad waiters pushed through the crush, hauling silver trays of hors d'oeuvres and bubbling flutes of champagne. Bartenders were set up against two walls, swiftly dispensing drinks. Party-goers clustered around a buffet spread over long tables.

When I glanced over my shoulder, Halkin wasn't there. I looked around the room, but I couldn't spot him. I tried to locate some elderly gentleman, surrounded by well-wishers, who might be our host. No one fit the bill. I wandered over to the buffet and helped myself to a couple of sea-fresh iced shrimp. Only the best. I asked the guy next to me where the host was. He didn't know. I asked a young couple. They didn't know either. I wandered down the tables, noshing on the buffet, and quizzing my fellow revelers about the host's whereabouts. Some said he never showed up at his own parties. Others assured me they had spotted him earlier in the evening. A few didn't know who their host even was. Then a trim redhead in an inspiring green cocktail-length dress caught my eye. Her dress showed off a pair of gorgeous legs. I felt more than a faint stirring of interest. I maneuvered my way through the crowd, and asked her if she'd run across Kelman Treister.

"Not yet," she said. "I'm looking for him myself."

"Probably gone to a better party," I said.

That got me a nice crooked grin.

"I'm Laura Faust," she said, and stuck out her hand.

I shook it. She had a nice firm grip.

"Max Weiss," I said.

Close up, Laura Faust wasn't just a redhead, she was a stunning redhead. Large green eyes, high cheekbones, crooked half smile, smooth vanilla skin. And she had a nice deep sexy voice, too. Maybe this party wouldn't be a total bust after all.

"I'm just going to ask him for an interview," Laura said. "He loves to talk about himself. He's his own favorite subject, I'm told."

"A writer?" I asked.

She nodded. "Freelance."

"So who wants a piece on Kelman Treister?"

She shrugged. "Everyone. No one. I see what the market will bear, then sell to the highest bidder," she said. "So tell me, Max, why do *you* want to see Mr. Treister?"

So I told her the whole story. Including the part about me being a private eye.

"What in the world made you choose *that* for a living?" she asked.

"Too many grade B movies as a child. Also, my great-uncle Morris was already in the racket. I graduated Columbia with a degree in sociology after switching majors five times. Don't ask me why. I found out pretty quick there wasn't much I wanted to do with it. Uncle Morris needed help, and I needed a quick way to earn a buck. And that's what I've been doing ever since. Blame it on lack of ambition."

"And your uncle Morris, he drifted into the profession, too?"

"Uh-uh. He filled a genuine need. When he was growing up there were still plenty of sweatshops on the Lower East Side. Husbands skipped out on their wives and kids—the long hours and low pay broke their spirits. So, Uncle Morris became a detective and devoted himself to finding the missing husbands, and then bringing their wives and them together. Sometimes it even worked out."

"Some story."

"Some life."

She grinned at me.

"So how," she asked, "do you plan to locate our host?"

I shrugged. "Well, I came here with a guy who was going to introduce me to Treister. He's a scholar who had worked with him. It was all set."

"And?"

"I seem to have lost him."

She shook her head and gave me her crooked grin. "Now that was very careless of you, Max,"

"Pretty careless of him, too," I said.

I got up on my toes, which, since I'm a fairly tall guy, allowed me to see lots of haircuts and the faces that went with them. None were Halkin. And if our host was on board, he wasn't getting much attention.

"Any luck?" Laura asked when I was flat-footed again.

"Uh-uh. Time to devise a new strategy, I think."

"That's where I come in."

She took me by the hand—a nice turn of events—and we began to shoulder our way back through the crowd. The party was in full swing, with plenty of alcohol lubricating the works. I wondered if Halkin had taken ill at the sight of all these people and was off in some bathroom regretting that he'd ever come here.

"I've done some research," she said. "He goes to his

private study. That's where our host likes to barricade himself during these affairs, along with a few old cronies."

"And where is that?"

"The second floor's a real good bet."

"You must be a detective, too."

She shrugged. "Read it in a magazine."

We started out, reached the second landing without a mishap. The crystal sconce lights were dimmed, showing off the ankle-deep green velvet carpets. The only sounds I heard came from below.

Unexpectedly, another corridor, more plainly furnished, opened up on our right. Laura and I exchanged glances. We turned down it, walking more quietly now. Somewhere up ahead I heard the murmur of voices. I nodded. We moved toward them.

A man stepped out of a dark open doorway to our left.

He was a thirtyish man, about my height, but big-boned and heavier. He wore a leather jacket, dark trousers, and a dark T-shirt. The jacket was tight around his chest. Clearly, this guy wasn't one of the revelers.

"Sorry, buddy," he said, "but this part of the house isn't open to guests."

I hadn't figured it was, but this wasn't the time to admit it. "We were invited up here to see Mr. Treister," I said. "He's expecting us."

The man shrugged. "I don't know anything about that."

Laura said, "We drove all the way from New York at his request."

I said, "We're friends of Leonard Halkin."

The murmuring voices from up the hall had suddenly grown silent, as if the speakers were avidly listening to our conversation. Maybe to distract themselves from their own, which had grown dull.

The man spread his large hands. "I've got my orders.

The boss doesn't want to see anyone right now. Even me. That's the way it is at these parties."

"I know he'd make an exception for us," Laura said loudly, as if appealing directly to Treister himself. "Just ask him, you'll see."

"Look, lady, I'm only doing my job. Why don't you two go downstairs and have a nice drink or something? You can come back tomorrow and speak to Mr. Treister all you want—if he'll see you."

Reasonable enough. I had to figure that Treister himself was taking all this in—and wanted no part of us right now. Twisting his arm would get us nowhere.

I glanced at Laura and shrugged a shoulder. To the guy I said, "When does your boss rouse himself after his parties?"

"Late."

"Okay," I said, "see you tomorrow."

I took Laura by the elbow, ready to steer her back the way we'd come.

"Help!" a man's voice screamed from somewhere up the hallway. "Help!"

I stopped dead in my tracks, eyeing Treister's sentry for guidance. This was his show, after all, what he got paid for.

The man blocking our way didn't even blink. As if someone yelling for help was an everyday occurrence here.

I took a step forward, ready to brush him aside, if need be, and run to the rescue. Though why *I* should be the one saddled with the job—in a house crawling with security—was beyond me.

In one movement the guy's hand swept his jacket aside, just like they do in western movies. A dark metal shape instantly appeared in it, the unmistakable snout of an Uzi machine gun pointed at my middle.

"Hold it right there, buddy," he said, hardly raising his voice.

That's when we heard the shot. From somewhere up ahead. Where the call for help had come from.

Laura yelled and made a move toward the guy.

The Uzi swerved in her direction.

I sprang at him, grabbed his gun hand in both of mine, twisted it toward the wall, and tried to take the gun away from him.

Easy enough usually for a guy my size. Only this guy was heavier with muscle to spare. He didn't give an inch. I began to regret my missed workouts at the gym.

The Uzi went off, spraying bullets in one-second bursts. Plaster flew. My ears rang. I smelled cordite.

I held on to his gun with one hand, balled the other hand into a fist, and hit him square on the chin.

He blinked and tried to twist the Uzi toward me again. Laura flung herself onto his gun arm and hung on tight.

I stepped back and uncorked a right uppercut, driving straight from the legs, the very same one our agency's resident pugilist, Uncle Morris, had helped me master.

The guy let go of the gun and fell down. Thank God. That was my best shot.

Score one for me and Uncle Morris.

I scooped up the Uzi, stepped over him, and ran down the hall to the closed door.

Logic, reason, and sanity dictated that I head the other way. No one had hired me to beat up Treister's help, let alone shoot someone. Or even worse, get shot myself. But my legs ran on, heedless of this native wisdom.

I found the closed door at the end of the hallway. Momentum carried me forward, up against it. The door wasn't locked. I almost broke my neck flying through it.

I pulled up short waving the Uzi in a wide arc. And took a long, amazed look at the scene before me.

Four elderly men sat in a semicircle on the floor, their hands cuffed behind them.

Leonard Halkin, also in handcuffs, lay stretched out on the floor, a pool of dark blood staining the beige carpet. Part of his head had been blown off.

CHAPTER 31

Morris Weiss—1948

Behind him Weiss could still hear Cora shouting.

"Quickly," he said, "before that woman comes out here."

The two men hurried down the stairs, Minsky a step behind Weiss.

"Your first case, Boris."

"Most hectic."

"You like it, eh?"

"I would not go quite so far."

"Usually," Weiss said, "things are very tame."

Presently they reached the ground floor. "This way," Weiss said, turning to the rear of the building.

"Where are we going?"

"Watch."

Behind the staircase Weiss found an unlocked door. He entered a darkened stairwell, felt around for the light cord, and gave it a determined yank. A bulb lit up directly over his head, revealing a flight of stairs and a dingy cellar.

"Come," he called to Minsky.

"Must I?"

"Have I ever led you astray, Boris?"

"So far you have not had the opportunity."

Weiss laughed. "True."

The pair made their way down the stairs.

The cellar floor was concrete, the walls cracked and damp. Mouse traps were scattered along the floor. Flypaper dangled from the ceiling. The whole place smelled of mold.

"To the back, Boris."

They passed a workbench, a coal bin and furnace, a rotting mop sitting in a pail of dirty water.

Minsky wrinkled his nose. "May I ask why we have chosen this route?"

"The other is worse."

"I find that hard to believe."

"I will soon make a believer of you."

Weiss halted at the back door, tried the knob.

"Locked," he announced. "Stand back."

Weiss again removed the Browning from his coat pocket, took a step back, and shot the lock off the door.

"An act of vandalism," Minsky said.

"But for a good cause."

The two men stepped out into the alley. Minsky followed the detective, who turned west. They passed overflowing garbage cans, assorted debris, and one frazzled cat as they moved toward the glow of a fog-shrouded street lamp. Soon they were back on Ninth Avenue.

"Now what?" Minsky asked.

"I will show you."

The pair strode rapidly to the corner of West Twenty-eighth Street, crossed to the other side. Cars, even at the intersection, were scarce and well hidden by the fog.

"Where are you parked?" Weiss asked.

"Around the corner."

"Excellent. I am parked diagonally across from Cora's building. Come. But make no noise."

The fog seemed to roll in from all directions at once, clinging to them as they headed east. Out on the Hudson, the foghorns kept up their mournful dirge. Presently, the detective put a hand on Minsky's arm and the two men drew to a halt.

"You see him?" Weiss whispered.

The figure of a man was barely discernible. He wore a peaked cap, long black coat, and stood leaning against the fender of a black Packard sedan, hands in pockets, a cigarette stuck between his lips, a foot up on the running board.

"That," Weiss said, "is one of Keller's hoodlums. And that is my car."

"How does he know it is yours?"

"He doesn't. It is simply a good place to watch from. He hopes we will walk through that front door."

"What does he want?"

"Us, I think."

"They are most persistent."

"To a fault."

Weiss handed the album to Minsky, and moved away.

The man leaning against the car was so intent on watching Cora's building that he failed to see the detective until he was at his side.

"Mister," Weiss said.

"What?" The man's head turned toward Weiss, and Weiss hit him hard across the jaw with his gun barrel. The man fell to the sidewalk.

If only, Weiss thought, *I could have hit like that in the ring.*

He unlocked the car door.

"Hurry," he whispered.

Across the street, from the doorways of two adjoining buildings, three men began to run toward them. Even in the fog Weiss could see they held guns.

He tumbled into the car, Minsky behind him, crammed the key into the ignition, and stabbed the starter button. The big motor sprang to life.

The Packard swerved out into the street, tires screaming, pointed directly at the three men, who scattered hurriedly, forgetting all about the guns in their hands.

The car shot toward Eighth Avenue, turned the corner, then slowed.

"We are done?" Minsky asked hopefully.

"Not yet."

"This is endless."

"Consider it your college course in detective work," Weiss said. "Already you are at the top of your class."

"I would rather go home."

"In due time. To the Jeep, Boris."

"My Jeep? It is only borrowed, you know."

"For combat, a Jeep is better than a Packard."

"Morris, if the Jeep is damaged I will be held responsible."

"Combat is merely a term of speech," Weiss said.

"I hope so."

They pulled up next to an olive-drab Jeep with a canvas top and side curtains. In less than a minute the cars had changed places and the Jeep was on the move.

"Back to Twenty-eighth Street," Weiss said. "Park as close to the house as you can."

"Is that wise?"

"More than wise, Boris. Inspired. Even in my car they would never expect to see us again. In your Jeep we are absolutely invisible."

The Jeep crept along until it hit Tenth Avenue, turned

north for one block, then drifted back to the same spot the Packard had previously occupied. It pulled up to the curb.

The street was empty.

"They are gone," Minsky said.

"More likely, upstairs with the woman."

"Why?"

"Why not? She has already betrayed her husband to them. Now they will worry she has betrayed *them* to *us*."

"Should we not assist her?"

Weiss shrugged. "She is one of them. Because of her, Blake is dead. She is not our concern." He held up the photo album. "This is. Let us take a quick look."

Minsky produced a flashlight as Weiss placed the album on his knees. Both men bent low, shielding the light with their bodies, Minsky focusing the beam as Weiss turned pages.

"Ah-ha," Weiss said.

"You have found something?"

A dozen snapshots were in the album, the same two men appearing in each one.

"You recognize him, Boris?"

"Who?"

"The tall one. He is our friend Keller without his mustache."

"I would not have guessed."

"The short one is the mystery. They are plainly in Paris," Weiss said. "Here is the Hotel Pax. I myself stayed there once when I was on three-day leave. It costs next to nothing."

"They seem unaware," Minsky said, "that they are being photographed."

"These, Boris, are the type of candid shots a detective takes when gathering incriminating evidence."

Weiss snapped the album shut, the flashlight went dark, and both men sat up.

The street was still empty.

"I think Blake," Weiss said, "was the photographer. With blackmail in mind. How and why we have yet to discover."

The two men sank into silence. Weiss folded his hands in his lap and sat back as comfortably as he could in the Jeep. Minsky seemed to doze. Only one car crept by in ten minutes.

The front door of Cora's building suddenly opened.

"Uh-oh," the detective said.

Through the swirling fog they saw Cora, surrounded by four men, one of them Keller. She struggled as she was half-carried, half-dragged to a waiting car.

Keller left them and strode to a red 1947 Cadillac coupe parked a few feet away. Without a backward glance, he climbed in and drove off.

Cora was bundled into the back of the other car, a big black De Soto sedan. The three men piled in after her, one in back next to Cora, two in front. The doors slammed shut. This car too drove off, heading toward Eighth Avenue.

The Jeep pulled out and followed.

The De Soto turned on Eighth, drove one block, and turned West toward the Hudson.

"This is not good," Weiss muttered. "They are going to kill her."

"You are sure?"

"West is the water," Weiss said. "What else is there?"

"Merely a moment ago," Minsky said, "you were unconcerned about her possible demise."

Weiss sighed. "I thought they would only manhandle her. How can we stand by and see her murdered?"

The De Soto turned a corner.

The Jeep put on a burst of speed and made the turn.

Half a block away, the De Soto had come to a stop. Its

back door was open, and one of the men was hauling Cora out.

The Jeep pulled to a screeching halt behind the car.

Weiss jumped out, Browning in hand.

The man let go of Cora and reached for his pocket.

Weiss shot him, and watched as he fell away into the fog.

Cora lay in a heap on the street—motionless.

Weiss flattened himself against the side of the Jeep.

Minsky crouched behind it.

Both men trained their guns on the De Soto. The driver inside didn't hesitate. The car took off, its back door flapping, and disappeared down the block.

The gunman Weiss had shot was also gone, crawled off somewhere in the fog.

The two men ran to the fallen woman.

"Cora," Weiss said.

There was no response.

"We must," Weiss said, "rush her to a hospital, Boris."

"She will be grateful."

"Let's hope so," the detective said.

CHAPTER 32

A beautiful woman, provided she is not too great a distraction, can be a true asset during a difficult case. At the very least, she could come up with a good idea or two. At best, she might even solve it.
From the casebooks of Morris Weiss

Max Weiss—The Present

Laura came in and said, "Oh, my God!"

We stood gaping at the semicircle of men seated on the floor, their hands cuffed behind them. And the unlikely body of Leonard Halkin next to them. I kept expecting him to grin, put his head together, and get up off the floor, as the elderly bunch jumped up and joined him in a breezy chorus. I was losing it.

"Which way did they go?" I demanded.

"That way," one of the men said, nodding at an open doorway across the room.

I ran into the next room. It was empty. A staircase behind another door led down to the rear of the house. I went with it. I figured the Uzi gave me an advantage. Unless, of course, they had one, too.

I needn't have worried. Only darkness greeted me. I peered in every direction as though the night itself might give me a clue. It didn't.

I turned and ran back up the stairs.

"Where are the keys to the cuffs?" Laura was saying as I burst into the room.

Her captive audience stirred, as if the mere mention of a key might do the trick and set them free.

"They took it," one of the victims, a very tall, thin man, croaked.

"Help us," another begged in a jittery voice. He was short, with sparse gray curly hair and gold-rimmed spectacles, which had fallen halfway down his nose.

The rest—almost comically—nodded their heads in unison. Except for one, a white-haired man in immaculate evening dress, whom I instantly took to be Kelman Treister. He looked up at me and said in a clear, calm voice, "Call the police."

Smart advice. Laura used a phone on a mahogany stand over by the far wall. Right next to an open wall safe. The painting of an elderly rabbi that must have covered it now languished on the floor.

I ran out into the hallway. The big ape I'd slugged was gone. I went back to the room, stowed the Uzi on a small end table. Laura and I helped the four men off the floor and into chairs. Except for our host they still didn't look any too comfortable. Maybe it was the handcuffs. Or the fact that they had been scared witless. At least I was earning points here. Treister could hardly turn me down now. Or could he? Or was that even the issue anymore?

Seated in an overstuffed easy chair, the white-haired man said, "I am Kelman Triester. Who are you?"

A question I could answer. In my current state of mind I wasn't up to much more.

"Max Weiss," I said. "Halkin's friend."

He nodded, sighed, and glanced down at the body as if hoping it might yet put in a good word for itself. "A tragedy."

"I should have kept a better eye on him," I said.

"How could you know?" Triester asked.

He was right. Despite my years in the business, this turn of events had shaken me. I was going to get my big lead here, and maybe wrap up the Margoshes business. Not have my contact murdered in a holdup. I couldn't forget I was the guy who had dragged him into this.

"And you, young lady?" Triester asked.

"Laura Faust," she said. "I'm with him."

I put a protective arm around my new redheaded friend and was amazed at how good it felt. I was being waylaid by conflicting emotions. An irrational urge to sit *shivah* for Halkin, whom I hardly knew, and a mad desire to romance Laura, whom I knew even less well. These feelings didn't even belong in the same day, let alone the same hour. *Pull yourself together, Weiss,* I told myself. *Duty first.* The thought of duty brought an immediate image to mind, that of the stalwart founder of our agency. Unfortunately, I pictured him in the act of placing a two-dollar bet at the local racetrack.

Triester nodded toward his fellow victims. "My colleagues," he said. "Forgive them for not shaking hands."

The small guy with the gold-rimmed glasses—which Laura had helpfully pushed back on his nose—was Isaac Jaffee, who was assisting our host with his memoirs. The string bean, Jack Lipman, was a Triester crony from way back. The stout sixtyish guy with a full head of silver hair, Carl Mendelbaum, turned out to be an executive in Treister's business empire. Mendelbaum was the youngster in the group.

"Well," Treister said, "I am indebted to you both."

"What did we do?" Laura asked.

Treister said, "The men fled when they heard your voices."

"Yes, and shot Dr. Halkin," Lipman said bitterly, as if we were somehow to blame. I hated to hear him voice my own irrational thought.

"Do not mind Jack," Treister said. "His tongue is sharper than his brain."

"There would have been no bloodshed," Lipman insisted, "if they had not made a disturbance."

"Be still," Mendelbaum said. "Halkin called out. He would be alive this very minute if he had not lost his head. These men did not come here to kill, merely to rob."

"Who were they?" Laura asked.

"Criminals," Jaffee yelled. "Gangsters, thieves, murderers."

Treister nodded toward the body. "There is their handiwork."

Saratoga Springs is a small town. The uniformed cops showed up in less than five minutes. They treated Treister and his guests like royalty, and had the cuffs off in a matter of seconds. A plainclothes detective breezed into the room on their heels, a short, stout man with slicked-back black hair, whose name was Ford. He wore a gray checked sports coat, yellow tie, and pink shirt. A guy like our host obviously rated the top brass. Ford was a lieutenant. Though he looked more like a racetrack tout. In this town it was probably an asset.

"Tell me what happened," he said.

Treister stood up and told him. He described three men with cartoon masks over their faces: Popeye, Bugs Bunny, and Batman. The trio had come bursting in, made everyone sit on the floor, and then handcuffed them. Popeye and Batman leaned on our host, convincing him to give up the combination to the safe by holding a gun to his head. The pair then went through the safe while Bugs held a gun on the lot. When Halkin called out, Bugs shot him. Then all three fled down the back staircase. "These two," Treister said, gesturing our way, "rescued us before they could empty the entire safe. Or shoot us all."

The lieutenant gave us a sour look. As though we were horning in on his act.

"Not rescued," I said.

"Who are you?" Ford demanded.

Laura and I gave him our names.

"What did you do?" he asked.

I said, "Leonard Halkin heard our voices in the hallway and called for help. By the time we got to him he was dead and the killers gone."

Ford shook his head as if he held us responsible for all this mayhem. He went to the back staircase door, opened it, and looked down.

"Back door jimmied?" he barked at one of his cops at the bottom of the stairs.

"Yes, sir."

"Alarm wires cut?"

"Yes, sir."

Ford's expression was grim. He returned to our midst and turned to Treister. "You rate a whole lot better security than this, Mr. Treister, sir."

I was hoping Ford might resign from the force right then and there and offer his personal services to our host.

"I was under the impression," Treister said, "that I had

the best protection that money could buy. Obviously, I was wrong."

"One of your men," Laura said, "pulled a gun on us when the shot sounded."

Treister looked startled. "Which one?"

"He didn't give a name," Laura said. "Max knocked him silly and took his gun away."

Ford gave me another dirty look.

"Where did this happen?"

"Up here," Laura said, "in the hallway."

"To my knowledge," Treister said, "no one was stationed there."

I described the guy.

Treister shook his head. "This man was not employed by me," he said.

"One of *them*," Ford said.

"Maybe," Laura said, "there was more than one inside man here."

Treister nodded sadly. "It is possible."

"And you two were just guests here?" Ford asked.

"We both had business with Mr. Treister," I said.

"Business? What business?"

Laura and I told him as Treister listened in. Not the best way to introduce the topic. But it would have to do under the circumstances. Especially since we had no choice.

"A private eye and a reporter," Ford said when I was done.

"Freelance journalist," Laura said.

"You two were invited together?"

"No," I said. "We just met here tonight."

Laura took my hand. "That's not a crime, I hope?"

Ford frowned. Maybe it was crime in his book. He turned to our host. "You still want them here, sir?"

"Yes."

"Tomorrow I want both of you at headquarters."

"Should we bring a lawyer?" I asked.

"Just bring yourselves. I want you to go over some mug shots."

"Sure," I said.

"And what of the party?" Ford asked our host.

"Let it go on. Why should our misfortune ruin their evening?"

CHAPTER 33

Morris Weiss—1948

The phone woke Weiss from a deep sleep. His head turned to the bedside clock. Six-thirty. His hand reached for the phone on the nightstand.

"Weiss," he said.

"And a grand good morning to you, Mr. Weiss."

"Detective O'Toole?"

"It is, indeed."

Weiss sighed. "Merely because I woke you at three this morning is no reason to wake me at this ungodly hour."

"Mr. Weiss, as the good Father Reilly often tells his flock, no hour is ungodly."

"I am glad to hear that, Detective O'Toole. May I go back to sleep now?"

"Wait til you hear what I have to say."

"Business, eh?"

Weiss sat up in bed, adjusted the pillows under his head.
"Go on," he said.

"Well," O'Toole said, "after you called, Mr. Weiss, I
alerted the lads at the precinct. And they swung into action.
First they went to the hospital. The Blake woman had suffered only a mild concussion. But the nurse on duty flatly
refused to wake her. The lads soon put the fear of God into
her; they took her aside and instructed her on what happens to those who obstruct a police investigation. Their
eloquence won the day. The Blake woman was groggy but
only too willing to talk. She gave us some half-dozen of
Keller's henchmen. Most were picked up within the hour.
We've been grilling them all night. If some shyster lawyer
turns up in the morning with court papers, we'll simply
move the whole lot out the back door to another precinct
and keep sweating them til they come across. The Blake
woman gave us Keller, too, a York Avenue address. But he
was out when the lads came calling. I'm still at home, Mr.
Weiss. I'll soon be showing up at the station house and see
for myself what progress we've made. I will keep you informed."

"Thank you, Detective O'Toole."

"Be on your guard. This Keller bears you some animosity," O'Toole said. "And he's loose in the city."

Weiss threw together a breakfast of hand-squeezed orange juice, scrambled eggs, rye bread and butter, and two
cups of steaming black coffee right out of the percolator.

When he was done eating, he washed his dishes in the
sink. Then, hanging his silk robe in the closet, he donned a
black chalk-striped three-piece suit, put on a pair of highly
polished black wing-tipped shoes, and chose a red paisley

tie. Again, seating himself at the kitchen table, he used the phone.

It rang twice before being picked up.

"It's Weiss," he said.

"So, Morris," Fineberg said, "you have made progress?"

"A little."

"You are being modest?"

"That, Fineberg, is not in my nature. But we will know more this afternoon."

"What happens this afternoon?"

"You and I are going to visit Joey Ginzberg."

"Morris, already I have a full day."

"You want to put a finish to this business, Fineberg, or not?"

"Finish?"

"Finish."

"For this I will make time, Morris."

"That is good of you," Weiss said.

The detective hung up.

He returned to the closet, shrugged into his trench coat, went to his dresser, removed the Browning, and jammed it into his coat pocket along with an extra clip. Hand in pocket, Weiss left the apartment and walked down three flights of stairs to the street below.

Grand Street was bustling with workers on the way to their jobs. He was surrounded by Jewish faces, all of them familiar, even if he had never seen them before. Except maybe for two hurrying toward him. These were standouts, big, beefy men, who pushed their way through the crowd, never taking their eyes off the detective. He looked right and saw two more who could have been their brothers.

Weiss put two fingers in his mouth and whistled shrilly. Two long, one short and high-pitched.

From out of the bakery ran Abe the Ox, still wearing his white baker's apron, his hands white with flour. Abe was almost seven feet tall. They called him ox for his strength. From the candy store ran Manny Glutton, who weighed two hundred and thirty pounds but was only five foot five. Manny liked to eat. But much of his girth came from muscle. From the laundry ran Itchy and Benjy. In Odessa, they had been gangsters. Here, they were honest workmen, except when they needed an easy dollar. Benjy carried a monkey wrench, Itchy a hammer. Keller's boys had almost reached Weiss when they were intercepted. The detective winced as the hooligans were pounded to the pavement.

Itchy stepped over to Weiss.

"What do we do with them, Morris?"

Weiss gave him O'Toole's number. "Call him. He will take them off your hands."

"You're here again."

"What else can I do?" Weiss asked. "About what happened in Yugoslavia, Mr. Sykes, you are the expert's expert."

Sykes grinned. He had on a wide-shouldered checkered sports coat and blue tie replete with tiny yellow wings. "Gonna make that colonel guy real happy, I bet."

Weiss pulled a chair up to the side of the insurance agent's desk, seated himself. "Colonel Minsky," he said, "is already happy with you."

"Too bad I'm not still in the service. They'd've given me a medal, I bet."

Weiss smiled. "At least two."

"That'll be the day," Sykes said. "Okay, chum, you won me over. Whaddya wanna know?"

Weiss handed him a snapshot. "Do you recognize either of them?"

Sykes took one look at the snapshot and grinned.

"Go on, ask me a tough one," he said. "The big lug's Sergeant Keller. And the little squirt, this Colonel Rutledge, is the guy running the show in the woods."

"You are sure?"

"Like I told you, that day's stuck in my mind for keeps. Along with all those guys."

"Excellent." Weiss held up Joey Ginzberg's mug shot. "And this one?"

Sykes took a longer look, then nodded.

"Yeah, he's put on some weight, but I know him all right."

"Who is he?"

"That's Corporal Leon Asher."

"My thanks, Mr. Sykes."

"Hey, wait a sec."

"Yes?"

"What's the story here? That's a mug shot, isn't it?"

"Absolutely."

"What happened?"

"Nothing that cannot be fixed," Weiss said. "I'm working on it."

"So answer me this one. The sergeant and colonel hanging out together? When did that happen?"

"It will be my pleasure to tell you, Mr. Sykes, as soon as I find out."

"So, Joey," Fineberg said, "you are well?"

Joey Ginzberg, in his cell, seemed to be sitting in the exact same spot as the last time they had visited him, as if he had not moved since. But his short, muscular body looked as though it had shrunk in the intervening days.

Ginzberg stared at the lawyer.

"The Ritz," Fineberg added heartily, "it is not."

"Listen," Ginzberg said, "I had enougha you guys screwing up my life."

Fineberg seemed astonished. "*We* screwing up your life?"

"You heard me."

"You want, Joey, to screw it up even more?" Fineberg said. "Go ahead, help yourself."

"Go screw yourself."

"So tell me, Joey," Fineberg said, "you are going to be your own lawyer now?"

"The court's gettin' me one. At least he'll speak good English."

Weiss frowned.

"You are making a big mistake," Fineberg said.

"Yeah, sure. It won't be the first one."

"On this point," Weiss said, "you are right."

"What the hell do you know?"

"For one thing, Joey, I know about you and this Colonel Rutledge."

"Who?"

"Also about Leon Asher."

Ginzberg's face turned white.

My deserted wives, Weiss thought, *are worth a hundred of this one.*

Hands hanging limply by his sides, eyes fixed somewhere on the wall, Ginzberg began to speak.

"It looked like a swell deal," he said.

"Such deals, Joey," Fineberg said, "have put you in here."

"Shhhhh, Irving," Weiss said. "Let him speak."

Ginzberg sighed. "It's like this," he said. "Rutledge and me go way back to before the war. The guy imported cut-rate fabrics, had maybe half a dozen shops around town. The one on Orchard Street was run by Jews. I was their part-time delivery boy. Rutledge useta drop around sometimes. That's how I met him."

"Fabrics?" Fineberg said. "From this he made such a fine living?"

Ginzberg shrugged. "Even then I was sure he was smuggling. I figured the stuff had to come into the country hidden in the fabrics. Listen, it didn't take long for him to wise up I had a juv sheet."

Weiss said, "And he put you to work for him."

"Me and some local boys."

"You did what?"

"Hijackings, break-ins. We busted heads on picket lines, too."

"Shame, shame," Fineberg said.

Ginzberg just looked at him.

Weiss said, "You stole what sort of things?"

"Radios, phonographs, clothes. A little here, a little there." Ginzberg grinned. "It adds up."

Now he has even forgotten where he is, Weiss thought. *He takes pride in his achievements.*

"In the army," Weiss said, "you changed your name."

"Not me. Rutledge did that."

"Why?"

"Look, he knew I'd had some run-ins with the law. Two-bit stuff, but he had plans for me. He wasn't a lieutenant colonel yet, just a lousy major, but he knew how to pull strings. He had this guy in records could fix anything. He slipped me my new papers. I had a week's leave comin' after basic. I'm still Joe Ginzberg. But when I turn up at my new company, I'm this Leon Asher guy. I go through the whole lousy war using that dumb name. I think, if I'm killed in action, no one'll ever know what happened to Joe Ginzberg. Only I ain't killed, and the war's almost over. Then, I get special orders. The army flies me to Yugoslavia. And that's when I meet up with my

pal Rutledge again. In some damn forest. Other guys are
there, too. The only one I ever seen before is Earl Grasser
from basic. I seen him but we ain't buddies. I take him
aside anyway and cue him in about my new name. Turns
out we both know Rutledge from the old days. So do the
other guys, all except the second looey. Because of him,
the colonel warns us to act like we was all strangers. What
we gotta do is babysit some Kraut outta there. What happens next, the Kraut steps out where we can see him, and a
truck blows sky-high. It's gone, he's gone, one of our guys
is dead, another hurt bad."

"What," Weiss asked, "was the German bringing out?"

"Diamonds."

"You are sure? Not dope?"

"Diamonds. And with them he paid for the dope.
That's how the racket began."

Fineberg said, "How do you know this?"

"That fat prick Rutledge told me. This was like three
weeks later, when he gets me transferred to him. The Kraut
is an old pal, too, he tells me. They did business together
before the war. Right away, I think smuggling. I'd lay odds
he got out okay, along with his diamonds. It was all a setup
from the word go."

Weiss nodded. "And this new assignment?"

"What he wanted is I should talk my way into this
smuggling racket he got wind of. It's run by enlisted men,
and he needs a guy on the inside. I figure he's angling for
a cut, or plans to take over. That's the kinda guy he was. I
say sure. But after a while, I start doing some thinkin'."

Fineberg said, "You were by then, Joey, a member of
this smuggling ring?"

"Knee deep. But all that thinkin' paid off. I tell our
pal I've had it. I want out, the rackets ain't for me no
more. Rutledge tells me things've changed on his side
too. My undercover job's gone legit. He says he and his

commanding officer, General Wilner, are gonna crack the
ring wide open, and I should stay put. The next thing I
know the MPs are all over me. That's when I find out the
bastard's transferred out and left me holding the bag. At
the court martial I tell 'em about Rutledge. And they tell
me that he got himself killed on the way to Germany. This
General Wilner, he's never hearda me. They kick me outta
the army with a dishonorable discharge. See, I squealed
on the other guys and that's what kept me outta the brig.
Back home I take back my own name and after a while I
land a job at the college. But you know about that."

Weiss nodded. "What happened at the college?"

"What didn't? I'm goin' straight now. Then I spot this
gimp pushing dope on campus. I make him easy. It's the
guy lost a leg that swell day we spent in Yugoslavia. I
brace him, say I'll kill him if he ever shows his rotten
mug here again."

"But he came back anyway," Weiss said, "didn't he?"

"How'd ya know that?"

"A witness."

"There are everywhere witnesses," Fineberg put in.

"He knows, Irving," Weiss said. To Ginzberg he said,
"You and Earl Grasser met together with Blake."

"Sure. At a greasy spoon near the college. He told us
his boss, Keller, wanted a deal. This Keller, he was another of the five guys. Earl and I were buddies by then, so
I asked him along. Earl had been a pusher once, worked
for Keller, but, like me, he figured he'd had enough. We
met with Blake about three times. He said Keller wanted
us to lay off his boys, said there was always room for guys
like us in the outfit."

Weiss said, "He offered money, of course?"

"Sure. But me and Earl were just stringing him along.
We were gonna turn in the whole bunch. Then Earl got
himself killed and I landed in here."

Fineberg stared at the prisoner.

"Why, Joey," he demanded, "did you not tell us this be-fore? Why?"

Ginzberg laughed bitterly. "You crazy? As Ginzberg I never even met Earl Grasser. What's my motive for killing him? I still gotta chance to beat the rap. So someone dumped him in my car? Big deal. But as Leon Asher, I was in basic with the guy. The army kicked me out 'cause I was a dope dealer, right? What kinda chance you think I got?"

Weiss and Fineberg exchanged glances. Weiss reached into his coat pocket, pulled out an envelope, removed a snapshot, and showed it to Ginzberg.

"Shit. It's that fat prick Rutledge." He paused. "I know the other guy too."

"Keller," Weiss said.

"Yeah, Keller."

"This, Joey, was taken in Paris. By your friend Blake. I think he was planning to blackmail them both. But he couldn't find the colonel and the best he could do was get a job with Keller."

"What're you giving me?" Ginzberg said. "Rutledge died."

"Do you read French, Joey?"

"Sure. Like I read Turkish."

"I will translate. See the cinema in the background?" Weiss pointed a finger at the marquee. "It says *La Belle et la Bete. Beauty and the Beast.* A very famous movie, it is already a classic."

"What's that to me?"

"The picture came out in 1946," Weiss said. "When did our colonel die?"

"Forty-five," Ginzberg said slowly.

Weiss smiled.

"Shit! Earl called me the day before he was killed, said while he was makin' the rounds looking for work, he'd spotted Rutledge or his double in some office. I told him he was crazy."

"And he said?"

"He'd show me."

"This colonel, he has framed you twice already," Fineberg said excitedly. "In the army, and now here."

"But this time," Weiss said, "will be the last."

CHAPTER 34

*The past always gives a clue to the present. But
sometimes it is the wrong clue.*

From the casebooks of Morris Weiss

Max Weiss—The Present

Laura and I had briefly returned to the party downstairs
with a pair of cops. But we couldn't spot the phony body-
guard anywhere. He'd gotten up off the floor and beat it.

Ford and his crew had quizzed Treister's three pals,
gone over the stories Laura and I had given them, gotten
the guest list, then put the screws on the security chief and
his crew. Cops were busy questioning guests and searching
the grounds. Forensics showed up to do their work. The assistant M.E. arrived, gave the body the once-over, then had
it carted off to the morgue.

Treister's three guests didn't hang around long after that.

As soon as Ford gave them the go-ahead, they excused themselves and almost fell over each other trying to get out the door first.

I couldn't blame them. It had been a tough night.

Always the gentleman, I suggested we leave, too. But our host wouldn't hear of it. He escorted us away from the murder scene—still teeming with cops—and into a smaller study a few doors down the hall.

The merrymaking downstairs continued unabated despite everything. Sounds drifted up to us every time a door opened somewhere. The guests were getting their money's worth out of all this excitement.

Treister said, "The young lady, I am afraid, will have to come back tomorrow for her interview. But you, Mr. Weiss, I can satisfy right now."

"If you'd rather," I said, "we can easily put this off for later."

"No trouble. It will not take much time."

All three of us settled back in our chairs. Soft lighting, ivory walls, and vases full of silvery China mums accented a room that smelled of pine.

Our host was seventy but looked a good fifteen years younger. His hair was white, but he had a full head of it. His face was all but unlined. Hazel eyes, graying eyebrows. His body hadn't gone to seed, but appeared to be the product of lots of workouts at the gym, good genes, and, no doubt, first-class medical advice.

"Dr. Margoshes and I met in late August," he said, "right here in this very room."

"He asked to see you?"

"Yes, and I was honored. My practice these days is to avoid most visitors. But he is a great scholar. And he had helped me no end with my archive. We spent the entire afternoon together."

"What did he want?" I asked.

"Something very simple. To hear about my experiences in the Warsaw Ghetto, firsthand. You two are familiar with what happened there?"

I nodded.

Laura said, "Not really."

"Well," Treister said, "it is important that you know, my dear."

Laura agreed.

"I will be happy to tell you," he said, "provided you have the time."

I said, "Of course we do."

Laura said, "May I take notes?"

"By all means."

Laura produced a small notebook and pen from her purse.

"I was only a teenager then," Treister began, "but one grows up fast under such circumstances. On September the first, 1939, the German Army crossed the Polish borders. There was a battle, but it did not last long. At the end of the third week, Warsaw fell. On the thirty-first of October 1940, the Germans created the ghetto."

Treister looked at Laura and smiled.

"So," he said. "I am giving you your interview now, after all, it seems."

Laura smiled back.

"Some of it," she said.

"Women," Treister said, "have a way of getting what they want. Take good notes," he told her.

"I'm getting it all down," she assured him.

He leaned forward in his chair. "By 1941," he said, "the death rate due to starvation and typhus had reached thirty percent. How I managed to live, I am still not certain. It helped of course that I was young. And resourceful. There were tunnels dug by our people. I volunteered to go to the Polish side. There, at night, I stole food and other items that could be used for barter, and brought them all back. Others who crossed over had more important roles to play."

"Why didn't you just stay there?" Laura asked, pen poised above her notebook.

Treister smiled bitterly. "There was no place to hide. The Poles did not hesitate to turn over anyone suspected of being a Jew to the Nazi authorities.

"I became a good thief for the cause. I went many times, and always the risk was great. To be caught meant death.

"By March of 1942 the Nazis had calculated that the half-million Jews in the ghetto would all be dead. But we surprised them. We lived on. And that, my dear young friends, was when the deportations began. You are acquainted with the term 'The Final Solution'?"

"Yes," Laura said.

"Well, this was it. Six to ten thousand a day. To Auschwitz, Maidanek, Treblinka, Belzec, Chelmno, Sobibor—the death camps. The Nazis called the deported 'Jewish war industry workers' and claimed they were being shipped to factories. Word got back. But who could believe it? No one at first. It was too bizarre. It was utterly unreasonable to think that during a war, the Germans would divert so many resources to the annihilation of noncombatants. They would have to be insane to do so. But of course they were. Slowly we realized the truth. But what could be done by starving, untrained, and unarmed civilians against the German Army? Many gave up all hope. Others still would not believe. But those who were members of political organizations, Zionists, Socialists,

Bundists, Communists, they put aside their differences. And began to prepare. This in itself was a miracle.

"On January 18, 1943, the orders were given for the liquidation of the ghetto. By then, of the half-million, only forty thousand were left. An SS detachment marched in to make a routine selection of deportees. Instead they were met by bullets—Jewish bullets. The fighting lasted for three days before the Nazis fled."

"Where did you get the weapons?" Laura asked.

"Smuggled into the ghetto, my dear. Very quietly. This was the mission of those others who had crawled under the wall. We called ourselves the Fighter Organization of the Jewish Underground. We dug bunkers, underground shelters. We made incendiaries, bombs, grenades. I was sixteen, but our leader was a mere twenty-three. His name was Mordecai Anielewicz. I will spell it for you."

Laura scribbled furiously. I was beginning to feel that for all my efforts to get hold of this guy, I was going to come up empty. Laura was getting the windfall. I didn't take it to heart. Treister was the genuine article: a true hero. I was glad to have met him.

"At dawn on April 19, 1943," he continued, "under the command of SS Major General Jugen Stroop, the German troops again moved into the ghetto. Himmler himself had given the order for its final and complete liquidation. We were ready. From the rooftops, from basements, from behind brick rubble and shattered windows, we gave our answer. Step by step we drove them back. The Nazis brought up artillery and flamethrowers. Again they entered. And again were driven out. By the twenty-eighth of April, the SS had thrown thousands of heavily armed troops into battle against us. Planes, artillery, and tanks were used. But we held. Now they turned to extra-military means. They set fire to the ghetto. Day and night it burned. Still we fought on, house by house. Then, when there were no houses left but only rubble, we moved down to the sewers, to underground shelters we had prepared. There was no food, no air. The SS brought up dynamite and gas shells. Police dogs were unleashed. The sewers were flooded. One by one the shelters finally fell."

Treister paused and sighed. Beads of perspiration were appearing on his forehead. He continued.

"The battle lasted forty-two days and nights. Anielewicz did not survive. But a handful of us managed to escape. We made our way through the few remaining sewers not yet flooded. We reached the other side. We could not stay in Warsaw. I myself hid by day and traveled by night until I reached Podlaski. I had relatives there, but they had all been deported. A Polish farmer who knew my family hid me. I stayed in his barn until Poland was liberated by the Allies."

Treister was done. He wasn't looking at us anymore but staring off somewhere into the distance. Probably at the ghetto or the barn near Podlaski. The guy must have told this story often over the years. But the anguish was still stamped on his face.

He shook himself, as if waking out of a bad dream. He smiled at us. "Well, there you have it, the story I promised you. I hope I did not take too long."

We both assured him he had not.

"Tomorrow, Miss Faust, I will be only too glad to bring the story up-to-date. Let us say a late lunch here, about two in the afternoon?"

"That would be wonderful," Laura said.

"As for you, Mr. Weiss, what can I say? You have now heard the shorter version of what I told Dr. Margoshes."

"Thanks," I said. "What was the longer version like?"

Treister smiled. "Long."

"Why was Margoshes interested in your experiences, Mr. Treister?"

"He was writing a book about the ghetto. You didn't know?"

"This is the first I've heard of it."

"Well, it is his major project now. Much has already been written about this topic. But let me assure you there is room for more. Our fighters were not just Socialists or Zionists who agreed to get along this once. These are merely umbrella terms. Under each umbrella were many political parties, all at odds with one another, each convinced that their ideology was the only correct one. The Revisionists and Labor Zionists, for instance, were both Zionists. But they hated each other more than they hated the anti-Zionist Bundists."

"But not more than they hated the Nazis," Laura said.

Treister smiled. "Quite right, my dear. Not a bad subject for a book. What Dr. Margoshes wanted to know was how individuals from these groups worked together."

"How did they?"

"Splendidly, considering the great animosity these people bore each other."

"Most of the resistance fighters were political?" Laura asked.

"Yes, many were."

"And you?" she asked.

"I, my dear, was one of the exceptions. I knew that to stay alive I must join the resistance. A boy of sixteen alone had no chance. But I could not figure out which party was the sole representative of truth and virtue. I could not figure that out then, and I still cannot. That is why I am a businessman and not a politician. And why Dr. Margoshes needed my story. I have no ideological ax to grind, you see. I was the outsider looking in, the objective observer. From me he could get a fresh viewpoint, even at this late date. That, in any case, was his hope. You will have to ask him if I was a success."

"You haven't heard from him since?" I asked.

"I have not."

"Did he tell you what he planned to do next?"

"Of course. Continue research for his book."

"Any idea where he might have gone?"

"Europe, I think. That was my impression."

"Nothing more specific?"

Treister spread his hands. "I had no reason to ask him. Do you really think he is in some kind of trouble?"

"Yes, that's a distinct possibility."

"Then I hope you find him quickly."

"So do I. One more question, Mr. Treister, if I may?"

"Of course."

"What was Halkin doing with you and your friends in that room?"

"Doing?"

"Yes. He'd come here specifically to introduce me to you. But he vanished from sight almost as soon as we got past the front door."

"I am afraid he sought me out on your behalf."

"Mine?"

"I am sometimes short-tempered with strangers at these gatherings," Treister said. "I know it is a failing. In any case, Leonard was anxious that I give you my full attention. So he came to my study to speak up for you."

"But he never got back to me."

Treister shrugged. "We began to talk. Soon we were discussing my archive. What can I tell you? We simply lost all track of time."

I was about to rise and bid our host good night when a thought struck me. "Mr. Treister, do you know a Leo Kanufsky?"

"Who?"

I gave him the name again.

"Offhand I would say no. But I have met so many people over the years that it is quite impossible to say for certain. Who is he, if I may ask?"

"A man who may know something about Dr. Margoshes."

"Then good luck," Treister said, "when you speak to him."

Laura and I strolled back hand in hand toward town. It was a beautiful Indian-summer night, up in the sixties maybe. A nice warm wind blew at our backs. And Laura's hand felt warm and snug in mine. But for the life of me I couldn't restore the feeling of well-being that I'd carried with me to the party.

"At least you'll get your story," I said.

"Some way to get it, Max."

"I still don't believe any of this happened," I admitted. "Halkin deserved better. I keep telling myself that it's not my fault. But somehow I can't make myself believe it."

"It isn't your fault," Laura said. "You may feel guilty, but being a rational guy, Max, you know you're not. And I know it, too."

"Thanks."

And just like that, we came into each other's arms and kissed. A long luxurious kiss that left us both breathless. The zing—which was now humming inside me—was reaching new heights. There's a time for talk and there's a time for action. Action won the day. I kissed her again. It felt just as great the second time. We stepped apart, gazed at each other in wonder and silently continued our walk. After a while, Laura asked me, "So what's next?"

"Next?"

"You going after the killers, Max?"

"Me?"

"Who else?"

"You mean like the Masked Avenger?"

"Yes, only without the mask."

"I look like a comic book hero?"

"I think of myself as Brenda Starr," she said.

"And so you should. It's me you're confused about. What I do is find missing people, stolen property, go after swindlers, mundane things like that. And all on behalf of a client. Going after these four thugs is heavy-duty stuff. I wouldn't know where to begin. And even if I did know, the cops do these things so much better, it's no contest."

"Our Lieutenant Ford does it better?"

I laughed. "He's not the whole police force, Laura. For all we know he may not handle this investigation himself. Or he may actually turn out to be a good cop."

"Let's not be ridiculous."

"Well, the bottom line is Treister didn't say a word about hiring me. Which only goes to show how smart he is. And I doubt the Foundation will even think of it."

"You could give them a push."

"Sure. But they'd be throwing their money away. I wasn't kidding when I said there are better ways to go about this job. And without full cooperation from Treister and the locals I'd never get to first base. Even with their help I'd be in over my head."

"So what are you going to do?"

I put my arm around her. We kept strolling.

"What I set out to do," I said. "Finish this Margoshes business as fast as I can."

"And Halkin?"

"Attend his memorial, I guess. Try to remember your words of wisdom about not feeling too guilty. And hope whoever did this gets nailed fast and put away for keeps."

The Sheraton Hotel loomed on our left as we reached Broadway and Van Dam. The City Center building and civilization were right beyond it.

I tightened my hold around her waist. She put an arm around my shoulder.

The Adelphi Hotel was dead ahead. Inside, the place is an antique eyeful and always worth a gander. I ignored it. Before I knew it we were in her room on the second floor. There was time for one last searing kiss and then we were ripping off our clothes and tumbling into bed. The zing was going nuts.

It wasn't the only one.

CHAPTER 35

Morris Weiss—1948

"Well," O'Toole said.

Morris Weiss nodded, glumly.

"It will teach us," O'Toole said, "not to bet beyond our means."

Weiss reached for his coffee cup on O'Toole's desk.

"It's too late for that," he said. "We will never learn."

"Who would've thought it?" O'Toole said. "Cerdan beat him fair and square."

"Zale is thirty-five, Detective O'Toole, an old man in boxing."

"You're right, Mr. Weiss. Tossing in the towel before the twelfth round was the right thing to do. More of a shellacking and Zale could have been badly hurt."

Weiss took a swallow of coffee and began sifting through the items piled on top of his friend's desk. The station house around him seemed unusually quiet this afternoon. As if crime had taken a sudden holiday. Or the police were simply lying low, waiting to pounce on some hapless miscreant.

"Nothing else?" he asked. "You are sure?"

"It's the crop, Mr. Weiss. If you're looking for something to get your boy sprung—"

"I wouldn't mind."

"You won't find it here. The lads searched Grasser's place from top to bottom and came up empty-handed."

Weiss had already examined Grasser's wallet, which contained only a driver's license, eight dollars in singles, and a ticket to the Irish Sweepstakes.

Both men now eyed the ticket.

"Care to try your luck, Mr. Weiss?"

"I never liked the odds, Detective O'Toole."

"Nor I."

Weiss pointed a finger. "And this pile?"

"Want ads. Our boy was hunting for work. These were with some magazines in the kitchen, so the lads brought them along."

"Very thoughtful of them."

"Don't be getting your hopes up, Mr. Weiss. You'll find no leads there, I'm afraid."

Weiss picked up the ten loose pages from the *New York Times Classified Help Wanted* section—each for a different day—and leafed through them. The subheadings read *Sales Help Wanted*. The ads that Grasser had followed up were circled, then crossed out.

"He saved them, I see," Weiss said.

"So he wouldn't go to the same place twice," O'Toole said. "This top one was found in his coat pocket."

The page was from last Tuesday, Weiss saw. As on the other pages a number of ads were circled. But only a few here were crossed out.

"The day he died," Weiss said.

"The very day."

"Were any of these places checked?"

"For what?"

"Maybe Grasser met his killer in one of them?"

"The D.A. thinks Ginzberg is good for it."

"He's made up his mind already?"

O'Toole nodded. "They're ready to move on it."

"Do you mind if I borrow this page?"

"Keep it, Mr. Weiss. But I'll wager you'll not find a thing."

CHAPTER 36

If the police are so smart, why are there so many private detectives?

From the casebooks of Morris Weiss

Max Weiss—The Present

Laura was already gone when I woke up. I dressed and beat it back to the Holiday Inn. I shaved, showered, got into a pair of khaki slacks and a blue denim shirt, slipped into my jacket, and let my walking shoes walk me out of the place. Nine-fifteen. The sun was rising in a slightly clouded sky. A mild westerly wind rustled some dried leaves across the pavement. It was starting to feel more like autumn.

I had breakfast at Compton's Diner, then continued on to the City Center building, and presently found myself seated at a small table with a Sergeant Malone, a young sandy-haired guy, flipping through mug shots. I came across plenty of tough-looking customers, but no one who seemed familiar. No surprise. The guy I'd grappled with wasn't a homegrown product, someone who hung around Saratoga Springs street corners waiting for a victim to mug. He was a stranger just like the rest of his colleagues, me, and most of the people who hit town during the course of a year.

I spent another forty minutes with a cop artist who put together a composite drawing of our suspect based on my description—Laura hadn't shown up yet to add her two cents.

"Can you Xerox a copy of this for me?" I asked the artist.

"Sure."

He went away. I was just settling down to wait when a voice said, "Weiss."

I turned, and there was Lieutenant Ford. He was one of those guys with a tough blue-black beard who would always look like he needed a shave, the bane of the razor blade industry. This morning he had on a checkered green suit, yellow tie, and red shirt. Probably waiting for a casting call from *Guys and Dolls*.

"This way," he said.

I followed him into a small office. A pair of windows faced Broadway and looked out at the post office across the street. He motioned me to a seat next to his desk.

"Your girlfriend hasn't shown up yet," he said.

"Yet is the operative word," I told him.

"And another thing," Ford said. "I don't buy that story of yours about being at Mr. Treister's house just to get a lead on some guy you say you're looking for."

"Call the Jewish Historical Foundation in New York. Ask for Dr. Shavinsky, the director. He'll back me up."

"He your client, Weiss?"

"My client is Dr. Margoshes's niece. I told you all of that yesterday."

"Yeah, but you didn't give me her name."

"She has nothing to do with this."

"I don't buy that either."

"Ask Treister," I said. "Better yet, go find Margoshes and ask him."

"Don't be a wise guy, Weiss. I already called this Shavinsky guy."

"And?"

"He says what you say."

"So?"

"You two could've cooked it up together."

"Us two aren't that smart," I told him.

"He gave me the niece's name, too, April Freid. Whaddya think of that? I called her."

"What did she say?"

"What you and this Shavinsky say."

"Yeah, we could've all cooked it up together. Like three master chefs. Only we didn't."

He gave me a hard stare.

I said, "How's Shavinsky doing?"

Ford opened a desk drawer, took out a cigar, removed the cellophane, and lit up. I hate cigar smoke, but I decided to give the guy a break.

"Not so hot," he said. "Once I gave him the lowdown on his pal Halkin."

"I can imagine. What happens to the body now?"

"He's having it shipped to the widow."

That brought me up short. Somehow, I'd never thought of Halkin as married. In fact, I'd never thought of Halkin as anything more than a potential lead. The man probably had kids, too. The thought did not cheer me.

"Anything else?" I asked him.

"Keep your nose clean, Weiss."

"That's it, your words of wisdom?"

Ford waved a hand. "Go on, beat it. I'm done with you for now."

The cop artist handed me the Xerox copy of his sketch on my way out. "Thanks," I said, folding it and stuffing it into a jacket pocket.

I stood in front of the City Center building, looked in both directions, and weighed my options. It was only a short walk to Treister's mansion. I took it.

The butler didn't answer my ring. The man standing in the doorway was Carl Mendelbaum, his full head of silver hair glittering in the sunlight. He had on a gray pinstriped suit this morning, as befit a kingpin in Treister's business empire. He looked a lot more together than last night. In fact, he was exuding self-confidence. But then, his hands weren't cuffed behind his back.

"Good morning, Mr. Weiss," he said gravely.

"Morning, Mr. Mendelbaum. Has Laura Faust been by yet?"

"No," he said. "And I am not sure her coming here is the best idea."

"You've got a better one?"

"Yes. That you and your friend respect Mr. Treister's privacy and have the decency to leave him alone at this time. I think it is not asking too much when you consider what happened last night."

"Look," I said, "I'm not here to see your boss. But he expressly invited Miss Faust over to interview him."

Mendelbaum nodded gravely. "Mr. Treister has suffered a great shock. I myself am none too well this morning, and

Mr. Treister is a good decade older. You can imagine how he feels."

"Yes, I can. But he was doing just fine last time I saw him. What happened?"

"He is simply exhausted."

"Uh-huh."

"As one of his oldest friends, I have taken the liberty of appointing myself keeper of the gate."

"And no one gets in."

"Unless it is an absolute emergency."

I shrugged. "Whatever you say."

"Thank you."

"Sure," I said. "When Miss Faust gets here, could you tell her I'm looking for her?"

"Of course."

"Ask her to leave a message at the Adelphi, if we don't connect before mid-afternoon."

"I will inform her."

"Thanks."

I walked back to town none the wiser about anything, including where Laura was.

I tried the Adelphi. With the same results as before. I wasn't worried. She'd show up in her own good time. And I had business to attend to.

Margoshes didn't drive. So the obvious question was, how did he get out of town? I made the rounds of the cab company, bus, and railway station. Only a sixtyish lady clerk might stand a chance of remembering him after all this time, and none, as it turned out, had been on the job that week.

I showed his photo at each stop. Everyone I questioned gave me a no. I wangled the names and phone numbers of the off-duty personnel from the guys in charge and called them. Some of them were even home. I described the man I sought. No one had seen him.

I briefly considered trudging out to their homes to flash my snapshot, but thought better of it. Even here, in Saratoga Springs, where the long shot reigns supreme, this was too much of a long shot.

Back at the Adelphi, I went up to the reception desk. A different clerk was there this time. I gave him my name and asked if there were any messages from Laura Faust. He looked through some paper slips in a cubbyhole. And found one.

"Thanks," I said.

It was a two-line note. I read it standing by the desk:

Dearest Max: Called away on really urgent business. Will get in touch back in the city. I miss you already. Lots of love, Laura

CHAPTER 37

Morris Weiss—1948

It began to rain.

Weiss put up his collar, stepped under a green awning, and looked again at his now soggy page. He had briefly considered giving O'Toole Ginzberg's story but had decided to keep this news to himself. It could only hurt Ginzberg to have his army career brought to the prosecutor's attention. What Weiss needed was more evidence.

So far he had been to nine of the circled companies, small wholesalers selling men's ties, vacuum cleaners, encyclopedias, even toys. Grasser was versatile if nothing else. He was remembered at all of these places, a young man with a nice smile. But Weiss drew a blank when it came to Rutledge.

The next firm was Opta Imports on Canal Street.

The reception area was empty except for the young

blonde behind the small desk doing a crossword puzzle. She put down her pencil and asked, "Can I help you?"

"I hope so," Weiss said, showing her his license.

She stared at it blankly as if not certain which city agency he represented or what he wanted to inspect.

Weiss helped her out. "I'm a private detective," he said. The license went back in his coat pocket—in its place he produced the police shot of Earl Grasser. "Have you seen this man?"

The girl's eyes lost their indifference.

"What's he done?"

"He has done nothing. He is a victim."

"What happened?"

"He was murdered," Weiss said.

"Oh, no." Her hand went to her mouth. "That's awful."

"I am in full agreement. He was looking for work here?"

"Yes."

"He spoke to someone?"

"Our vice president. He sees all the job applicants."

"Then I wish to see him, too."

She used the intercom.

A moment later a young man hurried into the reception area through an inner door. He was no taller than Weiss himself, with a full head of wavy black hair and the pale complexion of someone who spends much of his time indoors. He wore a black and beige checkered sports coat, striped tie, and orange slacks.

"I am Kelman Treister," the young man said, in heavily accented English. "How can I help you?"

Weiss held up his license.

"What is this?" Treister asked, as though unable to identify the document in the detective's hand.

"My credentials."

"So? What do you want?"

"To speak to you about him," Weiss said, brandishing the Grasser photograph. "You met with this man last Tuesday?"

Treister eyed the snapshot. "I did, but it was only business. He wanted a job."

"He was murdered later that day."

Treister's face showed dismay. "I'm sorry, truly. I liked him. But what does this have to do with me?"

"His death may be connected to this company."

"How is that possible?"

"We should speak privately," Weiss said.

Treister swept his arm toward the inner door. "This way, please."

Weiss followed the young man down a beige corridor and into an office containing six green metal filing cabinets and a map of the world. A pair of windows looked out on a redbrick wall.

Not quite like a prison, Weiss thought. *But too close.*

Both men seated themselves.

Treister leaned forward from behind his desk, stretched out a hand for his guest to shake, and said in Yiddish, "You are a *landsman*?"

"It doesn't take a detective to figure that out," Weiss answered, also in Yiddish.

"Where is a Jew from?" It was the traditional greeting, phrased in the traditional manner.

"Lukov. But I left there when I was seven."

"Warsaw," Treister said. "I had family in Lukov, too, before the war. The Shapiros. You remember them, maybe?"

"It was a long time ago."

"True."

"Tell me," Weiss asked, still in Yiddish, "why didn't you hire Grasser if you liked him so much?"

"Between you and me, we are not doing so well right now. Opta Imports buys cheap and sells cheap. The market these days is flooded with foreign goods. So we are having trouble. It is bound to end sooner or later. I took Mr. Grasser's name and address and said I would remember him when things got better. And now you bring me this tragic news." Treister sighed deeply. "You see, we only had a quick talk and then he left. I am the one he saw here, and I know only what I have told you."

"Maybe," Weiss said, "you know more than you think."

"What do you mean?"

"It is possible he recognized someone here."

Treister thought it over. "Who knows, maybe . . ."

"And if he did," Weiss said, "this is the very man I am searching for."

"He is a criminal?"

"So it appears."

"He has a name?"

"Milton Rutledge."

Treister shook his head slowly. "I do not know this name."

"He may be using another."

"Can you describe him?"

"Gladly. He is short, fat, and has a mustache. And he was a lieutenant colonel in the U.S. Army during the war."

"Well, we have a few short men; some even have mustaches. One has a long beard, too. You say your man was a colonel. A nice corporal we have, but no higher. And while our corporal is not short, he is fat."

In Yiddish Weiss said, "Take a look at this."

From his pocket, the detective withdrew one of the snapshots Blake had taken in Paris. It showed Rutledge alone, walking on the Champs Elysees. He handed it to Treister and sat watching as the man studied it.

"So, in Paris?"

Weiss nodded.

"He picked a good city. When was this taken?"

"Three years ago."

"Well, my friend, I regret to say, this one does not work here."

"You are sure?"

"Who can be sure of anything? What I see in your photograph is a round little man with a mustache. But what can't happen in three years to change him? Tell me, you had face-to-face dealings with him?"

"Never."

Treister shrugged.

He's right, Weiss thought. *What I should have done is taken Ginsberg along; he at least knows this Rutledge from before. But even O'Toole can't be expected to work miracles and pry a murder suspect loose from his cell. Sykes, of course, spent a few hours with the colonel. But he was already grudging in his help the last time we spoke. I'd have to bring back Colonel Minsky to make another call, and hope that Sykes hasn't lost his reverence for authority. Still, if Grasser was able to recognize the colonel, maybe I can, too.*

"I need to look at your staff," Weiss said.

"My staff? Why not? We also have a warehouse next door."

"That, too."

"I will take you."

"Excellent."

"You think this colonel is truly here?"

"I think nothing. But it is easier looking here than going back in the rain."

"He knows who you are?"

"Not by sight."

"Good. Trouble on the premises would be bad."

"It wouldn't be so good for me either," Weiss said.

The two men stepped out into the corridor.

Treister, with the detective by his side, went from office to office, opening doors. "My friend here is taking the grand tour," Treister told a short, fat man who bore not the slightest resemblance to the colonel. To a much heftier man pecking at a Remington typewriter, he said simply, "He's inspecting." A stout woman warranted only a wave.

They came to a locked door.

"This is the boss's office," Treister said. "Mr. Janner is in Europe buying up more job lots. He looks like a football player. That much your colonel could not change."

"So who's in charge here?"

Treister beamed. "I suppose I am. But the business, to tell the truth, runs itself."

Soon they were done with the entire floor.

"What did I tell you?" Treister said. "Colonels don't work here. Why should they? There are better jobs for such people."

"I'm sure you're right."

"You still want to see our warehouse?"

"No. But that is what detectives do."

Opta had three floors of an eight-story redbrick building next door.

Treister opened the street door with a key.

"I'm afraid you'll be disappointed."

"I will live through it."

The two men entered a small lobby and took the freight elevator up.

"How," Weiss asked, "did you come to this business?"

"I answered an ad."

"Only in America. Someday you could own a building like this."

"Who wants such a building?"

They got off on the fourth floor.

Light from overhead lamps shown down on wooden crates piled high, one on top of the other.

Treister made a megaphone of his hands. "Hello!"

No one replied.

"They are upstairs."

"What's in the boxes?"

"Junk."

"But good junk, eh?"

"If you say so." He waved an arm. "Here we have army sweaters, there, army surplus shoes. Over by the far wall, army field jackets. Overcoats we also have. Where would we be without your army? You have maybe seen enough?"

"Too much."

"Follow me."

Again they took the elevator up.

The fifth floor had more wooden crates. "Women's wear," Treister said. "Skirts, sweaters, blouses. Made dirt cheap in Egypt or India. We mark them up two, three hundred percent and still they go straight to the bargain counters."

"Not a bad business."

"For the boss."

Six workmen were unpacking crates.

Weiss recognized the unmistakable smell of army clothing. Treister led him across the floor for a closer look at the six. While Treister exchanged a few joking words with them, the detective looked them over. *I am wasting my time,* he thought. Two were stocky, middle-sized men. Three were obviously too young and neither short nor fat. The sixth man was a Negro.

"This is your whole workforce?" the detective asked.

"We have more."

"Then let's go."

This time they took the stairway, which was nearer. Again they stepped out under bright lights. Crates were stacked even higher here, some almost to the ceiling. There were also benches and long worktables scattered haphazardly among the piles of crates, obstructing a clear view of the loft. But from the staircase and elevator, a good part of the floor could still be seen.

At first Weiss saw no one. Then he spied two workmen on the far side of the floor.

"Only two workers?" Weiss asked.

"Business is slow."

"What is this place?"

"Where we pack and ship orders to our domestic market. Is your colonel here?"

Weiss moved closer to the pair of workers. One almost fit the man in the snapshot. But he was in his late sixties. The other was tall, muscular, and in his twenties. *The wrong men,* Weiss thought. *At least I have spent a pleasant half-hour in a dry, warm place speaking some Yiddish. It would be ungrateful to complain too much.*

The detective spied a door across the room. It did not look like a bathroom.

"What's there?"

"Our coordinator, Mr. Bert. It's his office."

"It pays to look?"

Treister grinned. "He is not your man. Mr. Bert is taller than I am, not fat, and he is a redhead. I don't think he was even in the army—flat feet, they say. And he has been with the company longer than I have. I think the boss himself hired him."

"What does he coordinate?"

"Our shipments. Every week or two, when he prepares for orders, a part-time assistant, a Mr. Harriman, comes to help him. He is here today. So if you want, you will be able to see the whole Opta family. Except, of course, for Mr. Jenner."

Weiss glanced at the closed door and then imagined the rain falling outside. "What have we got to lose? Let's take a look."

"Why not? He won't mind."

The two men went to the door and Treister opened it. The room was dark and empty.

"They are at lunch," Treister said.

"Well," Weiss said, "I have seen enough."

"Then maybe you will join me for a bite? There is a good cafeteria next block."

"A quick one. I must still find the colonel."

"Your colonel, he is worth all this trouble?"

"Nothing is worth all this trouble."

Both men laughed.

"Come," Treister said. "If you want, you can return to look at Mr. Bert after. He and Harriman will enjoy the company."

The two turned and began making their way back to the elevator. Weiss could hear it moving up. They were halfway there when the elevator stopped and its doors slid open. Out stepped Gordon Keller and a redheaded man in his mid-thirties. Keller casually glanced down the makeshift aisle between boxes, crates, and tables at the detective, and stopped dead in his tracks.

"The assistant," Treister said, and began to wave in greeting.

Keller, very fast, reached behind him under his jacket and came up with a Colt 45.

Weiss, grabbing Treister, hurled himself sideways behind a wall of wooden crates as Keller fired. The shots boomed out in the confined space. The crate began to fly apart like papier mâché, spraying a hail of fragments over the detective.

Weiss, on hands and knees, propelled himself forward from crate to crate, Treister crawling frantically beside him, his face twisted in panic.

The detective yanked out his Browning, jumped to his feet, and, over the crate tops, fired diagonally toward the aisle where he'd last seen Keller. The gun bucked in his hand like a living thing, shells popping out and smoke pouring from its muzzle.

Weiss didn't wait to see what damage, if any, he'd done. Instantly, he dropped back to the floor. Slugs tore up the crate to his left. He hurtled forward, one second ahead of the onslaught.

Catching up with Treister, who had kept crawling, Weiss pulled him sideways across an open aisle and behind a very tall pile of crates—perfect cover for at least an instant.

The detective sprang to his feet, gave Treister a hand.

"What in God's name is happening?" Treister whispered.

"I've found my colonel."

"Who, the assistant?"

"The redhead. With elevator shoes, red hair dye, and after a good diet."

"Then who is the assistant?"

"A killer. You carry a gun, Treister?"

"Are you crazy?"

"Probably, to have walked into this."

"They will kill us."

"They will try."

"What should we do?"

"Not let them."

Weiss stuck the Browning in his waistband, leaped up on a workbench, and rising on his toes, hoisted himself up to the crate tops. The crates began to wobble under him.

He lay prone—and very still—but could see nothing. Taking a deep breath, he managed to rise to one knee. And saw Keller below him far over near the left wall.

Keller saw him, too.

Weiss dropped flat as Keller fired and slid off his unsteady perch. Forsaking caution, bent almost double, he

sprinted around crates and packing tables to the far wall
where he had last seen Keller, and hurled himself against
the tall stack of boxes. He heard a satisfying cry from the
other side as they went crashing down.

Before Weiss could catch his breath, Treister screamed.
"Look out!"

Weiss fell flat, rolled under a table in one motion. As
he rolled, he heard two shots, felt the table splinter above
him.

On hands and knees, he scurried from one table to the
other.

Twisting around, he saw a pair of dungaree-clad legs
in the aisle behind him, saw the body that came with it,
bending for a better look.

He shot at both body and legs.

The tall, muscular worker, gun in hand, fell to the floor.

He and Weiss stared at each other.

Weiss shot him again.

Treister scrambled across the floor and snatched up
the man's gun.

The other worker began racing for the stairs.

Weiss, rolling out from under the table, yelled, "Stand
where you are!"

The man ignored him and plunged through the staircase doorway.

"Over there!" Treister screamed.

Weiss turned. The colonel, he saw, had popped up on
the far right and was sprinting furiously toward the same
door.

"Stop!" Weiss yelled.

The colonel whirled and squeezed off three rounds.

Treister, by the detective's side, cut loose with his
newfound gun.

The impact sent the colonel crashing against the door.
It flew open, and he toppled backward down the stairs.

Weiss took a deep breath.

"Where is the other one?" Treister said, gasping.

"Under the boxes."

"He is dead?"

"Who knows?" Weiss said. "Call the police. This is their job now."

CHAPTER 38

I always begin with the premise that no one is telling the whole truth. Occasionally, this even works. But not as often as one would hope.

From the casebooks of Morris Weiss

Max Weiss—The Present

Back in my room at the Holiday Inn, I was busy packing when the phone rang.

"Mr. Weiss?"

"Yes," I said.

"It is I, Isaac Jaffee, Mr. Treister's biographer."

That perked up my interest.

"What can I do for you, Mr. Jaffee?"

"I am in the lobby of your hotel. I must see you."

"Sure, I'll be right down."

"No, no, we cannot be seen together."

Better and better. Maybe I was actually going to learn something. Either that or he had seen one spy movie too many.

"Come on up."

He was at my door in less than a minute. Here was a man who wasted no time. I let him in and waved at a chair, but he remained standing, pulling anxiously at his fingers as if trying to see if any were loose. He still wore the same gold-rimmed glasses, only now he'd swapped his black evening jacket for one that was professorial brown tweed.

I seated myself on the edge of the bed.

"What's on your mind, Mr. Jaffee?"

"As you no doubt know I am a professional biographer."

"So Treister said. You're helping him with his life story."

"Not helping. I am writing the whole book. Mr. Treister may have many virtues, but organizing a coherent narrative is not one of them. He talks, I listen, and then I write."

"How come you picked him as a subject?"

"Oh, no," Jaffee said, "I did not pick him. It is always the subjects who pick me. They phone me at home or they write me. That is all there is to it."

"You must have quite a reputation."

He smiled. "For some I am far and away the biographer of choice. Of course, the field is very limited. And the subject himself must pay for the book's printing."

"How's that?"

"My biographies are all in Yiddish."

"Mr. Jaffee," I said, "why would Treister want his biography written in Yiddish?"

He smiled again. "Perhaps Mr. Treister is more comfortable telling his story in Yiddish, which was, after all, his first language. In his case the book will, of course, be translated into English, and put out by an American firm as an autobiography; it is written in the first person. My name will not appear on the cover and I will not share in these profits, but my fee was quite substantial. I have no grounds for complaint."

Jaffee was silent a moment. He sighed, glanced around, and suddenly plunked down across from me in the chair. When he spoke it was in a lowered voice.

"This is what I wish to tell you, Mr. Weiss. My book is based on Mr. Treister's memory of events and my own research. I have been quite unable to independently verify many of his war experiences. There is nothing to flatly contradict them, either. Those were chaotic years and many witnesses were lost, or simply did not survive. In a book of this type, the subject's memory is verification enough. So I have no motive to look any deeper. But perhaps you do. Dr. Margoshes sought information about those years, and now, I hear, he cannot be found. In all likelihood there is no connection whatsoever. Yet, I felt it my duty to inform you. . . ."

"Thanks. I appreciate that."

"You are quite welcome." Jaffee rose to his feet. "Having now done my duty, my conscience is clear. Good day, Mr. Weiss, and thank you for sparing me these few moments. I know your time is valuable."

I rose, we shook hands, and Jaffee left me.

I stood there chewing over what he'd said. Not bad. It could mean that Margoshes had found out the truth about Treister, and had, as a consequence, been killed. There was, however, a slight problem with this. My missing scholar, hardly a slouch in his chosen field, had been in charge of the Treister archives for years. Why had it taken him so long to figure out that something was wrong?

I put another shirt in my suitcase. The phone rang. I walked around the bed and answered it. A guy again.

"I must see you immediately."

"Sure." My popularity with guys was at an all-time high. "Who are you, incidentally?"

"Jack Lipman."

"Right. Where are you calling from?"

"Your lobby."

"I'll come right down."

"I would rather come up."

Of course. All the junior G-Men would rather come up. He'd probably brought his Captain Midnight decoding ring with him, too.

"Come ahead," I told him.

Lipman hurried through the door a minute later, his tight tan jacket making him look even skinnier than the first time we met.

"Jaffee has been here to see you," he said.

I nodded.

"I demand to know what he said about me."

"That's easy, not a word."

Lipman scowled. "You are lying for him."

I almost laughed. "Come on. Why would I bother? I don't even know the guy."

"Then if not me it was Kelman he maligned."

"Why do you say that?"

"Because I know him."

I shrugged. "Why don't you sit down and tell me about it?"

"I will stand. I must urge you, Mr. Weiss, to disregard everything that Isaac Jaffee tells you. The man is mentally unbalanced. He has been spreading lies about me and Kelman Treister for years. And not just us. Others too have fallen victim to his twisted mind. No one is safe. But it is the oldest friends who have suffered the most. Do you know that Jaffee has twice spent time in mental institutions? It is true. He has nervous breakdowns. He has obsessions and delusions. What doesn't he have? He pretends friendship, but once your back is turned he is merciless. What did he say to you?"

"I'm afraid it was said in confidence."

"Bah! The man is a vicious purveyor of slander. He is unworthy of your trust. He should be ignored, shunned, ostracized, but you are coddling him. I insist on knowing what he told you."

"Look, Mr. Lipman, if Jaffee is so crazy, why is Treister letting him do his biography?"

"Why? Because he is so soft-hearted. I have warned him time and again about Jaffee, but always Kelman makes excuses for him. It is I who must always run to undo the damage."

"That's nice of you," I said, keeping a straight face.

"But I must. I am one of Kelman's oldest and most trusted advisors. I am his right hand."

"So what can you tell me about Felix Margoshes?" I said. "He was here a few months ago."

"Margoshes? A meddler. There is no end to his prying. And all in the name of scholarship." Lipman shook his head in disgust. "All these so-called scholars with their useless titles and degrees, all they know is how to put on airs, puff themselves up with their importance. They understand nothing."

I nodded as though we might be in perfect agreement on this important issue. "What did he want with Treister?" I said.

"What do they always want? More gossip, more worthless stories, more garbage. Who cares? But Kelman has the patience of a saint. He puts up with them."

"Maybe you can give me a detail or two about their conversation?"

"Never! I do not concern myself with such trash!"

"You know nothing?"

"I have no more to say to you. Remember what I told you."

"Sure."

He left without another word.

I sighed.

I finished packing, went down to the lobby, and checked out. I retrieved my Saab and headed up Broadway, past the shops and restaurants and into the residential district. But not very far.

I pulled up in the Treister driveway, climbed out of my car, and hiked to the front door. This time a servant answered my ring. I gave him my name and asked for Carl Mendelbaum. I was told to wait, the door closed, and he went away. I spent the time admiring the trees and houses of North Broadway, always a pleasing sight. I took a deep breath of clear air. It was starting to get dark.

Mendelbaum himself opened the door.

"Mr. Weiss, what a great pleasure."

We shook hands as though we were old buddies and I followed him into the house.

"I hope," I said, "I'm not disturbing your evening?"

"Not at all."

He wore a maroon smoking jacket, white shirt, paisley ascot, gray slacks, and brown leather slippers. Somehow, he seemed taller this time. He carried himself like a man used to giving orders.

"So, Mr. Weiss," he said, a broad smile on his face. "Still looking for the elusive Miss Faust?"

"Not this time. I'm here about two of your colleagues."

"Really? Which ones?"

"Jaffee and Lipman."

"Ah, those two."

"You don't seem surprised."

"I am not," he said. "They are, I presume, up to their old tricks."

"And what would those be?"

"Come with me, please, Mr. Weiss."

I came. We went down a short hallway and into a small library. He motioned me to a chair and took a seat across from me.

"You were," he said, "paid a visit."

"So I was."

"But, of course, they did not come together."

"Right again," I told him.

He leaned toward me. "And what world-shaking news did they bring you?"

"Jaffee said your boss, Treister, may be hiding something about his past. He made it sound ominous. Though he did add there might be nothing to it. Lipman told me Jaffee was a mental case and a compulsive slanderer who can't be trusted about anything. He called Margoshes a meddler, then extended the definition to fit all scholars."

"And what do you think of these two gentlemen, Mr. Weiss?"

"A bit high-strung?"

He laughed. "You must understand, both are embittered men. Jaffee's livelihood consists of turning out unreadable vanity books in Yiddish. The fees are usually small and the clients old and disagreeable. What he does in revenge is spread insane stories about them."

"Yet apparently they keep coming."

"Who says so? Jaffee? Were it not for Kelman he would be destitute. As for Lipman, he is a ruined businessman, three times over. He blames everyone but himself for his downfall. His profession now is simply being Kelman's self-appointed protector, a mission he takes to absurd lengths."

"So if they're that bad, why didn't Mr. Treister kick them out long ago?"

"Because, my dear young man," a voice behind me

said, "they may be troublesome in some respects, but they also have many virtues, which Carl fails to recognize."

I turned my head and there was Kelman Treister standing in the doorway.

"Forgive me," he said. "I was passing and could not help but overhear."

"Kelman, come in," Mendelbaum said.

"My pleasure," he said, seating himself in an armchair near the wall. "It is good to see you again, Mr. Weiss."

Another fan. I was on a roll. He had on a black robe over a pink shirt and black slacks.

"And where is the estimable Miss Faust?" he asked.

"Being estimable elsewhere."

"Too bad," Treister said. "When Carl speaks of Jack and Isaac, you should know, Mr. Weiss, that he does so as a businessman. A brilliant one, I should add."

"Thank you, Kelman."

"For my friend Carl, it is simply inefficient to deal with such people. I, however, view the matter in a different light. These are friends. And this gives them privileges, as it were, for which others do not qualify. What does it matter to me if Isaac says wild things behind my back? How can this hurt me? And if Jack makes a nuisance of himself with others, he has never done so with me. When he berates my friends, they know it is not Jack but his troubled heart speaking. In the end what matters to me is our long-standing friendship. Over the years, as Carl can attest, it has been a great source of satisfaction to me."

Mendelbaum said, "I still do not like those two."

I said, "Jaffee told me that he hasn't been able to corroborate any of your ghetto experiences."

Treister nodded, a smile on his face. "Yes, that is one of the things he says."

"Is it true?"

"Certainly. Isaac is a historian like I am an astronaut.

Never would I ask him to do research. He would have no idea where to begin. All he does is transcribe my memoirs as I dictate them to him. But this, Mr. Weiss, is no small task. I dictate in Yiddish. And Isaac never makes a mistake."

"And for this," Mendelbaum said, "you shower him with money."

"If not I, who then? He would be a pauper were it not for the work I throw his way."

"At least he writes," Mendelbaum said. "What does the other one do to earn his money?"

"He advises me."

"In what, Kelman? What does he know? How to go bankrupt?"

"That does not matter. The advice is from an old friend. And it is in Yiddish."

"So?"

"It warms my heart, Carl," Treister said. "All my wealth cannot do that. It is simply priceless."

CHAPTER 39

Morris Weiss—1948

"You keep turning up," Gerry Sykes said, "like a bad penny."

"This," Weiss assured him, "is the last time."

"I've heard that one before. And you've brought your pals," Sykes said.

"Detective Ryan," Weiss said, "and Detective Flynn."

Ryan was slender and hatchet-faced, Flynn, square-faced and stocky. *A nice combination,* Weiss thought, *if you don't get them riled.*

The two detectives nodded amiably. Flynn produced a badge, then both men stood impassively behind Weiss as he seated himself.

"Okay," Sykes said. "I know what you want, more dirt on that crazy mission—like always. What do they want?"

"To arrest you."

Sykes laughed.

Ryan said, "We have a warrant, Mr. Sykes."

The insurance man managed a half smile. "And a screw loose. What's this about?"

Weiss said, "I'm afraid there was a small problem with the story you told me, Mr. Sykes."

"What kinda problem?"

"Well," Weiss said, "to begin with, it was all a lie."

"Obstruction of justice," Flynn said gravely.

"Just for starters," Ryan said.

Weiss thought, *It's a good thing this Sykes isn't a lawyer.* What he said was, "Thank you, gentlemen. When I first came to your office, Mr. Sykes, you thought it was for insurance business. When you learned what I wanted, it put you in a quandary."

"A what, chum?"

"A fix," Ryan said.

"A jam," Flynn said.

Weiss smiled. "I am sometimes carried away by my own eloquence. You had no idea, Mr. Sykes, how much I already knew. How could you? So you attempted to stonewall. You claimed your Yugoslav mission was classified. Colonel Minsky put a quick stop to that. No wonder you were sweating. You were now forced to improvise on the spot, to come up with a story that would cover most of the facts, but leave you blameless. You needed time, so you suggested we go out to lunch."

Sykes looked at the two detectives. "I want you guys to remember all this. He's raving."

"My friend," Weiss said, "it never made any sense for Colonel Rutledge to place a stranger in charge of his hand-picked crew. Such a move would have undermined the whole operation. What he needed was an overseer, some-one who knew precisely what was going on."

"And that someone was me?"

"Who else?"

"Go prove it."

"Fortunately," Weiss said, "that has already happened. Keller talked. To save his own skin."

"Keller? I ain't laid eyes on the guy since that day. What does he know?"

"Everything. He and the colonel were partners. And partners speak to each other. The diamonds the German brought out helped finance their smuggling operation. Keller says before the war, you were the colonel's insurance agent. That's how you knew him. And fell in with him."

"He fingered me?"

"Precisely."

"So where is the bastard?"

"In a hospital. Alive, if not exactly well. He will, however, recover. Which is more than can be said for poor Colonel Rutledge."

"What's with him?"

"He died."

Sykes eyed the three men silently. "Hey," he finally said, "I get it. You're looking for a fall guy. That's what this is all about."

"We don't need a fall guy," Ryan said. "We've got you dead to rights, Sykes."

"Play ball," Flynn said, "and we'll give you a break."

"To hell with that. I want to speak with my lawyer."

"Sure," Ryan said.

"You get one call," Flynn said. "You can make it from the station house."

Weiss rose. "I hope you have a good lawyer, Mr. Sykes," he said. *But not too good,* the detective thought to himself.

CHAPTER 40

Max and I both share a love of cars—I coming by mine belatedly. If only we could teach cars to solve our cases, we would both be retired by now.

From the casebooks of Morris Weiss

Max Weiss—The Present

The night slipped by my car windows. I was halfway back to the city and glad of it. Treister and his cronies were starting to get to me. They had all managed, miraculously, to cancel each other out. Treister couldn't care less what I said about Jaffee. And Jaffee knew he could say anything about his boss that he wanted to. Only Lipman cared, and Lipman was crazy.

I clicked on the radio. Schubert filled the car. I settled in and let Schubert keep me company. At least he was sane.

The road had emptied out. I'd chosen U.S. 50 to avoid traffic, and for once had made the right choice. I was now alone except for a couple of cars behind me.

One of them, I saw, was moving up fast. I eyed the car idly as it gained on me. It dropped back as headlights appeared from the other direction. No way to pass me. I put on a burst of speed myself. And, suddenly, the car was reduced to a slow-motion crawl.

Another minute of loose living at high revs and I let reason reassert itself and eased up on the gas pedal, slipping back into fifth.

Behind me, the car began creeping up.

Some car.

I popped open the glove compartment, reached for the Browning, and laid it down on the seat beside me.

The car pulled even with me, but declined to pass.

It was a gray Honda, just hanging there.

And the pair of guys in it were all but wearing masks. Hats pulled low. Collars turned up. Their faces in shadow. Shades of the Lone Ranger. Except I was the good guy here. I had testimonials back at the office to prove it.

Still, nothing bad had happened yet.

The guy in the passenger seat had his head turned my way. His car window began rolling down.

My hand closed over the Browning and clicked off the safety.

I saw a flicker of metal in the guy's hand. In my mind's eye I saw a small red hole smack in the center of his forehead. Then I saw one in mine. That did it. Too much imagination. I didn't wait around to see which one of us got killed.

I down-shifted, pressed hard on the gas pedal, and sailed off into the night.

Through my rearview mirror I saw the Honda fading

back. I couldn't make out the license plate, so I turned my attention to the road again.

A good thing.

A brand new SUV, headlights still blazing, had driven out and parked smack across the roadway.

I twisted the wheel, almost busted my left headlight on the SUV's flank, careened over the shoulder, and bounced down a shallow slope. Thank God it was an embankment. I braked hard and the Saab obediently skidded to a halt.

My hands were shaking as I unclipped my seat belt. I reached for the Browning. Of course, it wasn't there. I groped on the floor and found it lodged near the clutch pedal.

I tumbled out of the car, and flattened myself behind it. I was still in one piece. But not for long if I didn't get busy.

A pair of headlights from above lit up the terrain like searchlights. The Honda was parked right above me.

Bracing my arms on top of the Saab, I shot out both headlights, then put a hole through the windshield.

The hole probably did it.

The pair of guys leaped out as though their car were on fire. An instant later they were gone, part of the landscape.

I squeezed off a couple of rounds in their general direction. It was just for show. I couldn't see them. But they knew exactly where I was. Right here, crouching behind my car, waiting for them to creep up and shoot me. And where was the SUV driver? Did he have any company along for the ride?

The hell with this.

I crawled down the embankment, away from the Saab, using shrubs, trees, and bushes to hide me.

I turned to my right, keeping low to the ground. Stones, roots, branches, and lots of earth got in my way.

Who were they? I wondered. The stick-up guys from Treister's party? The bunch chasing after Kanufsky? The guys Margoshes was running from? Or maybe the whole lot of them together, with me as their intended new victim.

I pulled up behind a tree. Enough crawling around. To find me they'd have to move, too.

I waited.

Presently, sounds reached me. An animal creeping through the underbrush? Or something more promising?

The sounds came from my left.

Very quietly I began inching toward them. I tried to make no noise at all. My early years as a Boy Scout must have paid off. I saw him—a dark shape bent double—before he saw me. He was making such a racket getting through the underbrush that he hadn't a clue I was anywhere near him till I stuck my Browning up against his temple.

"Shhhhh," I whispered in his ear.

Shhhhh it was. I took the gun from his unresisting fingers.

"How many are you?" I whispered.

"Five."

That was four too many.

"Who are you?"

"Hired help."

Right. "Who hired you?"

"Guy called Chuck."

"Big blond guy?"

"Yeah, that's him."

"What were you supposed to do?"

"You don't want to know."

"For how much?"

"Three hundred apiece."

"Cheap."

"Look, it's nothin' personal. Gimme a break, mister, I got a wife and kids."

"Sure. Don't worry. Just yell, 'I got him, he's here.' "

"You crazy?"

"Go on, do it."

He shrugged.

And did it.

I smashed my gun barrel over his head. He went down. And out of the game.

Flashlights lit up the terrain above me and began moving down toward me.

I got out of there as they grew closer. I crawled uphill as fast as I could, giving the lights a wide berth.

A short guy was standing near my Saab. No gun was visible in his hand. I stepped over and showed him mine.

"Raise 'em," I whispered.

He raised 'em.

No heroes on this job, I was glad to see. I patted him down. And came up with two knives and a short length of pipe taped over on one end.

They went into my pocket.

"Who's in the SUV?" I whispered.

"No one."

I took hold of his shoulder and gave him a good hard shove. He went sprawling downhill.

I dived into my car, twisted the ignition key, and stepped on the gas pedal. The Saab came alive. I backed up, taking half the shrubbery with me. Lights were now waving in my direction from below.

I heard shots as I hit the highway.

I stopped just long enough to put a few rounds into the front tires of the Honda and SUV.

Then I peeled off into the night, still in one piece. Uncle Morris, it seems, had raised an apt pupil.

CHAPTER 41

Morris Weiss—1948

Morris Weiss called Fineberg.

"It's done," he said.

"You have cleared Joey?"

"Of this crime, at least."

"Thank you, Morris."

"Thank you, Fineberg."

"For what?"

"For the big check you will send me."

"It is that big?"

"Bigger."

"Why?"

"Why not? I risked my life for this Joey. I admit, cash is a meager reward for such services," Morris Weiss said. "But in this case it will have to do."

CHAPTER 42

Expect many surprises in the detective business, some of them unpleasant. When the surprises turn out, after all, to be nice ones, it does not mean that the detective has done everything right, merely that he has been very lucky.

From the casebooks of Morris Weiss

Max Weiss—The Present

The alarm clock jolted me awake.

I managed to crawl out of bed, an effort that would have won an award if only the judges had been around to see it. I stumbled into my bathroom. Some twenty minutes later, shaved, showered, and reasonably alert, I grabbed a quick bite and went over my current agenda. Find Margoshes, find Kanufsky, and call Laura. And

maybe, while I was at it, find out who killed Leonard
Halkin, just in case it had anything to do with the other two
guys, but mainly because it seemed the right thing to do. It
also wouldn't hurt to find out who had run me off the road
last night, and why. Just in case they decided to have another go at it.

I put on a black turtleneck sweater, charcoal-gray
slacks, strapped on my holster, stuck my gun into it, and
was almost ready.

I looked up Leonard Halkin's number in the phone
book, slid into my gray sports coat, locked up my apartment, and went to reclaim my Saab at the corner garage.

It was a short ride to West End Avenue and Ninety-
ninth Street.

Finding a parking spot was something else again. It
took longer than the ride itself, which gave some thoughts
time to rattle through my head.

Halkin had been Margoshes's guy Friday, privy to
whatever the Foundation archives contained. Even more
so when he took over the job as chief archivist. And since
Kelman Treister's personal papers, now residing at Skidmore, seemed to be of special interest to Margoshes, I
should probably find out why.

I finally parked on Riverside Drive and 102nd Street
only because some lady was pulling out as I cruised by.

Hiking back to Halkin's building, I again mulled over
his death. Had he been killed because of a gunman's itchy
finger? Or because he knew something about the archives
that someone wanted kept under wraps?

Then there were the guys who'd gone after me on the
highway. Why bother? Unless Treister, Margoshes, and
Halkin were somehow all tied together and I was coming
close to untying the knot.

A uniformed doorman greeted me in the lobby of

Halkin's building. I gave him Mrs. Halkin's name along with mine.

The doorman used the intercom, said a few words into it, and told me, "8A."

I took the elevator up, glad that I'd left my jeans and T-shirt in the closet and had come suitably attired in jacket and overcoat for meeting a recent widow. Weiss and Weiss had its standards.

I walked down a short hallway and pressed the 8A buzzer.

I waited, heard footsteps from inside, heard the click of a lock. The door opened.

Laura Faust stood in the doorway.

She was wearing a pale green suit, white, frilly-collared blouse, and brown suede pumps. Her red hair was tied back in a businesslike bun.

"Beaten to the punch again," I said, after getting over the shock, "by the power of the press."

"Actually," she said, "I'm a private eye. Just like you."

"Not just like me," I said. "You're prettier."

"You figured it out?"

"I was getting ready to."

"Come in, Sherlock."

She turned and I followed her through the doorway and into a darkened living room. The heavy purple drapes were drawn and only one table lamp was lit. A short, slightly plump, round-shouldered woman in her early forties sat on a yellow sofa, dabbing at her eyes with a tissue. She had on a simple brown dress and fuzzy pink slippers.

"Mrs. Halkin," Laura said, "this is my colleague, Max Weiss."

Mrs. Halkin looked up. "Weiss? Max Weiss? You are the Weiss who phoned my husband?"

"I am," I said, offering her my hand.

"Assassin!" she screamed, half rising. "Murderer!"

I withdrew the offer of my hand. It seemed the wise thing to do.

She sank back onto the sofa, buried her face in her hands, and began weeping.

I stood there, wishing I were somewhere else—almost anywhere else would do just fine.

Laura moved to the woman's side, embraced her, started murmuring and making cooing sounds. I hoped the cooing sounds would somehow exonerate me, but I had my doubts.

Her sobs finally subsided. She wiped her eyes and blew her nose. She looked up at me. I braced myself for another storm, but she surprised me.

"I know you are not responsible," she said. "I know. Forgive me, please. He is completely to blame. It is his fault entirely, not yours."

"Whose?" I asked, truly stumped.

"Leonard," she said, "my husband. I begged him. But he would not change his mind. Now see what has happened."

"Begged him?"

"Not to go to those people."

"What people?"

"There, where you were, the place with the racehorses. He went to see them. He said it would make us rich. I told him I did not want it—"

"He give you any names, Mrs. Halkin?"

She let out one loud sob, shook her head.

"Do you know how he planned to get this money?"

"He knew things," she said. "He had found out about them. Things they wanted no one to know."

"What things?"

She shrugged.

"He never told me," she said.

"That's it?" I asked.

"Yes," she said. "You now know everything I know. Everything. Which is nothing. Only that my husband is dead."

She spread her arms in a gesture of utter defeat.

I opened my mouth to ask another question. Then closed it.

Laura and I exchanged glances.

I nodded.

Laura gave the widow her hand, told her we had taken up enough of her time, and again offered her our condolences. I muttered something suitable. We headed for the door, the widow still glued to her sofa.

"No kids?" I said in the hallway.

"One, a daughter in her first year of college," Laura said. "She's flying in from Berkeley."

The elevator came, carrying a stout woman and a little girl having an argument. We tabled our discussion. The little girl was winning when we reached the lobby.

We went out on the street and Laura turned to me. "I think we should talk."

"I think what you think," I said. "I know a place."

The Key West Diner was only a few blocks away on Broadway. That's where we went.

I ordered a bowl of chicken soup with noodles, a burger medium rare, home fries, and coleslaw. Laura had the Caesar salad with grilled chicken.

She took a few forkfuls of chicken, then said, "Guess what case I'm on."

"There's more than one?" I said.

I finished my burger, signaled the waiter, and ordered blueberry pie with vanilla ice cream and coffee. Laura was still working on her salad, but asked for the same. It's irresistible.

"So who's the lucky client?" I asked.

She fixed me with her luminous green eyes. "Dr. Margoshes."

Dessert came but I let it stand.

I said, "He hired you to find himself?"

"He wasn't lost."

I reached for dessert and followed it up with coffee, hoping my morning cups were out of my system by now. I raised my cup to Laura. It looked as if I'd have a favorable report for my client April, after all.

"What did Margoshes want?" I asked.

"Proof that Kelman Treister had worked for the Nazis."

I whistled. "Jaffee, his biographer," I told her, "hinted that something might be wrong."

"Margoshes suspected the same thing," she said.

"Find anything?" I asked.

"Nothing conclusive," she said, and started in on her dessert.

I said, "You could have told me all this in Saratoga Springs."

"No, I couldn't."

I nodded. She was right. Not without her client's say-so.

"You asked him?"

"Of course. He wouldn't hear of it. He is a very stubborn man."

"So I've heard."

"My client felt he might be in danger. He hired me to keep looking, and made himself scarce. No one knew his plans, not even his friends. He didn't want them to become possible victims."

"Very thoughtful of him. I gather he finally gave you the go-ahead about telling me all, or we wouldn't be having this chat now."

"Not quite."

"How's that?" I said.

"Dr. Margoshes vanished out of his hotel room two days ago. Under the circumstances, Max, I don't think he'd object very much to our working together."

"Not very much," I agreed.

CHAPTER 43

Morris, what are you doing here?
Helping you solve this case, Max, what else?

Max and Morris Weiss—The Present

I parked in a garage in Tribeca.

Then Laura and I spent twenty minutes on foot looking for Boris Minsky in his favorite haunts, all to no avail. I used my cell phone on the off chance he might be at home. Perish the thought.

"Guy has a way of disappearing," I told Laura.

We hit Hudson Street where the Weiss and Weiss agency hangs out, entered the lobby, and rang for the elevator.

"Maybe he left a note," I said hopefully.

"What was he working on?"

"This Kanufsky business I was telling you about."

We'd filled each other in on developments of our now mutual case on the way down here.

"All we have to do," I said, "is find Kanufsky and get him talking."

"According to you," she said, "that didn't work too well the last time you tried it."

"This time I've got a foolproof plan."

"What's that?" she said.

"You just bat an eyelash at him," I said. "He'll sing like a jaybird."

She smiled.

"You say the sweetest things," she said.

The elevator came and carried us up to the third floor.

The smell of coffee from somewhere invitingly trailed after us as we went down the hallway. The door to my office was slightly ajar. I reached for my Browning before pushing it open.

"Don't shoot, dear boy," Boris Minsky said. "You will find no one who works as cheaply as I."

He had on a double-breasted, tan chalk-striped suit, pale-green and yellow speckled tie, white shirt, and a boutonniere in his lapel. His black hair was, as always, parted dead center down the middle. He was seated at my desk, his eyes, behind thick black-rimmed glasses, gazing up at me placidly.

I was amazed.

The guy almost always worked out of his home.

"What are you doing here, Boris?" I asked.

"I came to write you a memorandum," he told me. "But it was so cozy I decided to stay."

I put my Browning away, ushered Laura into the office and introduced her to Minsky.

"She's a colleague," I said.

He rose, leaned across the desk, and took her hand in his. "It is a great pleasure to meet a colleague of such beauty."

"Why thank you, Boris. I've heard so much about you," Laura said, smiling.

Minsky reseated himself. "Pay no attention to that, my dear. Maxwell tends to exaggerate my failings and ignore my virtues, such as they are. It is deplorable, but I have learned to live with it." He beamed at me. "It is his only fault."

"Thanks, Boris," I said. "I like you, too."

"You are a nice boy, Maxwell."

Minsky made as though to evacuate my chair. I waved him back.

"Relax," I said. "We're only here for your Kanufsky report."

"It was the subject of my memorandum."

I pulled up two client chairs from against the wall and Laura and I made ourselves comfortable.

"Fire away," I said.

"Your Mr. Kanufsky hardly presented an insurmountable problem, Maxwell."

"Then you made progress?"

"I found him."

"You did?" Laura said, her voice full of admiration. I could see these two were going to get on famously.

Minsky nodded. "I canvassed his block and interviewed as many neighbors as were available."

He leaned back in the desk chair and made a steeple of his fingers.

"The area," he said, "as you know, has undergone numerous changes through the years. The Jews, as a rule, have departed. But Mr. Kanufsky and his sister chose otherwise. No one knows their present whereabouts. Indeed, few know them at all. My search there proved fruitless."

"But you weren't beaten," Laura said. A few more like her and Minsky would be taking over the agency.

He smiled. "Far from it. I have been in this business too long, my dear, to be deterred by minor stumbling blocks. It occurred to me that Mr. Kanufsky's former business, his fruit and vegetable store, was located on East Houston Street, only a few blocks from his domicile. Their proximity to one another suggested a visit was in order. I went down to the site of his former store and made inquiries. Mr. Kanufsky, I learned, had not only owned his own store, but the entire building as well. In fact, he still does."

That surprised me.

"I thought the guy was living on Social Security," I said, "and barely making ends meet."

"He is better off than that, Maxwell. The building on Houston Street, however, is an ancient relic. An elderly resident informed me that Mr. Kanufsky bought it dirt cheap many years ago. He never made the necessary repairs, and the city rent control board ruled he could not raise rents until he did so. Despite that, every apartment is taken, but for a loft on the fifth floor. He used it for storage. But according to the gentleman who acquired the store from him, Mr. Kanufsky has recently returned to it, both he and his sister. It appears they rarely venture out, and then only to purchase food downstairs. No doubt he is at this very moment ensconced there." Minsky smiled. "I trust this was the information you sought, Maxwell?"

"I'll say. You've done a great job, Boris."

Laura nodded. "Very impressive."

"Thank you both. I am sure your thanks, Maxwell, will be reflected in a generous bonus."

"Count on it."

"Then I shall repair for lunch with a light heart," Boris said. "I wish you both success in your encounter with Mr. Kanufsky."

* * *

Laura and I drove past Orchard Street, the onetime bargain mecca of the Lower East Side. On the corner was
Katz's Delicatessen, where the tireless Uncle Morris used
to pounce on errant husbands. We drove on for another
five blocks.

"Over on the left, Max."

"I see it."

It was a weathered five-story building, indistinguish-
able from the other tenements that filled the block, except for the mom-and-pop fruit and vegetable store on its
ground floor. Middle-class housing projects hovered in
the distance, but time seemed to have bypassed this street.
It took ten minutes to find a parking spot, and another five
to walk back to the tenement.

I used a lock pick. It worked even faster than a key,
and made our visit a true surprise before Kanufsky could
find some convenient place to hide.

We entered a short hallway. Gray paint had chipped
off the walls. Rap music filtered down to us from somewhere above, mixed with traffic noise from outdoors.

We hit the top floor and headed for the rear of the house.

The doorbell was out of whack. It would be. I used my
knuckles.

A resounding silence followed.

I pounded again with the same useless results.

I raised my voice.

"It's Max Weiss, Mr. Kanufsky," I yelled. "Open up,
we've got to talk."

Silence.

If he was in there, my argument hadn't impressed him.

"Look," I said to the door, "if I could find you, so can
they. You're in trouble here, Mr. Kanufsky, you and your
sister. Let me help you."

Laura and I exchanged glances. The magic words, "Let me help you," had worked wonders with his sister when I went calling on her that first time.

We waited.

I was beginning to think I'd misjudged my man or he really wasn't home when a lock clicked, then another, then a third. This guy was taking no chances. Unless you counted hiding out in your own building as taking a chance.

The door opened an inch. A nose and one eye showed through the crack.

"Why have you come here? You have put us in terrible danger."

"You weren't listening, Mr. Kanufsky. You're easy to find."

"Of course you found me. You are a trained investigator."

"Don't kid yourself. Anyone can do it."

"He's right," Laura said.

Kanufsky turned and gasped. "Who is this? What have you done?"

"Cool it," I told him, trying to keep the irritation out of my voice. "We're all on the same side here."

"Please, Mr. Kanufsky," Laura said, "open the door. Dr. Margoshes would want us to work together."

"Dr. Margoshes? How do you know this?"

"I saw him last week," Laura said.

"You saw him?"

"He hired me."

"For what?"

"To investigate Kelman Treister."

"You are a detective, too?"

"One of the best," I assured him.

Kanufsky hesitated, then opened the door, leaving just enough room for us to push by him. Quickly, he shut it again and snapped all three locks into place.

We were in a damp loft. The floor was bare, the walls made of brick. The place still looked like the storage area it had once been. Junk was piled everywhere: old furniture, clothing, pillows, blankets. Light came from two windows in the rear and a floor lamp by the wall. Still, everything here seemed dark and uninviting. Probably because it was.

Kanufsky addressed Laura.

"Where is he, Dr. Margoshes? You must tell me."

"I wish I knew," she said.

"But you met with him." He turned to me. "Did she not say so?"

"I did," Laura said. "We were supposed to see each other again."

"And?" The little man was almost jumping up and down with impatience.

"He didn't show up the second time," Laura said.

"How is this possible, Mr. Weiss? She says he hired her."

"He has a habit," I said, "of taking off without notice."

"When did this happen?" he demanded of Laura.

"Yesterday."

"Where?"

She gave him the name of a midtown hotel.

Kanufsky wrung his hands. "It is the same story all over again. With me it was last week. I was to meet him in a boardinghouse on West Twenty-fourth Street. But he was gone when I arrived there. It is a catastrophe. Mr. Weiss, the evil ones seek me. You have seen their work. Without Dr. Margoshes, I have nowhere to turn. What is to become of me?"

"Everything's going to be fine," I told him, taking him by the arm and gently steering him toward the table and chairs near the center of the loft. I sat him down. Laura and I took chairs across from him.

I smiled reassuringly.

"It's okay," I said. "You're in good hands now."

He nodded uncertainly.

"Your sister still with you?" I asked.

"How else can it be? I have dragged her into this. She is a helpless victim. They will hurt her to get at me."

"We won't let them," Laura said.

"Just where," I asked, "is she now?"

"Downstairs shopping. We must still eat, must we not?"

"When she returns," I said, "we're getting you both out of here."

"To a safe place," Laura added.

"Now," I said, "what's all this about?"

"Kelman Treister. What else should it be about?"

"Almost anything, considering the runaround you've given us."

"What could I do? I would gladly have come forward sooner, but I was sworn to secrecy. I gave my word to Dr. Margoshes. He told me, 'Run like the wind if you are asked a single question.' Now you see?"

"Not quite," I said.

"I will tell you everything. Listen. In Europe, after the war, I met a man. His name was Rudolph Fisher and he was a waiter. This man told me a story. It was, you understand, just talk to pass the time in a railway station. Mr. Fisher was working at the Grand Hotel in Geneva, Switzerland, when the war broke out. He stayed there. In Geneva he was safe and making a good living besides. No one even knew he was a Jew.

"During the war the city was full of German officers out of uniform, businessmen, vacationers. And of course, spies. Many spies. One table in the hotel dining room was only for the Germans.

"One day, Fisher saw a young man at this table he had

never seen before. He was maybe seventeen or eighteen.
Fisher was stunned. He looked Jewish. How could this be?
The German table was full of Nazis. Among themselves
the waiters called this 'the spy table.' Fisher looked and
listened. He learned the boy's name was Helmut Liedke, a
good German name. But this also could not be. The few
times the boy spoke, it was in broken German with a Yiddish accent. Fisher made it his business to stay close to
this table as much as he could. He felt he must solve the
riddle. But he never did. By keeping his ears open, however, he found that the young man was sometimes called
by another name as well, a Jewish one. It was Kelman
Treister."

Laura asked, "You kept in touch with Mr. Fisher?"

"No, I never saw him again. What happened was this.
His story was so strange that I myself began repeating it
over the years. A month before I got my visa to America,
I was sitting in a Paris café with my dear friend Alex
Bloom. I mentioned the story again. This time Alex looked
strangely at me. He had seen the name Kelman Treister in
a newspaper only the week before. He called me that night.
Treister, that devil, had bought a bottling plant."

"Why do you call him a devil?" Laura asked.

"I call him worse," Kanufsky said. "He was there with
the Germans at their table. And now, only ten years later,
he is rich enough to buy plants. How does one explain
that?

"I sailed to America. And from time to time I saw stories about this man in the newspapers. He had made millions. There were stories in magazines about how he had
been in the Warsaw Ghetto. Then how could he have been
in Geneva at the same time? I ask you?"

"The same time?" I said.

Kanufsky squirmed. "The waiter was not so sure of the
time. All right. But my friend Alex made a study of this

man. He collected facts about him, sought out people who should have been where he was in the ghetto. But did they know him? Never. Kelman Treister is the man who wasn't there. You understand now?"

My understanding was somewhat remiss. "No one else asked any questions about this guy?"

"Who would ask? Why should they? He is a hero. He gives money with both hands."

"So," Laura said, "the issue never came up."

"Never."

She said "There were books written about him."

"And?"

"Fighters in the ghetto spoke of his courage."

"Liars."

"Why would they lie, Mr. Kanufsky?"

"Money."

"They were all bribed?" I asked.

"All, Mr. Weiss? Did you read any of the books about Kelman Treister?"

"No," I said.

"Actually," Laura said, "I did."

"So, you tell me, Miss Faust, how many of these witnesses were there? You maybe kept count?"

"There seemed to be many."

Kanufsky grinned. "Not so many as you think. Maybe eight. Other testimony comes only from diaries."

"What's wrong with that?"

"Forgeries."

"You know that for a fact?" she asked.

"*His* people found them. The writers were long dead. Who could say by this time that these were false writings?"

"Mr. Kanufsky," Laura said, "a war was going on. Six million Jews perished. Eight witnesses is a lot."

"Not these. Some were plain criminals. Others could

not have been where they said they were. A few were in
the right place at the right time. They lied."

"How do you know?"

He laughed bitterly. "Suddenly, they are all rich men."

"No women?" Laura asked.

"Two. They are also rich now. Vouching for Kelman
Treister is good business."

I said, "You've kept track, I see."

"No, Alex did. It was he who begged me to see Dr.
Margoshes. So I made an appointment. I went to his office and told him what I have told you. He is a good man.
He paid attention to my every word. He took notes, too.
When I was finished, he shook my hand warmly and said
I had just done a very important thing. He promised to
contact me. He said we looked so much alike we could
have been brothers. But weeks went by and I heard nothing. I had almost given up hope when suddenly he called.
He asked if it were possible for Alex to microfilm the evidence and send it to me."

"Not him?"

"No, to me."

"Why?"

"I have no idea, Mr. Weiss. Is it important?"

"Yeah, it's important." I turned to Laura. "Are you
thinking what I am? Margoshes thought his house might
be watched. And if the package showed up at the Foundation, he was worried that someone would tip Treister."

"A spy," Laura said.

"A spy," I said. "And it couldn't be just anyone in the
building either. It had to be someone who could search
through Margoshes's files and mail without attracting attention and know what he was looking at."

"Leonard Halkin!" Laura exclaimed.

"Sure, the assistant archivist. No one would think

twice about him digging through the files or opening the mail. It was part of his job."

Kanufsky sat looking confused. "Just a second more," I told him. To Laura I said, "Treister must have gotten to Halkin when they were both at Skidmore setting up his archives. He needed an inside man at the Foundation, which houses the biggest collection of Holocaust material. It would be the logical place to check out information about him. But Halkin got greedy. He must've overheard some of the conversation between Kanufsky and Margoshes. He decided to put the squeeze on his new meal ticket and turn up at the party with me at his side to prove that he meant business. He called ahead. That was a mistake. Treister was ready for him. He staged a phony stickup with his spy as the intended casualty. In the last minute, Halkin saw it coming, heard our voices, and called out for help."

"Plausible," Laura said.

"Even to me," Kanufsky said. "And I do not even know who this Halkin is."

"Thanks. On with your story, Mr. Kanufsky."

"The microfilm came."

"And you called Dr. Margoshes," Laura said.

"Immediately. But he was no longer at the Foundation. I was bewildered."

"You tried his home number, of course?" she said.

"Of course. I found it in the phone book. But it was disconnected. I ran to his apartment. He had moved out."

"Sounds like our boy," I said.

"I returned home," Kanufsky said. "I did not even open the package. What could I do with this microfilm?"

"Give it to the press?" Laura said.

"This was for Dr. Margoshes to decide. I knew he would contact me. How could he forget me? I was right. A letter came three days later. It contained cash. Dr. Margoshes told me to hide. He left a number where I should call every Wednesday at three. If he was not there, I must call the next Wednesday. But I refused to hide. Why should I? Who knew I even had this thing?"

"So how did you end up at Mannerdale?" I asked.

"My mind, Mr. Weiss, was changed for me. You see, they killed my friend Alex. He was hit by a car in mid-afternoon while crossing the street. His wife called me with the terrible news. I was shattered. The same day his files were stolen. I called Dr. Margoshes's number. There was an answering machine. I told him what I planned to do. Then I ran. I have been running since. Mannerdale was already known to me. Dr. Margoshes told me about it. He had found it for just such an eventuality. So I went there. Of course, I took with me the microfilm. How could I leave it behind?

"The next morning," Kanufsky said, "I left Mannerdale. I did not take Alex's package with me. It was safer where it was. I came back for it one night, but the devils were there, as somehow were you, Mr. Weiss. You fought them, and I was able to escape with my package. I will always be grateful."

"All in a day's work," I said modestly.

"Again I ran. I found refuge in an awful house by the Brooklyn Bridge, where a friend of mine had once lived. Somehow they found me there, too. I heard them coming and jumped out a window. I had become expert at this. But now I truly had nowhere left to run. So finally I took my sister and I came here. Until a half-hour ago when you knocked on my door I felt I was safe."

"You'll be okay from now on," I said. "Pack some things to take with you."

"The microfilm, too?"

"Especially the microfilm."

Kanufsky left us.

"Where," Laura asked, "are we going to take him?"

"We'll put him with the cronies."

"Yours?"

"My uncle's. He's got friends all over town. And they're the right age for this guy, too."

Soon Kanufsky returned to the table with two bags, one filled with personal items, the other the red bag I'd seen at Mannerdale.

"We'll have you back in circulation in no time," I told him. "Once this goes public, you'll be off the hook."

"It would be a great relief."

We sat and waited for the sister to arrive. Kanufsky told us more about his life. How he had been parted from Stella just before the war, and how they had found each other years later.

It took some while before we heard fumbling at the door.

"She is here at last," Kanufsky said, jumping to his feet.

Keys clicked in the locks three times.

The door opened.

Stella Kanufsky stood in the doorway. No shopping bags stuffed with groceries were visible. But something else was. The blond ape I'd knocked cold at Treister's party stood right behind her, his left arm wound tightly around her neck, his right hand holding a gun, its muzzle pressed against her temple.

Two more guys were visible right behind them. That made it three guys too many.

Kanufsky screamed.

I almost screamed myself.

Reflexes took over. I was halfway out of my chair and groping for my Browning before it occurred to me I was going to get us all killed.

I froze.

"Good boy, smartass," the blond bozo said. "Stay smart and maybe I let you live."

I stayed smart. Though I wasn't too crazy about the maybe part. I wasn't ready to toss in the towel just yet. Laura's hand was only inches away from her purse. I knew what she had in there. My own gun was still stuck in my shoulder holster. To bring it out, before it got taken away from me, I needed Kanufsky's help.

They came in together, the two guys, their guns out, bringing up the rear, the sister in front, still in the blond guy's stranglehold. Her face was turning a bight red. She was making small gagging noises.

Kanufsky jumped to his feet. "Fiends!" he screamed.

"Shut up," the guy told him. "Where's the film?"

"Never!" Kanufsky screamed.

The ape tightened his hold on the sister. Her eyes began to bug out. "She dies. Then we find it anyway. You call it."

Kanufsky tried to run to his sister's defense, a true sign of dementia. I grabbed him by a scrawny arm, jerked him to me. I could almost hear the beating of his heart.

"It's here on the table," I said. "In the red bag."

"Aieeee!" Kanufsky screamed.

Three pairs of eyes darted toward the red bag.

Kanufsky tried to squirm loose. I held him back. "Let me go!" he screamed.

"They'll kill you," I yelled at him. And with his body shielding mine, I pulled the Browning out from under my half-open jacket.

The ape shoved the sister aside. She fell to the floor, gasping. Gun in hand, he trotted to the table and reached out for the bag.

Behind them a figure quietly stepped through the doorway.

He wore an open tan trench coat and brown fedora. Under the coat he had on a pair of charcoal-gray slacks, a dark-blue jacket, light-blue shirt, and paisley tie.

A Browning Hi-Powered automatic was in his hand.

"Drop your guns," he said, raising his voice only slightly.

The ape turned fast, open bag in one hand, gun in the other.

The man in the doorway shot him twice.

Then, in one swift motion, he was back in the hallway out of the line of fire.

The other two guys got off one shot apiece before Laura and I cut them down.

The white-haired man gingerly stepped back into the loft. He covered the three downed men as Laura and I scooped up their hardware.

"Are you two all right?" my uncle Morris asked.

"Much better," I said, "than a minute ago."

"We need to get help for these men quickly," Laura said.

"Absolutely," Uncle Morris said.

He whipped out a cell phone from a coat pocket, punched in a number. "Captain Mike O'Toole, please," he said. "Tell him it's Morris Weiss, his father's friend. We have an emergency here."

"Uncle," I began.

He smiled. "It is perfectly simple. Boris called me. I flew in yesterday."

"Why?"

"He remembered your Kelman Treister from our case in '48. He thought I would be interested."

"But how did you find us here?"

"I have been following you all day. These men, I saw, were following you, too. So I ended up following them. It was, as they say, a merry chase. But here I am."

He smiled broadly.

"Now, if you will introduce me to this young lady," he said. "She is not only beautiful, but an excellent shot."

CHAPTER 44

After you, my dear Morris.
No, no, after you, my dear Max.

Max and Morris Weiss—The Present

It was a four-story limestone town house in the Gramercy Park district. The name on the bell read Kelman Treister.

I rang the bell and Laura, Uncle Morris, and I waited a long moment.

The door opened and a short, bald-headed man in a black jacket and trousers was standing before us.

"We're here," Laura said, "to see Mr. Treister."

"He is expecting you?"

Laura gave him her name. She added, "I called a half-hour ago." Which was a few seconds after I called Saratoga Springs and learned that Treister was back in New York.

Because the butler remembered that I had rescued his boss from the bad guys, I was given Treister's unlisted city number.

"And these gentlemen?"

"My associates."

"This way, please."

We stepped inside.

"Your coats?"

"We'll hang on to them," I said.

He showed us to an elevator and we rode up to the second floor, where a maid was waiting for us. We followed her into a softly lit book-lined study. The dark parquet floor gleamed except where it was covered by an ornate cream-and-blue silk oriental carpet. Chagall, Modigliani, and Matisse paintings gazed serenely from the walls. Mahogany Sheraton chairs, a matching desk, and a pair of leather Beiedermeir sofas were also on display.

Along with Kelman Treister.

Our host was dressed in a trim black pinstriped suit and dark-blue tie, and looked like someone in a glossy fashion ad. He broke the pose by rising. His smile dimmed only a fraction when he saw who Laura's company was.

"Ah," he said, "the detective."

"Not just the detective," Laura said, beaming as though she were bringing him a very rare gift, "but his uncle Morris, as well."

"His uncle?"

"Mr. Weiss is also a detective," she said. "Together they are the Weiss and Weiss Detective Agency."

"I see," Treister said, sounding as if he saw nothing.

He stepped forward and dutifully shook hands with us all, lingering longest to peer at my uncle. Then, turning, he strode to the long, narrow desk behind the sofa and seated himself. The rest of us pulled up armchairs facing him, my uncle directly in front, Laura and I over to the side. The red bag was on my lap.

Uncle Morris said, "You don't recognize me?"

"You do look familiar," Treister said. "We have done business together?"

"Big business."

Treister examined him. "You must help me out."

"Of course. You remember Opta?"

"Opta?"

"Yes, the import-export company. This was in the forties. You were vice president. I never learned exactly what you really imported." My uncle paused. "Drugs, wasn't it?"

Treister turned white. "What are you saying?"

"I am saying that drugs were Opta's main business."

"I don't know where you heard this, but it is a lie."

"You still do not remember me, eh? You killed a man that day. I was with you."

Treister stared, wide-eyed. "*You* are that young detective?"

Uncle Weiss smiled. "The same."

"I am so very glad to see you again."

"Thank you."

"But I know nothing about drugs."

"I will remind you. The man you shot was a former army officer, a Colonel Milton Rutledge. But there, at Opta, he used another name—Mr. Bert. It was this clever fellow who did the smuggling—he, and his good friend Gordon Keller."

Treister looked aghast.

"During the last days of the war," Uncle Morris continued, "the colonel, an army intelligence officer, arranged for the defection of a high-ranking German officer. No one suspected that before the war this von Richtler had been a professional crook, a smuggler, and that one of his

American buyers was none other than our good colonel. The colonel and the German met secretly. The German told his friend how they could become very rich. He had confiscated enough diamonds during the occupation to set them up in a fine business—peddling dope."

"I know nothing of this."

"Of course. This dope business," my uncle said, "was only step one to great wealth. Other steps would follow. But if their scheme was to succeed they had to move quickly. Once the war was over there would be plenty of competition."

"Why are you telling me this?"

Uncle Morris raised a hand. "Wait. This pair needed new identities. Also, they needed a figurehead to run the legitimate end of their business. Von Richtler had just the man. He and some fellow officers had already been grooming him as a front for the diamonds. But this was better. His name was Kelman Treister."

Treister stared at him. It was quiet for a moment.

"You are insane," he said evenly.

"But then so are others," Laura said calmly. "Dr. Felix Margoshes, for one."

"Margoshes? He never said a word about this," Treister said, visibly more agitated. "Not a word! You are making it all up!"

"Dr. Margoshes," Laura said, "knew enough about you to go into hiding. He feared for his life. He hired me to uncover the truth."

"He hired a magazine writer?"

"A private detective," Laura said.

"And today," I said, "Margoshes is still alive. A man in Paris named Bloom wasn't so lucky. He made you his hobby. Now he's dead."

"You can't be serious," Treister said. "This is some kind of joke."

I raised the red bag in both hands, and shook it. "Here is your joke."

"What is that?"

"Evidence—where you actually spent the war years. Not in the ghetto. But under Nazi protection, first in Warsaw, then in Switzerland. We have witnesses."

"What witnesses? What are you talking about? For every one of yours, there will be ten of mine. And mine will be telling the truth. You have nothing."

Uncle Morris said, "There is more."

"What more?"

"Von Richtler disappeared," Uncle Morris said, "and was based in Europe after the war. He was well-known because of his war exploits, not to mention a prewar police record. So when you killed the colonel you thought you were free—"

"I saved your life!"

Uncle Morris smiled thinly. "At the time I was sure he was shooting at me. Now I'm not so sure. I think the sight of us together convinced him he was being double-crossed. It was you, Treister, he wanted to kill.

"Now the colonel was gone," my uncle continued. "Janner, the so-called president of Opta, was one of them, but took his orders from the colonel. He could be handled. The other stockholders were former Nazis, now businessmen, living in Germany and Switzerland. The sale of dope was winding down at Opta. It was becoming a legitimate business. The Germans received their profits through stock dividends. You were finally free to run the company as you saw fit. Then something unexpected happened. Von Richtler sent his son over here. And the son took over where the colonel left off."

"What son? There was never any son."

"No? Boris Minsky, our colleague, looked up three of your associates when Max was in Saratoga Springs.

Along with biographies he also found photographs. Boris has a photographic memory and recognized one of the men. In our files he found an old snapshot. Our friend Rutledge and his henchman Keller, are seated in a Paris bistro. In the background a man is walking toward them. Through all these years this man meant nothing to me, or to Boris. But Boris never forgets a face." Uncle Morris reached into his jacket pocket. "Here is the enlargement." He tossed it on the desk. "You know this man?"

Treister studied the snapshot. "He looks like Carl Mendelbaum."

"But he is not. This shot was taken in 1945. The man in the snapshot is Ludwig von Richtler—Mendelbaum's father."

Kelman Treister gave Uncle Morris a long look. For a moment there was dead silence. Then Treister shrugged, and settled back in his chair. "Very well, you are right. I was in the ghetto for less than two months. A group of German officers chose me to be their front man, as they say. They trained me. So what? Most of them are dead now. Their diamonds helped start me on my way, that is true. But I had no part in any illicit drug trade. That was *their* doing. And it ended with the death of Colonel Rutledge. *I* ran the Kelman Treister Industries, not the officers. What did they know about business? I took to it like a fish to water. I made millions. And with this money I helped Jews the world over. What is wrong with that?"

"The problem," I said, "is that it's just half the story."

"You mean the Germans? Yes, they became wealthy. But that was merely a drop in the bucket. Hundreds of thousands profited because of my industries."

"That's not exactly what I meant."

"Then what are you talking about?"

"The robbery I interrupted was a fake."

"A fake?"

"Yes. Its real purpose was to get rid of Halkin. He'd found out about you—"

Treister stared at me.

"You sent your goons after Kanufsky, too," I said. "He had the goods on you. So he had to die. Along with Bloom in Paris."

"Get out!" Treister yelled. "Get out! Before I call the police!"

"I'll call them for you," I said.

"I think not," a voice from behind me said.

I turned my head. Carl Mendelbaum, in white jacket and bow tie, stood in the doorway, a black Glock in his hand. Beside him stood the short, bald-headed butler. The little man had a long-barreled pump-action shotgun trained in our direction. He looked quite calm and efficient.

"Do I have to do everything for you?" Mendelbaum said.

Treister looked at him, speechless.

"The red bag," Mendelbaum said, "toss it over."

"What are you doing?" Treister finally said.

"Be quiet," Mendelbaum said. "I will take care of this. The bag. Now!"

"Carl," Treister said in a choked voice. "It was you! *You* killed Halkin."

"You always were a fool," Mendelbaum said.

"What?"

"He would have talked," Mendelbaum said.

"Talked?"

"If and when I found Margoshes, and I got rid of him."

"God forbid!"

"He would not have kept still. And everything would have been kaput!"

"You killed Bloom, too," I said, "didn't you?"

"I did whatever had to be done, my friend. I built this business, not him. I did the hard jobs."

"Shame! Shame!" Treister cried. "Who asked you to?"

"Shut up. The business is more mine than yours."

"An investigation," I said, "would have sunk you."

"Yes. But now there will be no investigation. The bag, or you die where you sit!"

"Sure."

I tossed it to him, and watched as he caught it one-handed.

"You will have to die anyway, of course," he said. "You three, and him."

"And how," I asked," do you hope to pull that off?"

"You tried to blackmail him. He wouldn't stand for it. He had a gun. Many shots were fired." Mendelbaum shrugged. "You all died."

"You wouldn't dare," Treister shouted.

I said, "Better look in the bag first. It's open."

"What?"

"Go on. You can shoot us after."

He gazed into the bag. "What is this, a cell phone?"

"Exactly," I said. "My uncle's."

"So?"

"The line is open. The cops missed your opening speech, Mendelbaum. But after I tossed you the bag, the phone was in perfect range."

He stared at me, then at the phone.

"The part about killing all of us was a nice touch," Laura said.

"You probably want to rethink that," I said. "Especially since there are three guns trained on you under our coats. And a bunch of cops waiting outside."

"You are bluffing," he said.

On cue, the phone on Treister's desk rang. He picked it up, listened a moment, then looked at Mendelbaum. "A Captain O'Toole. He says the building is surrounded."

There was a moment of dead silence.

The butler slowly turned and pointed his shotgun at Mendelbaum. "That being the case, sir, I must ask you to drop your gun."

Mendelbaum looked at him, his face ashen. The Glock fell to the floor as he raised his hands over his head.

"Very smart," Uncle Morris said.

All three of us pulled out our guns, which we'd been gripping in our coat pockets all this time, and stuck them back in their holsters.

"Some bluff, eh?" Uncle Morris said.

I wiped my sweaty palm on the chair, glad that I didn't have to shoot a hole through my coat pocket. I hate ruining a good coat.

"My lawyers," Mendelbaum said, "will destroy you."

"You bet," I said.

Laura turned to Uncle Morris. "How," she asked, "did you get the police to act so quickly?"

He shrugged. "I simply told the captain what I wanted. Years ago, his father asked him to always listen to me." My uncle smiled. "That was good advice. And, as you see, Michael is a very obedient son."

CHAPTER 45

A good day's work, Max? What's good about it? It only took fifty years to write "closed" to the case.

Max and Morris Weiss—The Present

I called my client April on the cell phone. And told her I expected her uncle, Dr. Margoshes, to surface very soon. We were knee-deep in uncles. But I wasn't complaining.

"What's soon?" she asked.

I explained about Treister and how he fit. "Right after the news about his bust goes public," I said. "It shouldn't take long."

That got me a bunch of thank-yous and the promise of a check in the mail.

Then Laura, Uncle Morris, and I went for a stroll, hunting around for an Italian restaurant. We found one on Third

Avenue, only a few blocks from Treister's Gramercy Park town house.

The place was almost empty.

Laura chose a bottle of wine for us, a nice 1996 Cabernet Sauvignon special reserve, and we settled down to wait for our food.

She said, "You two probably have a lot of catching up to do, after all this time away."

Uncle Morris shrugged. "I have only been away eight days."

"Ah," I said, "but it seemed like months."

"He used to say years," my uncle said. "How quickly the young forget."

I know a cue when I hear one, and raised my glass. "A toast to the master."

We all touched glasses and drank. "He used to say *grand* master," Uncle Morris said with a mournful face.

Laura and I laughed.

"So," she said, "what happens to Mr. Treister now?"

"Who knows?" my uncle said. "Millions make their own justice."

"Well," I said, "he *has* done a lot of good. And all this Nazi stuff happened when he was just a kid."

"A kid, eh?" Uncle Morris said. "He was sixteen at the time. In Europe that was already a grown man—Enough of this," he said. "I wish to offer a toast." He raised his glass.

"To a smart pair of young detectives," he said, "who can show my generation plenty of new tricks."

Laura and I held hands and beamed back. Who could argue with that? Not us. We were too busy trying to keep from blushing.

Jim Fusilli

CLOSING TIME

0-425-18712-8

In one brutal moment, Terry Orr's life changed forever. His wife and son were murdered, leaving him alone to raise his twelve-year-old daughter. But the killer still roams the streets of New York, and Terry will risk all he has left to find him.

"THIS IS A TERRIFIC BOOK."
—NEVADA BARR

A WELL-KNOWN SECRET

0-425-19280-6

Obsessed with a man he can't find, Terry Orr struggles with the reality that his wife and son's murderer may never be caught, and relizes he is failing the only person he has left—his teenaged daughter.

"STUNNING...A COMPLEX,
HAUNTING MYSTERY."
—PUBLISHERS WEEKLY (STARRED)

Also available
TRIBECA BLUES
0-425-19883-9